REDWOOD
and GOLD

**Center Point
Large Print**

Also by Jackson Gregory and available from Center Point Large Print:

Lonely Trail
Guardians of the Trail

REDWOOD
and GOLD

13-01-60

JACKS⊗N GREGORY

CENTER POINT PUBLISHING
THORNDIKE, MAINE

This Center Point Large Print edition
is published in the year 2009 by arrangement with
Golden West Literary Agency.

The text of this Large Print edition is unabridged.
In other aspects, this book may vary
from the original edition.
Printed in the United States of America.
Set in 16-point Times New Roman type.

ISBN: 978-1-60285-611-0

Library of Congress Cataloging-in-Publication Data

Gregory, Jackson, 1882-1943.
  Redwood and gold / Gregory Jackson.
    p. cm.
  Originally published: New York : Grossett & Dunlap, 1928.
  ISBN 978-1-60285-611-0 (library binding : alk. paper)
  1. Large type books. I. Title.

PS3513.R562R43 2009
813'.52--dc22

2009024423

To
LOUIS SPRECKELS
TO REMIND YOU OF
OLD CALIFORNIA DAYS

CONTENTS

REDWOOD
and GOLD

NEVER had Glennister been so astounded. He started wide-awake, misdoubted the evidence of his own eyes and rubbed them vigorously. A moment ago he had been fast asleep, lying where he had thrown himself down last night in the dark of an unknown forest; he wondered if he were awake even now, or dreaming one of those incredible, impossible dreams that obsess a man even after reinstated reason would banish them.

It was at that pearly fresh morning hour when, though night is reluctantly withdrawing, the day has not fully flowered. Somewhere the lusty young sun was up, but his direct rays would not penetrate this grove for another hour. Among the tree trunks, down through the intricacies of interwoven branches, seeped and filtered a dim, dusky light; an uncertain, vague luminescence with some intangible quality of the weird in it. So in Glennister's mind, rudely awakened, there existed for a moment a condition comparable to this twilight phase of the dawn; his mental processes belonged fully neither to sleep nor to wakefulness. Thus, sitting bolt upright and staring he saw clearly enough yet would not give credence to what he saw.

The straight-boled trees stood all about at generous intervals with clear open spaces among them. Yonder, glinting wanly like a misted mirror, a placid, cool pool was fringed with tall ferns and the lacy greenery of graceful shrubbery; beyond, so faintly glimpsed that its presence was suspected rather than known, and would not have been suspected but for its subdued voices, a waterfall came slithering down over polished rock and mossy bowlder to slip quietly into the pool. An ancient fallen tree, seeming to extend limitlessly into a region of lesser light, was slowly gathered back into the bosom of earth; here and there ferns and feathery young trees rooted themselves in it and made the old log appear to live again.

It had not been the falling water which had awakened Glennister; its voices had been in his ears all night and had been indistinguishable from the quiet breathing of the tree tops. There had been some newer, sharper sound; the crackling of dry leaves under some quick tread, the snapping of a dead stick.

He saw the doe first; then the second doe; then the buck. And Glennister, though a man who had slept more nights of his life under the stars than under any roof, gasped at what he saw. For surely, as he stared at the antlered deer, here was a thing to make any man rub his eyes! Superb, perfect deer—and no whit bigger than rabbits! He had never heard of such a thing; had never dreamed such a possibility—unless he dreamed now—and strove to see more clearly through the thin light and among the leafy greenery.

In a flash the deer were gone, vanishing, leaving the world quiet and empty. Something had startled them. What? He watched breathlessly.

Only now did the full, complete wonder smite him. Half seen through the still leaves, a glimpse, a gleam—as swift as a bird's wing—white uptossed arms, dusky hair—a splash in the pool—sparkling spray—appearing, vanishing like the deer. And it seemed to Glennister that he had caught the most fleeting of visions of a girl, superb, perfect, wonderful—a girl created to the same tiny scale as the deer—not tall enough to come up to a man's knee—so little, almost, as to stand, held in his open palm!

Silence again; the forest emptier now than ever. Then the far, faint drumming of a woodpecker, begun abruptly, stopped abruptly, an echoing note to call attention to the utter stillness.

Glennister sprang to his feet, flinging off his blanket and, bootless, dashed forward to the pool's edge. A series of ripples in concentric circles made ever widening rings, spreading out until they broke in tiny wavelets among the ferns. There was nothing else to see. Small wonder that he stood there uncertain, like a man bewitched; small wonder that he looked all about him with the sobered, marveling expression of one who has at a step quitted the world he has always known and come straight into the heart of some impossible fairyland.

A strange hush was in the air. He looked through vistas of tree trunks into a region of russet browns and Lincoln greens; glimmering softly beyond the pool that had been like a misty mirror were pale lilac hues, faint tinges of rose colorings, amethystine lights and vague purple shadows; the dark brown boles stood like pillars to the vault of the heavens, their lofty limbs lost in an aerial jungle; rare glimpses could be had of the sky which, seen in little fragments, was as deep a blue as any richly dyed silken fabric.

All of a sudden comprehension smote Glennister. Perhaps only now, after all, he was truly wide awake? . . . Last night in the dark he had come to the very edge of a grove of gigantic redwoods: he had awakened among them without realization. He stood now leaning against one of them, a mighty old fellow fully sixty feet in circumference. "Relativity!" That was what it had been, and all without warning or proper mental adjustment for him. These huge monsters dwarfed everything that wandered into their company! A noble antlered buck had looked as small as a rabbit: he himself, alone now, felt like one who had drunk from some magic draught which had shrunk him down from man's full estate to the stature of a pygmy.

He returned to the spot where he had made his

camp last night, and all the while that new sense of being suddenly dwarfed was on him. The strange, almost unearthly light, flooding everything about him in its purplish stains and lilacs and wan rose hues, seemed to pervade his senses. And still a flashing vision haunted him: the broken gleam of white, uptossed arms, the splash in the pool.

To break camp was the affair of little more than a moment. His blanket and square of canvas made a tight, light little roll: he was booted, his rifle was caught up and he set his face purposefully toward his journey's end. What had he, Jim Glennister, adventurer and gambler and now a man wedded to a stern purpose, to do with forest pools and their magic, and vanishing Dryads?

He hurried along, found a faint woodland trail, and swung into it with a determination touched with impatience. He would not even tarry for breakfast. Give him another hour or so and he would drop his bundle and make his cool, grim announcement:

"Well, I am here to take a hand!"

THE HOME IN THE DARK FOREST   CHAPTER II

JUST where that faint woodland trail led, though he had never trodden it before, Glennister knew right well. Threading as fine an extent of virgin wilderness as even he, a man of many wilderness wanderings, had ever glimpsed, it would bring him soon to the one solitary human outpost in all these forested miles. Broad highways run up and down through northern California, but they cling to coast and valley; between those busy rivers of human traffic were these remote, wild mountains with their headlong rivers and tiny, hidden valleys. Here were all but limitless solitudes, thick black pine forests, magnificent redwood groves, regions of wide-branched oaks that had no fear as they had no knowledge of the woodman's ax, but went on through the generations, dropping their brown, polished acorns into their own cool shadows lying athwart tall grasses; vivid groupings of the red-boled *madroños,* those sylvan cavaliers of California, true gallants among noble trees, the "captains of the western wood."

A man might wander here for days, for weeks on end, with only these and the soft-footed and quick-pinioned wild folk for company. Even the trails themselves, haphazardly hit, abandoned so often for a whim, were like pretty threads serving but to bind the sweep of this magnificent wilderness country into one perfect and harmonious whole; thin, faint pathways made by deer and bear, softly trodden by wolf and mountain cat, crisscrossed by the smaller, stealthier little fellows seldom seen, ever quiveringly alert. A quiet, peaceful land of tiny emerald meadows; creeks among whose smooth rocks and tumbling waters broad-leafed plants nod and rustle and make shadowy grottoes for strong-bodied trout; nooks where bright flowers and butterflies and honey-bees find their simple paradise.

But this morning Glennister, swinging along in haste from one pleasantly intriguing phase to another of this pristine wild, had no eye for its beauties and no wish to linger. He was like a man goaded along; he was all hot impatience to come to his objective. Another man, a man with leisure and a contented and peaceful soul, might have loitered, both mentally and physically. Four or five miles traversed with never a stop—and with never a glimpse of camp or cabin. He might have set himself to explain the girl, to analyze the vision— to answer the question: "Girl or Dryad or Dream?" "A fairy Creature of these silent, dim, dusky aisles who flitted and vanished; who, of a quiet night with a full golden moon, flashed along the mysterious pathways drawn by little running deer—deer as small as rabbits—herself so elfin small that a man might hold her in the palm of his hand!—"

"Ah!" said Glennister, a look of almost savage triumph in his dark eyes, "At last!"

He had come to the brow of a hill and, abruptly, to the edge of the wood. Down there in the lower lands was the place he had come so far—and so urgently—to set his heel upon, announcing: "I am here to take a hand!"

Here, before and below him, was so pretty a little valley that one might fancy it as having been conceived in an artist's brain, lovingly set down upon canvas and then, by some magic process, translated into material existence. Had a man, seeing it for the first time, not had his mind hard set on other and more sinister matters, he must have thanked God for color! Such colors as were found in regions like this one, vivid and aglow in the clear air of early morning. The serene blue of the sky; the deep, tender blue of the mountains locking the valley in, away from the outer world, their softened hues giving a look almost of translucency to bare rocky peaks and thickly-wooded slopes; the living green of the valley floor. Such might have been the Happy Valley of Rasselas; one born and bred in this seclusion might well dream of wings—might have the winged soul to lift him into the rare atmosphere.

Late yesterday afternoon Glennister had parted company with a racing mountain river; a regular scabbard-rattling, swashbuckling devil-may-care sort of fellow, dashing and flashing and thundering and challenging and flinging spray and laughter and bits of wild song to startle a hundred echoes into shouting back at him as he plunged bold and reckless, into a dark and deep ravine; tributary to some more lordly stream, the Trinity, Hay Fork or Mad River, but here a careless freebooter of a fellow, lording it in his own fastnesses. And now here again, and all without warning, Glennister came again upon the same stream—only to find it of altered mood and aspect in this altered environment.

Done with the black cañons, winding into the little valley, it made its entrance still with a flash as of unscabbarded steel, and with a dash in which there remained a hint of bravado—but a hint only. Like some bold adventurer who, by dint of his brilliant sword-play, had won his way clear of battle and danger, from which he now emerged triumphant and not averse to accept briefly of the placidity of peace and the laurels of victory, he sang out a little, he chuckled more, perhaps he boasted a trifle. But of a sudden, mercuric fellow that he was, his soul softened to grow infinitely tender; it was quite as though he had cut his way through all bristling obstacles to come to a tryst with his wildwood sweetheart—and she was here, awaiting him. The velvet meadowland, in her fresh green gown, flower-bedecked, was hushed and tremulous at the coming of her lover; now was his golden hour to loiter, dallying among the willows which, like timid fingers, caressed his cheek; to pause, turning backward, whispering softly; to grow broader and more contemplative, communing with the tender reflections treasured in the bosoms of still pools; to encircle and clasp in his strong young arms all this palpitant, virginal loveliness.

Glennister's glance sped across park-like fields

and groves of the valley floor; hastened where the river made its dallying bends; discovered the old footbridge far below, looking from here like a child's toy; sped on to the house itself, last of all details to assert itself, so did it blend and harmonize like a natural growth.

Glennister pushed on eagerly, following the downward-leading, zig-zag trail, and thus coming presently to the first hint of a road; scarcely more than a hint, so old and long disused was it, two tracks made long ago by iron tires of wagon wheels, become through the seasons mere ruts, rain-washed, grass-grown.

And now the house itself, an old, old house. "The House of the Madrones." The place which had drawn him from afar, with his own purpose to serve.

It was an enormous affair, sprawling under a sturdy weathered roof thick with gray-green moss, its walls of big rough logs reared upon low, massive foundations of unquarried field-stone. There were square, gray rock chimneys, four of them, like towers. An old-fashioned flower garden, unkempt, a place of stragglers, hollyhocks and honeysuckles, overflowed into the field and invaded the porches; it harbored the home-made sun-dial, huge block of stone with rusty iron finger pointing out the flight of time, and the rude rock fountain, cracked, dripping water everywhere, weed-grown, moss-green.

About the whole was a redwood picket fence, pickets missing all along, gates long ago vanished. Yonder an ancient pear tree; a spring-house looking to be but a hummock of turf with a little brown square door set in it; a dozen broad, vigorous old apple trees that had never known what pruning meant, but flourished naturally like any wild tree, showing the small, unripe fruit amid a thick growth of branch and leaf, with here and there an apple turning pinkish or pale red. Giving the house its name, a magnificent grove of tall madrone trees proudly and gracefully lifted their satin-soft, red limbs and shadow-dropping green leaves. An overflow from the spring gushed out under a monster log and began its pleasant journeyings among the madrones, threading a bit of kitchen garden, flashing and shining by an old stone hut in tumbled ruins, a potential Sir Gareth on his way to the court of kings.

Asleep, all this; plunged deep into silence, overlaid with solitude. No smoke from the chimneys; no bark of dog; no sight of domestic animals. Only a curious-eyed, impertinent tree squirrel, fluffing his tail over his gray back and sending forth his not unmusical, bird-like chatter; a crested blue jay, screaming distrust and a warning to all and sundry; a pair of king-fishers skimming the still pond. The drowsing valley appeared to have fallen under a spell long, long ago; in the all-pervading hush one was assailed by the very spirit of desertion.

All unexpectedly Glennister came upon an old man. He sat on a rustic bench under a sagging trellis of grape vines, head down, brooding. Like a gnome he was with his long white beard falling to his lap, his snowy hair, his small, slight stature. He did not turn at the sound of oncoming footsteps; did not stir as Glennister's shadow fell and stopped before him; did not even lift his head as he said in a quiet voice:

"Morning, Stranger."

"How do you know if I am a stranger?" demanded Glennister, his eyes bright and hard and keen, his voice curt and direct. "You haven't even seen me."

The old man stirred only enough to point with the gnarled red staff over which his veined and knotted hands were clasped; alike were they, hands and staff, as though from many years of companionship they slowly grew together. He moved, not weakly, but with an impressive leisureness, gesture and voice alike bespeaking an infinite, patient quietude.

"Your shadow," the old man indicated, "is that of a stranger. So was your step."

The old eyes were raised now, pale blue eyes set so deep under tangled white brows that they were half-hidden, half-revealed, shining mildly with an expression which may be glimpsed now and then in the eyes of very old men—something, oddly enough, akin to the ingenuousness of a little child.

Here was one who had passed onward from the innocence of ignorance to the innocence of understanding. He removed a torn, flap-brimmed old hat; a ray of sunlight gleamed on the white hair which framed the small, pinched face and fell to the stooping shoulders from which the ivory-tinted ends curled upward.

"This is Madrone Ranch?" said Glennister.

"Ah!" The one syllable only; yet it answered "Yes!" and went further—a flash of fervor in the hushed exclamation.

"You've a love for the place, eh?" Glennister, in whom, as yet, no love of home had played any part, looked mildly amused. "You've been here a long while?"

"I came here as a boy, not yet twenty; and not a single night since the old home was built have I been away from it."

"A long way back," said Glennister. Impatient as he was to come to a certain matter which had brought him here, he felt that he must match his step to the step of age. "A long way back for this part of California. Not many men, white men, hereabouts then, were there?"

"Precious few." The old man nodded after a little quiet pause in which, perhaps, he had turned back in his leisurely way to clasp hands with his own departed youth. "Just the two of us, to be exact. There was Daniel Jennifer: that's me. There was Dick Hathaway, a young Englishman; just the two of us. He's dead now; dead fifty years, poor Dick!"

Glennister's shoulders twitched; a queer quirk came to the corner of his mouth. How little of life itself, life with its zest and striving and doing, its battling and failing and triumphing, had come under the calm blue eyes of this old fellow.

He returned to his purpose.

"There's always something jogging us at the elbow or tugging at our sleeve," he observed with an assumption of carelessness; "driving or pulling us along into the out-of-way spots of earth."

"And I've noticed," said old Daniel Jennifer, "that, so long as we're young and often enough when we're old, it's the same thing. Gold."

"Gold hereabouts?" Glennister laughed.

The old man lifted his staff with slow deliberation and pointed to the house only a few steps away, yet seen only in fragmentary glimpses through the lichen-coated trees.

"What do you reckon built that—if not gold?"

Glennister's eyes did not alter; not a line of his face changed. He was not the man to have his expression say for him anything which he did not care to put into words. He merely said, as though little impressed:

"Gold here, in these mountains? Some little low-grade, maybe—"

The thin old shoulders achieved a listless shrug. But as the bowed head was raised again Glennister for the second time saw a flash as of pale fire in the deep-socketed eyes.

"It's here, man! High-grade; such ore as few of us ever looked on. And for what would amount to a long life for most folks I've been looking for it, day after day, day after day. Up at every daybreak, dark and bright, sure I'd find it before sunset. Until this morning. I got up late this morning. For now," and there was a faint helpless and hopeless flutter of the old hands, " I know it will never be Dan Jennifer that finds it."

Glennister, gold-seeker that he was himself, experienced a queer sort of contempt for the ancient Dan Jennifer. It was one thing for youth, headlong and hot-blooded, to yield to the urge of the eternal quest; let Twenty-One dream of gold, eager-fingered for all the precious metals to decorate his fine Castilian castles; what, though, had Ninety-Nine to do with it? But, speaking, he held to the main issue:

"If you used this gold building the house—?"

"Dick Hathaway's house. Dick's money; his gold. Lost now, these many a year."

He fell brooding again, seeming to have forgotten the stranger. Glennister, finding his philosophic-looking ancient turning out the ordinary greedy old money-chaser, grunted curtly:

"What would *you* do with your gold, if you found it?"

He was not in the least prepared for the rare,

peculiarly sweet smile which preluded the answer: "Do with it? Why, that depends!"

"On what?" demanded Glennister.

"On when I found it, of course! Suppose I'd got it the first year I started hunting? Young I was and upstanding and vigorous, and as wild as the head-waters of Wild River down yonder. Why, I'd have bought me champagne at fifty dollars a bottle! I'd have sent out for oranges, just to pay five dollars apiece for them! I'd have had special, hand-made boots if they cost me five hundred dollars; I've always wanted a pair like I saw once on a gambler, down on the Sacramento River. And I'd have had a diamond like his, only bigger. And I'd have found out all the gambling houses and dance halls this side the Rockies, cutting a path they'd long talk about as young Dan Jennifer's path!"

"I see," grunted Glennister.

"If I'd have found it later," said old Jennifer, "I'd have done whatever happened to call for doing at the time; a man changes, come his different seasons, like the woods change from Spring to Winter. Each year a man would do something different; one year I'd have given it to the churches! Which is different, you'll say, from handling it over in the dance halls? Oh, I've fancied having the spending of it many a time and in many a way, and it's still there—and now I'll never find it—"

Glennister saw now how it was. Here was a search which had begun in the hot heyday of youth

26

and had been prolonged into the very dead of life's winter; and it had been the ever changeful quest itself which had mattered to Dan Jennifer. A man, though he live out his life in the solitudes, must have his task, his day's work, his objective. It was like the angler's zest; the fish in the basket were nothing.

"Why give up hope—now?" he asked.

"I'll be dead, most likely, inside ten days," was the serene dispassionate rejoinder. "And I was always so sure I'd find it first. I've dreamed. Well, well, my boy, the waters keep a-running on, down to the sea."

"The place is to be sold?" said Glennister, sharply.

"Ah!"

Again and again Glennister had glanced toward the house; there seemed no one there.

"By the way," he said, abruptly, "I broke camp early this morning, four or five miles back, at the edge of the National Forest—"

"Four or five miles? No National Forest, then; that would be on Hathaway land. We call it the Dark Forest hereabouts."

Glennister's brows shot up.

"I didn't know your place was so big!"

"Not mine; I'm just a sort of pensioner, friend. Tolerated by young Andrew, who's still in the special-hand-made-to-order fancy boot stage." He laughed quietly. "Yes, the Hathaway place is fair-sized, taking in a piece ten miles by two; over twelve thousand acres."

"A principality," said Glennister and under his breath, "gone to the devil with a whoop!" Aloud he went on: "I broke camp without breakfasting. If it's all right I'll go down by the bridge there for my coffee."

The old man rose and waved toward the house.

"You're right welcome; come into the kitchen, stranger."

"Name of Glennister."

Dan Jennifer offered his hand that the introduction be made complete; his fingers were slight and cool but the grip firm and steady.

"Come on then, Mr. Glennister."

Deep were the lichens on the stone-paved walk; deep were the mosses upon the spreading roof. Logs sixty, eighty feet long made the valiant old walls. Imagine getting them into place in the old pioneer days! The door set in the middle of the front wall was deeply recessed, of proportions to accommodate a convivial giant bringing his boon companions home with him arm in arm; it stood wide open, and shadowy glimpses were afforded of the big house's interior.

They did not turn in here but went on through the dilapidated garden toward the kitchen door; Glennister, however, had received an impression of wide spaciousness, of cool bare floors, of that deep, shadowy silence of an empty house which is ever pervaded by a sense of mystery. Passing along the southern wall, with the faint commingled scents of mint and mignonette in his nostrils, he marked a window here with its heavy shutter, a door there stood ajar or wide open, and had yet other fleeting glimpses: now of an oak bench, hand-hewn, solid, massive and dark with age; now of a walnut table with its carvings of clustered fruit and leaves which no doubt had known what it was to buffet strong seas in the venturesome voyage around the Horn; once of a great square rock fireplace.

The kitchen, entered directly from the stone-flagged yard, was puncheon-floored; there was a generous old sheet-iron stove on which a fat buck might have been roasted whole; benches and home-made chairs; a fireplace with a row of black iron pots hanging from rust-red iron hooks.

From a little parcel which Glennister had carried in his roll he produced bacon, coffee, flour and salt; while he busied himself with breakfast-getting the old man sat on a bench and watched him. Glennister, with a sharp glance about, remarked a somewhat startling lack of just those things a man might look to find in a room like this. Ample cupboards stood bleakly empty. Everything was clean, but there were no tins nor boxes nor bags of provisions; no smoked hams depended picturesquely from blackened beams; no bulging chests stood in the open closet. On a table in a willow basket were a dozen apples; beside the basket a thick earthenware platter decorated with faint, faded garlands, held a couple of carrots, fresh from the soil. No flour; no sugar; no spices. It was as though no one had cooked or dined here for a long, long while. Yet the apples and the carrots insisted that this remained the kitchen.

What every glance outside had proclaimed, this clean-swept room repeated in its turn: Abandonment. Well, he had expected something of the kind casting its forward, advancing shadow. But it was here, and worse, far worse. Here where bounty had once ripened like a sugary fruit, bursting its rich, glowing skin in tempting, generous offerings, poverty had long usurped its place. Rank, dire poverty. But how explain that? An estate here, as he had said, like a principality, which should be sufficient unto itself in all its needs; broad wild acres, thousands of them extending over twenty square miles; the savor of an olden order of extravagant plenty—and now the impression of a bone picked clean!

His coffee bubbled over: its seductive aroma floated wide through the sunlit morning air. Glennister looked toward Jennifer invitingly. The old man only shook his head and smiled, saying simply:

"I've got out of the habit of coffee. We're out of the world a bit, Mr. Glennister. It's a good dozen miles out to the wagon road, and then a long way to any sort of store."

"No wagon to go in," was Glennister's silent addition. "No horse to draw it, most likely; certainly no money for provisions at the end. And that's why—" Aloud he offered casually: "So the place is selling?"

There was just the suspicion of a tremor in the quiet voice which answered him, just a hint of tears in the deep-set eyes.

"Being sold—to-day."

Glennister whipped about sharply, crying out:

"To-day? Not to-day, man!"

"Being sold to-day." The old hand was smoothing and patting the old familiar bench; patting it ever so softly. "Sold? Ah, give' away. That's why none of the folks is here. Andrew was off in a hurry—to sell to a man named—named Norcross. Well, well, I'm sorry; sorry that it had to be to a man like Jet Norcross."

He sighed and stopped there. Glennister stood rigidly still. There was no movement in the room save the gentle stirring of the old hand patting and smoothing the bench.

"I've told you how Dick Hathaway was an Englishman? Of a good old home-loving stock, too. Such have their traditions; they like to hold on to the old homes; to pass them on, father to son. So Dick, when he died—killed, was poor Dick, like Oliver after him—had left a will that gave every-

31

thing to Oliver, his oldest boy. And Oliver, when he died, left everything the same way to Andrew. And Andrew—Well, Andrew won't listen to anyone else. Andrew's young; that's all that's wrong with him. He wants his oranges at sixty dollars a dozen and his diamond and his cards. He's let things run down a bit; you couldn't help see how it is. Stock sold; place gutted. Mortgages.— Andrew restless, hearing the cities a-calling him. Norcross could have stopped all that, but Norcross had his own plans. He gets it all now. You see—"

He had been staring at the floor. He looked up. Glennister was not listening!—He was down on his knees, remaking his roll with a rush, his face dark with rage. And then, with never a word, Glennister was gone!

"THERE'S SOME MISTAKE HERE!"   CHAPTER III

NIGHT had shut down. The old Hathaway home, enwrapping itself in shadows as in a cloak, seemed to shiver in the uncertain, early starlight. It had stood through the many years, sturdy, valiant and serene, echoing to the tread of Hathaways, sheltering Hathaways through the many thousands of nights, awaking in the thousands of daybreaks to Hathaway voices. To-night it was as though the old house knew—and shivered with dread. It had been sold like an old slave who meant little or nothing after all these years to the young master.

But, quiet and hushed though it was, not yet was it utterly deserted. From the throats of four wide chimneys rose four wisps of smoke; within doors, throughout the many large quiet rooms a flickering light ebbed and flowed from the blaze of pitchy pine upon the four hearths. Not a single burning candle; there were no candles. No steady-flamed lamp; there remained no oil. It was well, entirely befitting, that upon this, a last night for the Hathaways, a night of farewells, the place was lighted as it had first been lighted under the first Hathaway. Such light is tremulous; there is a touch of sadness in it when, as now, the fires are small; dreams and sighs weave in and out among the quivering shadows and old ghosts start up.

On the old settle before the fire in the main room sat the old man, Jennifer, brooding. More like a gnome than ever did he appear now, his weazened form dwarfed by the big empty room. The firelight silvered hair and beard, the shadows made deep dark pools of his eyes, old eyes communing with the little ghosts of memory. There was not an ax mark in hewn timber which he did not know; not a floor board; not a bench or table.

Yet it had not been Jennifer who had lighted the four fires; he would not have had the heart to do so; he would have sat on in the dark, seeing it all with closed eyes. A quiet little figure stole through the silence to him at intervals; a hand came softly to rest upon his drooping shoulder or slipped down to his hand that was clasped upon the head of his staff, the warm fingers of youth tightening a moment upon the cool fingers of age. Neither spoke; what was there to say?

She it was who had lighted the fires that in the fire-glow she might go slowly into every room to stand gazing into every nook, to touch, as she had touched old Jennifer's hand, some beloved object, the dear old walls themselves. Her eyes were very bright when the fire shone in them, gleaming as eyes can gleam only when brightened with laughter—or tears.

She came and went on tiptoe, hushed, like one treading softly in a house where death is. Oh, if Andrew had only loved the place with one-tenth the love she had for it! She and Jennifer alone, he at one end of the long road, she at the other, were bound to it by ties which it would be like death itself to sever. There hung the old rifle, unmoved all these years, where her grandfather had put it for the last time. He had brought it with him across the plains and the mountains; there was many a remembered tale told of it. A useless old thing—to a man like Norcross! There was the cradle in which her mother had rocked her and Lavinia and Andrew and Bud. And Lavinia had been in such haste to go! Bud, too. But then Bud was so young and so eager and impatient to rush out to do battle with the world. When Andrew's note had been brought in by the messenger, it had been accompanied by Andrew's gifts in money to his brother and two sisters: fifteen hundred dollars in bank notes. Bud had waved his unexpected golden fortune above his head, whooping; Lavinia had clutched hers almost as excitedly. And within an hour they had started out to Eureka. Andrew was to meet them there; no doubt they were by now all on their way to San Francisco.

And she remained; with old Dan Jennifer. They, too, would have to go soon, of course. Norcross was expected now at every moment; yet it might be that he would not arrive before to-morrow. So it might be that they had all of to-night.

If Glennister could have looked in now, as she wandered through the empty rooms, he must have thought with a start of his Elf of the pearly dawn. For here, in their own way, these large silent rooms did what the giants of the redwood grove had done; by comparison they tended to diminish the stature of a figure which Nature had begun by casting into a slight, fairy-like mold; she stood musing by a fireplace so huge that she might have walked into its black, yawning jaws.

But Glennister had gone on and she had neither seen nor heard of him; Jennifer, naturally silent, had not so much as mentioned a stranger coming and going on a day like this. She touched many an object with lingering, caressing fingers, like Jennifer himself patting the old kitchen bench. She wiped her tears away and they came back afresh, bedewing eyes which were all unaccustomed to them; eyes in which gayety lived and laughter was always bubbling up. Never did a brighter spirit glance through these wilds than hers; she was one of those rare beings who seem created to gather happiness to them, to shed it all about them, adding to its sum total, enriching it with fresh spontaneity in its outpouring.

She was the youngest of this house of Hathaway and the very names she went by, pet names freely bestowed by a household which asked no more cherished possession, paid bright tribute to her sparkling joyousness. Two cumbrous Christian names had been bestowed upon her in her cradle days, but of them remained only the initials: "B.B." Her father, first of them all, when looking down into the happy little face, though accepting for her as necessary burdens the old family names, had been swift to call her "Wee Glee Hathaway." For from the beginning gleeful she was, and Wee Glee, Andrew still often named her. To Bud she was just "B.B." at most times; more affectionately, "Bonnie Bee"; and to Lavinia, oldest of the four, she was "Joy, dear."

But to-night Wee Glee Hathaway was grief-stricken. She had lived on all the while in hope, and maintained stoutly that something would happen to avert this dreaded disaster. And now, for the first time in her bright little life, hope itself lay smitten and could not lift its head. Andrew's brief note lay upon a mantelpiece; she had gone back to it to read it over a dozen times. And every time it was as though she heard the clanging shut of great iron doors, locking her out.

She lingered in her room; it had been her mother's and father's. She looked at the old walnut bed, the old walnut wardrobe and had to turn swiftly and go out. But they followed her. In the quiet she heard voices: voices which had been stilled many a year, some which she had never heard from living lips. Like Jennifer, every plank and puncheon had a meaning for her.—Andrew, at least, might have saved the furniture—

There were some things which she would save: the thick, steel-clasped family albums; the pictures; a certain old crazy-quilt; a drawer full of letters, yellowing with the years; the cradle; the settle where Dan Jennifer crouched now; the Mexican saddle and the side-saddle in the harness room; a few old books; the long dining-table about which on so many happy occasions—

She put her face into her hands. That all this was to go into strange hands,worst of all into the hands of a man like Norcross—

Quietly she slipped out of the house. It was but a few steps to the knoll rising gently from the floor of the little valley and Dan Jennifer, brooding, would not miss her.—How could Andrew sell?— She hurried on, then came to a dead stop. Old

Jennifer was here before her; he must have been all stealth in creeping out. There was the knoll, dark under the stars, shadowed by the trees which scarcely whispered, so still was the air; there the old fence about its small enclosure, broken here and there under the weight of the years but always mended by loving hands; and there, head bowed, beard and hair gleaming wanly, stood the old man. She began withdrawing; she knew his thoughts and felt ashamed, as though she had peered in through some key-hole. She knew that he had always thought that some day he, too, would rest here; near his old friend, Dick Hathaway; near Oliver and the rest—and that now he was saying his hopeless farewell and perhaps asking himself in listless unconcern where on earth he, very soon now, would lie alone under the stars.

"Poor old Danny," she whispered sobbingly. "Can it be that it is harder on him than on me even?"

For a week, though all the while hoping—yes, and praying passionately where she flung herself down with none to see in some beloved nook of the great, sprawling ranch—she had been making her pilgrimage of good-by; to little hidden meadows where her flowers seemed to be awaiting her and to be drooping in frail spiritless-ness when she made her lingering departure; to each one of the score of rivulets gushing away so merrily to march off under the glittering banners of Wild River; to a gallant old log fallen here or a tall centuries-old tree standing there; among the apple trees about the house; to the pond where the raft was; up and down in the flower garden; everywhere. It had been good-by old fellows, old friends, playmates; a long good-by to mean "God go with you." Jennifer, too, she knew, had made his own silent farewells; he was making the last now.

Like a little lost and wandering soul she went listlessly back through the glimmering starlight, back to the old house where the shadows stirred; she visited each of the fireplaces, renewing the fuel for the sake of the light. Again she resumed her pathetic little tour; the house, with Jennifer out of it, was even more silent and empty and sad now.

"I have the five hundred dollars Andrew sent," she said. "I can buy some of the things back from Mr. Norcross. I can have a man come with a wagon and haul them away—"

Haul them where? Herself along with them. Jennifer, too.

She returned to the shadowy living-room; the fire was almost out. She marked that the front door stood wide open; no doubt Jennifer had gone that way, not closing it after him for fear that she might hear and guess his errand. She stepped toward the fireplace—

"Nobody was around, so I just came in," said Norcross.

She started back and gasped. She saw him now. There he stood at the corner of the hearth, lounging against the mantelpiece, a dark, tall, sinister man; among the other shadows a blacker, more ominous shadow. He had strong white teeth; the firelight made the most of them now as he smiled; also it winked wickedly on the cruelly sharp rowells of his spurs. There was a little clinking of steel as he moved.

For her part she neither moved nor spoke. The final blow had fallen and stunned her. She had known that he would come; in her heart she had known that he would come to-night. It would have been absurd to think of Norcross, after all his eagerness and predatory scheming, waiting another day. Yet she had been absurd enough to hope. And now, like any dreadful thing which one may see casting its shadow before it, the actual fact crushed her.

He was regarding her steadily. She could not see his eyes but felt them. They were like insolent, prying fingers to which no closed door was inviolate.

"Has Andrew got back yet?" he asked.

"No. He is not coming back. He sent word. That's all."

She had spoken abstractedly, quietly, and tonelessly. At the end she sighed wearily. At last everything was over—

"What did he say?" demanded Norcross, sharply.

She pointed to Andrew's note upon the mantel-piece.

"He wrote that. He just said—"

But Norcross plucked the bit of paper down and stooped to hold it close to the dying fire. Even in this uncertain light it was but the matter of a moment to read the few words: "Sold at last. Have received the money, delivered the deed and am off to Eureka. Am sending five hundred to each of you. Better meet me at the coast." That was all.

She had never marked the man so particularly as now and yet, oddly, it was as though she saw him at some great distance. He was like an object which, while near by, was gazed at through a diminishing glass. He did not belong to her world, yet here he was in it; that was what made him seem at the same time close by and far away. He had black hair which curled in metallic looking rings; his hat was still on, pushed a bit back and to one side, a soft gray Stetson that looked white against the black hair. He was one of those men who, when close-shaved, have bluish-black jowls. Jet—Jet Norcross—

"Ah," said Norcross. He piled the fireplace high, dragged the settle closer and sat down, his legs thrust before him, his hands in his pockets.

"You have come to—to stay?" she asked faintly.

"I am here to take possession to-night—now!" he said bluntly. "I've waited long enough. Now it's mine."

41

"Yes. It's yours now. I'll go."

She was turning away when he called out:

"Go? At this time of night? Go where?"

"Danny Jennifer and I stayed on. We thought that maybe you would not come for another day. We'll go now, though."

"Where, I said!" said Norcross, insistently. "Where'll you two go? That's nonsense, you know. You'll stay here to-night, anyhow; you'll be all right here."

She smiled queerly. She'd be all right here!

"Wait a minute; I want to talk with you.— Where's a lamp or a candle?"

"We use the firelight instead—"

"Lord, what an improvident mess of helpless babies you are!" He laughed good-humoredly. "Andrew the worst of the lot, too. Well, it was a good thing that I was on hand; the place will be better off with me at that. Well, here's what I was going to say: You needn't be in any hurry to make off. Fact is, you can stay here right along!"

A quick, eager "Oh!" burst from her and she wheeled back toward him; for the instant there sprang up the wild hope that he was going off somewhere, that he would want someone, her and Jennifer, to stay and look out for the place. But that was only because she had let hope still tug at her thoughts. In a flash she understood; it was so obvious.

"Marry me," said Norcross. "That's it. Then you

stay here always. I know you like the old place; I know you are worried about old Jennifer, too." He chuckled. "Crazy, that old bird? Not so crazy after all, as I'm willing to admit now.—You see, a woman is needed to keep a place like this going; I've got nobody, as you know, but Judy—a topsy-turvy if there ever was one; she'll need looking after, herself. You'd be friends after a while, you and Judy—you'll take both her and the place in hand—"

He broke off suddenly there. As for Glee Hathaway, wearied with grief, confused by Norcross' sudden strange declaration, she was dazed at a new unexpected appearance. Here came Judy Norcross herself, who had been rummaging all the rooms, and who now burst in upon them with startling suddenness. Glee Hathaway knew her fairy tales; it was only recently that she had begun, lingeringly, given up living with them; and it was now as though the pages of the Snow Queen had opened like doors and the little Robber Girl had rushed out upon her, "as wild and as savage a little animal as you could wish to find."

"Who'll need looking after?" Judy cried, shrilly. "Who's going to take me in hand? What are you talking about, Jet Norcross?"

She created a small tempest about her; her short yellow skirts billowed and ballooned, her scarlet earrings vibrated and flashed, her black boots thumped noisily. She was darker even than her father, as dark as the young Indian girl whom Norcross had made her mother but whose wild blood he had never tamed. Her black eyes were snapping, her brown hands clenched, her breast swelling as she raced in upon them, all readiness to surrender herself to her characteristic fury at the first hint of a hand being laid on her.

The resinous pine which Norcross had thrown on the fire was blazing up brightly now, flooding the room in its strong, soft light. Judy, having centered attention upon her vivid self, a thing she was never content without having achieved, posed dramatically. Her roving black eyes challenged the world; they cut at her father, stabbed at the other girl whom for her softer and more truly perfect beauty she resented immediately and hotly.

"I've been looking through our new home, Jet," she said in the voice which her passions made shrill. "It's a peach, or will be when I get it fixed to my notion. I've already picked out my bedroom and dressing-room; I've got Modoc and Starbuck pitching stuff out of windows; listen and you'll hear 'em going smash with a bunch of junk old Noah would have heaved overboard because it made him seasick to look at it. And if anybody asks you who's mistress here, you can tell 'em it's Judy Norcross!"

"You'll have whatever room I give to you," said Norcross angrily. And lifting his voice he shouted: "You, Starbuck! Modoc! Come here."

They came in through the same door at which Judy had entered, two gaunt, shadowy, noiseless forms, Northern California Indians with the impassive faces of their race, the straight black hair and glittering eyes.

"You'll keep your hands off until you get orders from me," commanded Norcross.

"Oh, will they?" scoffed Judy, though she had stood biting her lip before the words came. Then she looked at her father intently; one sharp glance was enough. She had angered him and saw swiftly that this was not the moment to clash. Suddenly, with an affected change of mood, she flung herself down on the hearth where she lay with her chin propped in both hands, crying gayly: "Go on with the love scene, Jet! Make it stormy! Just as though you didn't know any country kid, pitchforked out of house and home would grab you quick."

Glee Hathaway began to laugh. Nerves at tension, shocked rudely, quivered and nervous laughter became uncontrollable. Into the midst of grief stalked the ridiculous. Here was her first wooing, a thing which in anticipation had now and then flooded her daydreamings with its golden light. Norcross, of all men, asking her to marry him—Judy sprawling on the hearth, prompting him— two stark Indians looking on—

"Miss Hathaway," said Norcross, "I shouldn't have brought this imp along to-night—"

"I brought myself," said Judy, in an undertone.

"But I'll see that she keeps in her place and her tongue in her head. As to what I was saying, I mean it. I'm a bit older than you, but that makes no difference. Judy there is only fifteen—"

"Sixteen," commented Judy, impersonally.

"I married her mother when I was little more than a boy. I'm young yet, only beginning the prime of life—"

"No, no!" came his swift answer. "I am going now, Mr. Norcross."

Norcross frowned. He had long had his eye on her; she could not help knowing that. He wanted the Hathaway place; he wanted the youngest Hathaway girl along with it.

"You can't go to-night; there is no place to go. You'll stay here; I've said you'll be all right. In the morning—"

"No, no," she said again, with a flash of fire burning in her quick rejection of him and all his offerings. To her he was nothing but a marauder, a beast of prey; long ago he had come under their roof as a friend and from the beginning had been a traitor, accepting their salt and scheming to take their all; playing upon Andrew, leading him into debt, taking mortgages and finally hounding him into selling—giving away, as old Jennifer always maintained.

She heard Jennifer coming now; there was his steady, quiet tread in the kitchen with now and then the tap of his staff. Norcross, too, heard; he

46

knew the love and sympathetic understanding which bound these two, and the love of both for the old home.

"I'd like to see you have a home here," he said quietly. "You and the old man, I'd be sorry to have the two of you lose it. It would be hard on you—" He shrugged, managing to imply that the responsibility of what might happen resided now, not on his shoulders, but on hers. "It will kill him."

Jennifer came on into the room and stood looking at them with calm, grave earnestness.

"Evening, folks," he said in a voice which matched his bearing in unemotional placidity. He had said his farewells out there under the stars where the old cedars dropped their shadows softly over the knoll and was not to be moved now by such earthly happenings as the comings and goings of a Norcross.

"Hello, Santy Claus!" cried Judy, and sprang up. "You show up just as Jet here is asking the milkmaid to marry him—so that you can spend your next hundred years sunning yourself on the old home doorstep!"

Norcross' hand tightened on his riding-whip. But his eyes were drawn away from Judy and to the old man who was speaking.

"Come along, Glee Hathaway," he said as though he and she were alone here. "We'll go now."

"Curse it," muttered Norcross. "You can't go,

Jennifer. There's no place to go this time of night—"

"We'll take a couple of blankets," said Jennifer. "There are the woods. They're like home to us; they're good to us just as God is good. We'll sleep better tonight out in the woods. And we'll move on again in the morning before you folks begin to stir."

He put out his hand to Glee Hathaway who took it tightly in hers.

"Yes," she said. "We'll go now."

Norcross stood looking at them curiously. He could not understand either. He had looked to Jennifer to grasp at any straw; he had thought that the girl would at least hesitate, then temporize, surely stay the night and, in the end, stay on as his wife. And now their quiet rejection of his offer aroused his hot resentment and at the same time put fresh steel in the stubbornness of his intent.

"So you're going to give up your gold at last, are you, Jennifer?" he mocked him, knowing that thus he flicked him on the raw.

The old man stiffened at that. He turned and they could see the pale flash of his sunken eyes.

"I've looked for it for more than seventy years," he said swiftly. "At least I know you'll not find it in another seventy."

"Oho!" exclaimed Norcross, viciously. "So you know that, do you? And what, do you think, made me so set on getting the place?"

"You got a fine place, and for next to nothing. And you thought that one day you would get the gold, too."

Norcross stepped forward. There was a sudden gesture; his hand went to his coat pocket and tossed something to the old table top. It struck heavily: a thump as of lead or any soft metal.

"I found it six months ago!" he cried out, his voice ringing triumphantly and still mockingly now. "That's why I bought and why I am here. And now that the place is mine, I don't mind telling you. I've got it!"

Jennifer, with the alacrity of youth, sprang forward. He caught up the specimen, carried it to the fireplace and peered at it. His hands began to tremble terribly; a spasm shook him from head to foot.

"Virgin gold!" he whispered hoarsely. He stared at what he held as though he could not believe what he saw. He looked up then and stood very still. "Dick Hathaway's gold! And—God—let—him—find it—"

It slipped from his fingers, thudding to the floor.

"Stirs you up a bit, does it?" Norcross taunted him, more triumphant and more mocking than before. "Yes; I found it. And here's something else for you to think about: It was you, Dan Jennifer, who led me to it!"

Perhaps Jennifer did not hear. If he heard he did not heed.

"Come, Glee Hathaway," he said, brokenly, for an old, life-long dream was broken. "We'll go now—"

"You old fool!" shouted Norcross. "Keep your hands off that girl. She—"

It was then that a voice spoke from the front doorway.

"There's some mistake here," said Glennister, coolly.

A SHOT THROUGH THE WINDOW CHAPTER IV

LITTLE was to be seen of Glennister standing just outside, leaning on his rifle and looking in through the doorway. But a new atmosphere, electrically-pervaded, flooded the room on the instant. In a profound silence every eye was turned upon him expectantly. The two girls, both speechless, strove to make what they could of the shadowy figure. Judy fancied that he might prove to be romantic-looking, and began preening, deploying her almost barbaric charms against the bright curtain of the firelight, flamboyant as to scarlet pendants, inky tresses, yellow dress and glistening boots.

As for the other girl, more vaguely revealed by the dimmer light where she appeared to withdraw, she, too, was athrill with some eager expectation of her own. This stranger's words, "There is some mistake here!" started up a wild hope in her heart. A mistake! Had something at the last moment happened to save them—

Norcross looked perplexed only and was the first of all to break the silence, starting forward and crying out angrily:

"Who the devil are you and what do you mean?"

For answer Glennister stepped swiftly into the room. The light now shone full upon his face. As dark as Jet Norcross, at the moment he looked satanic; there was a vindictive grimness about the hard mouth and in the quick black eyes a gleam of malicious triumph. He spoke with savage satisfaction as he saw recognition spurt up in Norcross' eyes.

"Got you this time, Jet Norcross. And got you right!"

"It's Lord Jim!" gasped the astounded Norcross.

Even old Jennifer jerked up his wintry brows and muttered wonderingly, "It's Lord Jim Glennister!" For this man had a reputation—of sorts. Go a bit further eastward, to the California-Nevada state line, mention his name in Truckee or down the river in Reno, and all men knew Jim Glennister.

"You two," said Jennifer, "Jim Glennister and Jet Norcross, are pardners!"

"Not any more," said Glennister, coolly, his narrowing eyes all the while upon Norcross. "We were. We had our little string of gambling hells together; I was down and out, in a Denver hospital with a bullet hole in me. By the way, Norcross, it's only recently that I've come to understand that if Stanley Burke did that for me, it was while taking your pay!—Anyway, Norcross here took his chance to cheat me out of my share; oh, he did a nice, clean job of it, cheating me down to the roots of the sage brush. And now—"

"You lie!" shouted Norcross. "And besides, I've something else to-night—"

"And now," went on Lord Jim sharply, "it's my innings. I've been patient, for once in my life; I've let Norcross line things up and just as he thinks to rake in a nice fat pot—why, I save him the trouble."

"Look here, you," stormed Norcross, his moment of consternation passed, his wrath flaming up, "I'll have you know that this is my place. I bought it—"

"You thought that you did! You've been ready for a long while; ever since you found that," and he nodded toward the lump of gold still lying where Jennifer had let it fall. "With everything loaded to go off all the while, just waiting for Andrew Hathaway to come to it; your check in the hands of a shyster out at the county seat; a deed in his hands for Andrew to sign. You waited for Andrew—and I waited for you." There came a sudden hot flash into his eyes, a look almost of wolfishness into the dark face as he cried out, ringingly: "And this time, Jet Norcross, I've got you and be dammed to you."

Norcross knew his man and looked frightened. Suddenly he snatched down Andrew's note from the mantel.

"Read that, you fool—!"

"Read it already," said Lord Jim, jeering at him. "Dictated it, in fact. I thought you'd fail to note that he doesn't say from whom he got the money? To whom he delivered the deed?"

"And—you—mean—that—you—"

Lord Jim laughed. His laughter was deep and hearty and not unmusical. Yet Glee Hathaway, for one, shivered. If she had been afraid of Norcross she was suddenly more afraid of this man; if she had grieved to see the old home go into the hands of one like Norcross, it brought her no lessening of sorrow to learn that this other man was before Norcross. They were like wolves; like wolves they glared at each other now.

"Which of you two is the Hathaway girl?" asked Glennister abruptly. "I've brought along a second note from your sweet fool of a brother, Andrew; we'll let Jet Norcross read it and then perhaps he'll see the light and drift along—"

But it was Jet Norcross first of all who read it. He caught it from Glennister's careless fingers; at the fireplace, from which his daughter Judy whipped back with a little sharp cry lest he tread on her in his excitement, he read, hastily:

53

"Dear Glee: I sold to-day to a Mr. Glennister instead of to Norcross. Glennister made me a better proposition and at least I've the satisfaction of seeing Norcross lose out; if Norcross is still there you can tell him so for me. In haste,

"ANDREW."

Judy was the second to read the few lines, snatching the paper from her father's rigid fingers. Her eyes blazed, her cheeks flamed like fire. She stamped her foot and cried out, shrilly:

"He's a dirty devil, Andrew is. You're a big fool, Jet Norcross; I hate you! Here I was already fixing up the rooms you promised me—" She spun about, confronting the newcomer who had wrought such havoc in her bourgeoning plans, and spat out her words at him like an infuriated cat at bay: "You low-lived card-sharp, crook, cold-decker! If I was Jet Norcross I'd fill you full of lead before I'd let you walk away with a thing like this!"

She lunged toward him at the end of her tirade, meaning obviously to strike him full in the face. But he was the swifter of the two and caught her wrist, spinning her about and lightly casting her off. He laughed at her as a moment ago he had laughed at her father.

"Better call off your kitten, Jet," he advised coolly. "And trot along yourself, while the trail's open. And many thanks for getting a claim all ready here for me to stake."

By now Norcross, a man not in the least unused to the blows and stabs of adversity, had pulled himself together. A moment he stood brooding; there came a sinister flash into his eyes and an implacable hardening to the thin lips.

"So, sneaking out of the underbrush and in the dark, you think to make your killing, do you, Jim Glennister? Well, I'll have an eye on you after this. I happen to hold a pretty big mortgage on this place; not paying that off to-night, are you?"

"Better be on your way, Jet."

"Bought on a shoe-string, didn't you?" jeered Norcross. "Took a chance on finding the gold, eh? A long, long chance that! By the way, I notice you've lost the pin out of your tie and the ring off your finger! Dug deep, did you, for a first pay-ment? and have to leave the mortgage—my mort-gage!—hanging. Oh, I'll get you yet Jim Glennister; and I'll get this place, too—and all that goes along with it."

"Get out, damn you," snapped Glennister. "And don't forget to take along your kid and your two aboriginal friends."

"Oh, I'll go this time," and now it was Norcross who laughed. With a mighty effort be had gotten himself in hand and now appeared as cool as Glennister had been at the outset. "A jack-pot lost doesn't mean a game lost. Starbuck, you and Modoc go for the horses. Judy, you'll have to wait a bit—not long—to take possession. We're going—but if you don't mind I'll take what's mine along with me."

But Glennister was before him and with a sharp, "Oh, no, you don't!" caught up the piece of rich quartz while Norcross was stooping for it. He tossed it to old Dan Jennifer, saying coolly:

"Make a study of that specimen, and you'll save me a lot of time in coming to the old mine."

"Not if I know it!" shouted Norcross, swept away again by an onrush of rage. "That happens to be my property—"

"So?" Glennister jeered at him. "Only I happen to have heard you brag that you found it on the Hathaway place—on my place."

Norcross was at the end of words. He hurled himself forward, thrusting by Glennister and catching Jennifer by the shoulder. Jennifer, the gold again in his hands, clutched it tight. Norcross, entirely borne along by his baffled fury, shook him terribly.

"You old fool, drop that!"

"Hold it!" shouted Glennister. "Hold on to it, Jennifer."

Before he had done barking out his command, Glennister had shifted his rifle to his left hand and, with his right, now caught Norcross by the collar and jerked him backward, breaking his hold on the old man. And now all of Jet Norcross's burning, bitter chagrin and venomous resentment flared high and hot within him like a pillar of sulphurous fire. Forgotten was the gold, forgotten the old man who gripped it so tenaciously; remembered only this Glennister, hated of old, who stood now between him and everything he wanted. He struck out furiously and there was the lust of murder in his eyes.

"Kill him!" screamed Judy, her own hands clenched. "Kill him!"

Norcross' blow might well have come close to killing had not Glennister been ready for it. As it was it did no harm, glancing off the left shoulder which was hunched upward and forward to fend it off. In turn and with all his might, Glennister struck back. Norcross swept along in a blind rage, failed to turn aside or to protect himself; he received the clenched fist square in his face and was hurled backward, staggering and toppling half-way across the wide room, lurchingly saving himself from falling.

"Starbuck! Modoc!" he shouted. "Kill the fool!"

"Kill him! Kill him!" Judy kept on screaming.

The two Indians came forward, their eyes shining like glass beads. There was the winking glitter of steel in Starbuck's hand, for an instant stained red by the fire. Modoc, passing close to the fire-place, put out a stealthy dark hand to the heavy iron poker. Norcross, steadying himself, wiping his face with a hasty hand, pressed forward with the others; he whispered something in Starbuck's ear.

Jim Glennister, seeing the three men bearing down upon him, whipped his rifle over and forward, and began mocking and jeering at them. Then he saw that the old man and the Hathaway girl might get in the way, and shouted at them:

"Out of the way, Jennifer! Take the girl with you; clear out!"

"No!" cried Glee Hathaway, her face dead white but her own eyes shining angrily; anger at a pack of wolf-men turning her own beloved home into their savage battle ground. "Danny, give Mr. Norcross his gold. Let him take it and go."

"Nothing of the kind," Glennister snapped. "Back up, Jennifer, out of my way. You Indian with the knife, drop it or I'll shoot your arm off for you. You with the poker—Call 'em off, Norcross!"

Norcross himself came to a dead halt. Starbuck and Modoc, seeing him hesitate, paused likewise, looking to him for all the world like two trained hunting dogs.

"Give him his gold; Danny, give him his gold and let him go," repeated Glee Hathaway.

"I say no," Glennister growled at her. "It's mine and I keep it. Now, Norcross, suppose you back out of this. I've got the top hand and mean to keep it. Gather your crowd and go."

Norcross pulled out his handkerchief and wiped his face; he stood a moment looking moodily at the rusty stains, then his eyes trailed away to old

Jennifer. In the end he jerked up his head, quick, defiant, determined.

"I'll get you, Jim Glennister," he said rather quietly. "And I'll get this place—and everything that goes with it! You boys go for the horses. Judy, come along."

Judy stamped furiously and broke into a shrill torrent of abuse.

"You big coward, Jet Norcross! You—"

Norcross paid no heed to her. He went to the settle, took up his hat which had fallen there and went out with never a backward look. The two Indians were at his heels. Thus the last of all to go was Judy.

She remained to do her bit of posing; she shot a blazing look of hatred toward Jim Glennister, whose snapping black eyes were jeering at them all. Then of a sudden she began to laugh. And now the expression in Judy's eyes altered swiftly as once again she found this newcomer good to look upon.

"I think I like you after all, Lord Jim," she confided, coming closer and looking straight up into his face. "I've heard a lot about you; I've been crazy to meet you for a long while, but Jet he always kept me back. You handled this affair man-style, and I like that. Jet Norcross ain't a baby, and he ain't the coward I called him either, and—"

"Judy!" called Norcross, from outside.

"Coming," retorted Judy—and made a sudden,

59

unexpected dive at old Jennifer, snatching at his hand. But he, though taken by surprise, only clamped his fingers the tighter about the nugget and Judy, making a face at him and naming him a nasty old white goat, sped by and vanished through the doorway, following her father.

Glennister swiftly closed and barred the big door after them, and returned to the girl and the old man who stood close together now, hand in hand.

"Now, then," he said curtly, "let's get down to business."

The youngest Hathaway stood looking at him as though at some strange, unknown savage beast. She needed no telling why men of mining camp and gambling hall, ever the readiest with nicknames, called him Lord Jim; handsome and dominant and arrogant, he differed in all essentials from any of the few men she had ever known. He and the men of her forests were as far apart as day and night; small as was her experience she understood that in a flash, instinctively. In him as in them, sheer manhood asserted itself boldly; yet she grasped vaguely that even manhood may be an unlovely quality, stark and passionate and fierce. Here was one who lived for himself alone, who came at his ends the shortest way, unmindful of what and whom he trampled.

Her first impulse was to shrink back, to turn and hasten away. Out of the room pervaded by his presence, away from the house. It was no longer home; whether Lord Jim Glennister or Jet Norcross had it, it was lost to her for ever. But she resented his air of proprietorship, and was angry with herself for being afraid of him, and cried out hotly:

"Business! There need be no business with either of us, Mr. Glennister. You and Andrew—and Mr. Norcross—"

"One a fool, the other a crook, and I'm done with both," he retorted. "While with you two I may be just at the beginning."

"Come, Danny. We'll go now."

"No. You'll stay here to-night; there's no place to go even were you set on it. And I've got to talk things out with you."

"We thank you for your hospitality," said Glee Hathaway, coldly. "But we are going now."

He stared at her frowningly; he came a quick step forward and stooped to peer into her face. She saw his brows shoot up; a new light seemed kindled in his eyes.

"We'll have a bit more light here," he said, and tossed an armful of pinewood into the fireplace. The flames licked at the dry splinters and poured out a sudden brightness. Glennister whistled softly.

"You little beauty!" he cried admiringly.

Redder went her face than the fire-glow alone could have made it. It was not only his words but the rare impudence that flavored them; her hands clenched at her sides. Glennister began to laugh.

"My little wild dryad of the forest pool!" he cried out as though delighted with a fresh discovery. "I'd bet a man."

Redder than ever grew her face; and as hot as fire her anger.

"Danny—!"

"Oh, come now," laughed Glennister. "No harm meant. I'll apologize. I hadn't had a good look at you, you know, and seeing you all of a sudden— well, it sort of bowled me over. For you are the prettiest little thing I ever saw and I've seen more than one or two. I'm just all the more willing to make you my proposition. Both of you."

She told him emphatically that here was no proposition just now that he could make to interest them.

"But there is," he said good humoredly. "Just listen to it. You don't want to be run out of your home; it hits you pretty hard to have to go. I'm going to fix it so that you can stay. I need you; I need both of you. Now wait a minute!" He flung up his hand against the interruption he saw coming. "I won't force myself on you; I've no time for that and no desire. There are times when a man loses nothing by putting his cards down on the table, face up. I bought this place because I have been watching Jet Norcross and he's crazy to get it. That means that there is gold on it; gold to the tune of a million or he wouldn't have been so set on it. Now—"

"Come, Danny This doesn't concern us any longer."

Glennister's good humor vanished.

"You'll stay until I'm through," he said sharply. "If I have to tie up the two of you and make you listen! Now, here's my proposition: You two stay and lend me a hand. You, Jennifer, with that specimen to go on, can save me a lot of time; you know every foot of this ranch and having that to go by can lead the way. You, little Miss Dryad, can have a home here; you can keep house and see that we don't starve. And for that I'll pay high; anything you want."

"Have you finished?" asked Glee Hathaway, in a voice which she found it hard to control.

"Not interested?" grunted Glennister. Again he leaned toward her, studying her flushed face, looking straight into her eyes, marking how she held her head. "Insulted you, have I, offering a servant's place and a servant's wage to an infernally proud and haughty maid? Confound it; I've got to arrange this with you. Look you, Jennifer! Now I'm talking straight to you. Norcross showed you the gold; what's more, he told you when he found it; six months ago. And what's most, he told you that it was you yourself who led him to it! You see now how you can help. I've got to have you!"

"He lied!"

"No; he didn't lie. I know Jet Norcross. It was

63

six months ago and you led him to it. We'll get our heads together—"

"Has it dawned on you, Mr. Glennister," said Glee Hathaway, as icily as she knew how to speak, "that we can no longer have the slightest interest in what happens to the ranch? Whether you or Mr. Norcross gets it—"

"Exactly," Glennister cut in. "Unless—"

The splintering of glass, the crack of a rifle and the impact of the bullet were like one sinister explosion. Glennister's rifle fell with a clatter and he went reeling backward, clutching at his side. They saw his face whiten, saw his hand turn red. He managed to reach the settle and sank down, glaring furiously.

"Now's your chance," he muttered savagely. "Better go while I'm down and out and can't stop you. You, Jennifer, hand me my rifle first."

"Help me fasten the shutters, Danny," said Glee Hathaway quickly. "Run, Danny."

When, a few minutes later, she hastened back to the wounded man on the settle, she surprised a queer, crooked smile on his cynical lips.

"What if Norcross did me a good turn?" he demanded curiously. "You can't go off and leave me like this—"

"If you'll get some warm water, Danny," she said briefly, "I'll go for some clean cloths."

Glennister lay back, staring up at the black-beamed ceiling.

GLENNISTER DRIVES A BARGAIN

DAYBREAK found Glee Hathaway and Dan Jennifer in the kitchen, preparing a frugal breakfast and talking in whispers, guarded in every word and every movement not to awaken the sleeper. He was at the further end of the big house, several rooms intervening and all doors shut, yet they went on tip-toe and spoke in hushed voices.

"He's a tough customer," said Jennifer. "I've heard enough of Lord Jim Glennister to know that. And you wouldn't need to be told who he was to come at what breed of dog he is. He's not hurt bad enough for us to have to stay and look out for him any longer; and the best thing for us to do is be off before he's about."

"He's worse than Jet Norcross!" she retorted in subdued passion. Even to speak of him put a hot flush in her cheeks. "Yes, we'd better hurry, Danny." Then she broke off and sighed. "I did want—"

Softly, melodiously, like gently tapped silver bells, the notes of a piano were wafted to them through the silence of the house. Their sleeper, then, was already up and about. For it could be no one else. His room, the "guest room," always in hospitable readiness though guests were almost as rare here as dollars, adjoined Jennifer's; had been

Dick Hathaway's in the long dead years; and gave entrance down a narrow hallway to the music room. He had wandered that way and the old square piano had caught his eye.

He was fingering the notes idly, carelessly, with one hand only. The two in the kitchen looked at each other curiously; then their eyes wandered away as though they could aid their imaginations in picturing him at the piano. He was not using his left hand; that was because of his wound. His whole side must be stiff and sore.

Yet there came the base notes now; the same idle carelessness yet a certain nonchalant sureness about the touch, too. A couple of haphazard chords; a pause; a rippling strain of melody. He had noticed the sheet of music where she had left it a week ago. She had not touched the piano for a full week; there had been so little singing in her heart.

He was singing now. His voice rose higher, clear and true and very sweet; it filled the house and overflowed it and again caused those who heard it to look strangely at each other. The girl stood a moment as if spellbound; softly she went to the door, opening it. The golden flood of his music pulsed more strongly now; it asserted itself compellingly, and yet was all lingering tenderness. When the last note died away and the house fell silent again, it was not the same silence as before.

They heard him coming on toward them through the empty rooms, his heavy boots sounding noisily upon the bare floors.

"What ho!" he called cheerily from a distance, with some two or three closed doors still to open before he came to the kitchen. "Ahoy, there, my two good friends, Doctor Jennifer and Nurse Hathaway! I'm lost, I tell you; lost in the sleeping palace of the—" He flung open another door and appeared to them, saw them and called out: "Good morning, Beauty of the Sleeping Wood! Good morning, most patriarchal Jennifer."

He gave them a new and unsuspected Jim Glennister to think upon. He was pale and haggard from last night's experience, yet neither of them marked that for some little while. For the striking thing about him was his gayety. He seemed actually to sparkle with rare good humor, to be a-tingle with some fine, spontaneous zest. He greeted them with a flashing, friendly grin and in a merry voice; he looked a full dozen years younger than last night and, with that swift smile illuminating his face, the harsh and sinister lines vanished; nor could any glint of hardness linger in eyes so utterly gay as his were now.

All too little music had Glee heard in the sequestered years of her life, yet music she loved as only do some few mortals out of many; it alone could awaken something deep, very deep within her and set it thrilling, making the heart-strings quiver, causing her to breathe deep, stirring in her breast that poignant, exquisite delight which is joy akin to a sweet, nameless pain. The song of a mocking bird opened the windows of her soul; with closed eyes she listened for hours to the rustle of the forests; in falling waters and splashing brooks she heard fairy orchestras. And no music had ever caught her so by the throat as had this man's singing at the old piano. A look of pure wonder was in her eyes raised to his. If she had first known him through his singing and his touch upon the piano keys, instead of as she saw him last night, it would have been very hard for her to accept Lord Jim Glennister upon the reputation which he bore. Even now she was finding it bewilderingly difficult to reconcile the musician with the predatory adventurer.

It is seldom that two young people exchange a regard so perfectly frank. He, too, was reappraising her. In place of last night's hurly-burly and flickering firelight, he had now clear daybreak and quiet. Yet, the reverse of what he might have looked for, hers was an even more piquant beauty in this clearer, fuller light. And for the moment there was a look in her eyes, turned on him as honestly as a child's, which he had never seen in any girl's eyes before; a deep gravity, a vague wonderment.

"Well?" he said curiously, "and what do you make of me?"

She started, blushed hotly, as realization swept over her, and turned away, the spell broken by his abrupt question.

"We were getting ready to go—"

"What were you two saying about me just now?"

She wished Jennifer would speak up. But the old man was content with silence, his deeply sunken eyes watchful of Glennister's every look and gesture. So with a hint of annoyance and without turning from the table where she bent over their simple breakfast preparations, she said:

"We were making our plans, speaking of—"

"Of me, along with other bothersome affairs," he insisted. "Only naturally, since I come in the role I do. You don't deny that, do you?"

She denied nothing.

"You know we were about to go last night, when—"

"Oh, I remember well enough. Going in the devil's own hurry, until I got in the way of a bullet. After that being human, of course, you had to stay and see me through."

"Your wound doesn't seem to be troubling you much this morning," she retorted. "And so—"

"You're free to go? Well, I suppose so." He came on into the room, and sat on the far end of the long table, one leg swinging. His eyes darkened and grew piercing; then a sudden cleared and he began to laugh. Obviously he was not only in a rare good humor this morning, but meant to remain affable. "Last night I threatened to tie the two of you up, rather than let you desert me, didn't I? Ever notice how a fellow who may be rational enough by daytime is apt to go to extremes by candlelight?"

Even though he had only an eloquent silence for answer, he remained unruffled. He did, however, lift his black brows quizzically, though his smile lingered.

"Oh, I'm not so bad as you two tried to make me out just now," he chuckled. "Just a roughneck. You'd get used to me, you two, if you'd only stick around. Who knows but that I'd even make your fortunes for you? By the by, Jennifer, do you mind if I fill my eyes with the glory of that piece of rock?"

Jennifer took it from his coat pocket and put it on the table.

"It's yours," he said quietly. But Glennister, watching him like a hawk, saw how lingeringly the old fingers relinquished it.

"You bet it's mine!" He took it up and fell to examining it closely. "I paid enough for it, to begin with; took a bullet for it on top of that, too. Oh, I say, Miss Hathaway; am I invited to breakfast?"

"What little breakfast we are having;" she said, with just a hint of bitterness, "comes from the garden. It's your garden, now, and—"

"Mostly apples," he commented amusedly.

"Apples and water and what else? If you'd stay on for lunch, I'd promise you better fare; I've a man coming out with a load of provisions. Oh, well, you know the old adage: 'Better a feast of herbs where love is—'" Again he fell to chuckling. "So you intend to eat and run, without ceremony? At least, do you object to letting me know where you are going? If ever there were two real babes in the wood, I see 'em here this morning! Have you really any place to go?"

She hesitated before replying. She came very close to glimpsing his real mood: beneath the laughing good nature there was a bit of soreness. His wound irked him doubtless far more than he gave sign of; it was now that she saw how drawn and haggard his face was. Further, he was blanketing his own inner irritability which she herself and Jennifer were furthering by their own attitudes. Hence, while he laughed at them he was not above a bit of enjoyment could he plague her. Yet, after her brief hesitation, she gave him an answer; for thus could she come the most direct way to that which she meant to say to him.

"We are not going very far," she said stiffly, "though you can scarcely be interested in what we do, Mr. Glennister. About four miles from here is an old cabin on a bit of land which belongs to me; it was my grandmother's, then my mother's, mine now and never at any time a part of the acreage which you are buying."

71

"In the redwoods—close by Dryad Pool, I'd bet a man!" he cried, watching for the rush of color which he knew must come.

She ignored that, going on more swiftly:

"In the old home there are a number of things which I had hoped to remove before Andrew sold. Things which, I understand, become yours now. I don't think you would care very much for them; they could mean nothing to a—to you, and could be of little use. I have some money of my own; I'll be glad to pay you anything you like for them, and move them to my cabin."

"Come, that's reasonable," he agreed heartily, yet there remained the sign of mischief in his eyes. "Heirlooms, eh? Precious trinkets never to fall into a vandal's hands! The old musket with which grandpapa killed the Indian; the family album and the cradle over which I stumbled this very morning? An old dressing table which came around the Horn in '67, and which has a secret drawer in it—Ha! Who knows! With maybe a yellow paper all covered with puzzling figures, the memoranda, long lost, which is to lead to the rediscovery of the Hathaway millions! A snuff box and a spinning wheel."

She bit her lip and turned away from him again.

"I think, Danny—"

"You'll never turn any big business deals, young lady, until you learn to suppress that raging temper of yours. I haven't said no, have I? And you've got some money, all your own, to pay for all this? How much, I wonder?"

She went to a shelf, took down a tin can and from it brought a pad of banknotes.

"Five hundred dollars, which Andrew sent from the proceeds of the sale."

"My money, asking to come back to me! Why, here's luck," laughed Glennister.

"You will allow me then to take the things I want?"

"You are not going to carry them on your backs, you two valiant adventurers?"

"There is a big wagon in the barn. There are the two horses—"

"All right," grunted Glennister. "All ready to go, eh? And in hot haste. Well, I'll drive a bargain with you. You take what you want, anything in the house—and I'll name the price! I can't swear to the legality of the transaction; but who cares about the law so long as we get what we want, both of us? There's the mortgage, but I fancy it's on the land alone, so Norcross has nothing to say about it and it's up to just you and me and brother Andrew. What about the piano?"

"Danny and I could hardly move it," she told him, her eyes level upon his own.

"So the piano stays; good. It's most devilishly out of tune, by the way, but I've a notion I can remedy that. Well, we'll nibble our apple and carrot. A bowl of strawberries? Better and better!

And then we'll harness our gallant steeds to the family chariot, load in our lares and penates, and be up and away. It only remains to agree upon the price."

"Anything which you say, Mr. Glennister. The articles which I want to carry away are priceless, to me."

"Oh, I'm the man to see that you pay a plenty," he laughed back at her.

Breakfast, on the whole, was a failure. Glennister alone had anything to say and presently he grew silent and thoughtful. He took up the bit of quartz with its streaks and seams and pits of soft yellow precious metal and seemed to forget his companions in his study of it. He carried it away in his hand when he left the room, stopping at the door to say over his shoulder:

"I'm off to my room for the makings of a smoke. You two will want to get your horses and wagon and start loading. Go as far as you like and when you've done come to me and we'll make our trade."

It was some three hours later when she came to him, leaving Jennifer outside with the horses and the wagon-load of furniture and odds and ends which she had chosen to take with her. She found Glennister lying on his back on the broad couch in the living room, smoking cigarettes and seeming deeply concerned with the little vanishing rings which he sent up toward the black oak beams.

74

He pretended not to be aware of her approach, and she knew that it was pretense; that he got some sort of impish pleasure in making her stand there awaiting him, in forcing her to announce herself. For an instant she was about to turn swiftly and go out. But she remembered the wagon-load of household goods, and said quietly:

"I am here, Mr. Glennister."

He turned, sat up and flipped his cigarette into the fireplace.

"Why didn't you agree to marry Norcross?" he demanded sharply.

She looked at him wonderingly, more amazed than indignant.

"I am ready to go now," she said.

"Wouldn't marry Norcross, even at the price he offered? Well, you showed your good sense there. But we have other considerations before us, eh?"

"Yes. If you will come out and see what things we have packed—"

"What was Jennifer prowling around in the night for?" he surprised her by asking in his abrupt way of introducing unrelated matters.

"I didn't know that he was. Hadn't you better ask him?"

"Oh, he was, all right. Even into my room, while he thought I was asleep. Well, hc didn't offer to cut my throat for me, so we'll let him go unhung. Didn't see anything of the Norcross crowd while you were out for the horses, did you?"

75

"No. I suppose they have gone."

"Where? Where would he go? Has he some sort of hang-out near?"

"I don't know." But, though she had intended to stop there, she did add briefly: "He could not stop within two or three miles without camping on our—on your ranch. I do know that some months ago he was prospecting or pretending to prospect upon government land off to the north of us. And now, Mr. Glennister—"

All the while he had not risen. Now he sat back the more comfortably, thrust his long legs straight out in front of him and regarded his boots thoughtfully. Of a sudden he looked up at her with his somewhat impudent grin.

"I thought that 'Wee Glee' was the devil of a name to give any real girl while I watched Andrew write it down—but it just suits you! Or would, if you'd just let yourself go a bit. You're mighty proud, prim and proper with me, but I'll bet by nature you're as gleeful as a cricket. It's both a joy and a surprise to find a girl like you way out in this wilderness, do you know it?"

He had the trick of making her blush. She hated herself for her confusion and him for being the cause of it. She was little used to men, her experience the slightest of young men who were disposed to be both frank and impertinent, no experience at all with a man like Lord Jim Glennister. She saw his eyes brighten delightedly.

She turned quickly and without a word went out. He sprang to his feet and came hurrying after her.

"Look here, young woman, we haven't done our business yet."

"I'd far rather have you keep the whole of my five hundred dollars than do any business whatever with you," she said hotly.

"How do you know that I wasn't going to demand the whole five hundred any way? Were you thinking to melt me with your dimply beauty and so beat the price down?"

She had not stopped and did not answer. He came up with her again in the kitchen and put a detaining hand upon her shoulder. She shook it off but stopped now, her eyes blazing.

"You agreed to pay what I asked," he said coolly. "You can't go off in a huff with all your plunder without keeping your word."

"I told you you could take as much money as you liked—"

"Money! Who said money? Money hasn't anything to do with it; there are other ways to pay! Think I am going to rob a poor little heart-broken country kid of her last nickel, and for a handful of such things as you are taking? I won't have a penny of your dowry, fair maid; but I will take my pay like any Shylock."

"I don't understand!" She drew back, frightened.

"But you think you do," he chuckled. "You think that surely the wicked man, having the innocent maiden in his foul clutches, will surely take all advantage of her distress and helplessness as any bold bad man should do; especially when he is as highly appreciative of your wild-woodsy charm as Jim Glennister is! No, Glee Hathaway; whether you will be relieved or only piqued that you are not asked to pay the price of beauty and sweetness, it remains that I have something quite different in mind. You are to be just merely decent to me for a short time; say a week in all. During that time there is to be no nonsense on my part, only business. I need your help and Jennifer's and you are to grant me that. For this consideration the wagonload and as many more as you like are yours. There's my proposition for you to take or leave."

He had her fairly there. She thought of her treasures to be saved thus from vandals; from him or Jet Norcross. She could have other things carried to safety; they meant nothing to him and so much to her.

"How can we help you?"

"By telling me a lot of things I want to know. By indicating to me the property boundaries. By answering my questions, some of which I have in mind already, others which will suggest themselves."

Still she hesitated; and though finally she did say, "All right," it was reluctantly. He merely nodded but kept on regarding her intently. Of a sudden, all unwillingly yet none the less clearly did she see that his was a position in which he might have easily made a greater demand; for at least he was refusing to take her money. And so she added hastily: "And I thank you, Mr. Glennister, for letting me have these things."

"Now, that's better," he laughed, and she knew then that he had been waiting and perhaps wagering with himself that she would or would not thank him. "You will be busy upon your own affairs to-day; I'll be loafing within doors, giving my hurt a chance to heal over. But to-morrow morning you and Dan Jennifer will drop in on me, to spend the day. Now, I'll step out for a word with him and you are free to go."

She slipped past him and hurried out to the wagon. Jennifer was on the high seat, holding the reins. Glennister came out into the yard as she climbed up to a place at the old man's side.

On the instant Glennister was given fresh matters to think upon. He was not three paces advanced toward the wagon when there burst upon the morning stillness the crack of a rifle, and a bullet cut whistling close by his head. Missing him so narrowly, it could have scarcely missed Glee Hathaway more than a yard or so. Both sprang to one side so that the wagon with its load stood between them and the edge of the forest from which obviously the shot had been fired. Old Dan Jennifer sat where he was, his hands firm on the reins, his voice quieting the horses.

Glennister's face went white; with fear, thought the girl, and small blame to him. Death had come very close to him. But as she now caught the flash of his eyes, burning like little fires under his drawn brows, she read in them only a terrible, unmistakable anger.

"You two be on your way," he snapped savagely. "There's no danger to either of you to go; the fool could have knocked either of you over before I came out, and he's apt to do it yet, shooting at me, if you stick around this morning. And don't come back until I say: I'll look in on you when I am ready."

She looked at him wonderingly; before his few words were uttered his anger had seemed to pass, his color was normal, he was cool and quiet.

"I—I don't know what to do! To run away and leave you—to leave anyone—"

"Go," he said, and was very curt about it. "I can look out for myself."

"At least one of us will get word to the sheriff—"

His laugh was short and crisp; this was not the deep musically rumbling laughter of the early-morning Glennister.

"No, thanks! In the first place, I don't want the law sticking its nose into my business when that business has to do with Jet Norcross. And secondly, there's nothing a sheriff could do here. Who'll swear that it was Norcross who fired either shot? Who'll swear that he was even on the job here? Or think any sheriff on earth is going to spend his summer here, keeping men off? You just simply keep out of this, young lady."

"Oh. All right!"

She climbed up beside Jennifer and did not look back. But she heard the door slam shut, and knew that Jim Glennister had leaped back to shelter— and by now would be running through the house for his own rifle.

A DOOR REMAINS CLOSED   CHAPTER VI

"DANNY, oh, Danny dear! Try to remember!"

But the old man only shook his head and looked at her with sad eyes.

"It's no use; no use," he muttered. "How can a man remember what he doesn't know? What he never knew?"

But she was insistent. New hope thrilled her. He had never seen her so eagerly in earnest.

"But, Danny, you must! They say we never truly forget anything; you remember what Andrew was reading us only a week ago? How there are two parts to our minds; how it is as if a little gate locked one from the other, and how it can click back like the shutter of a kodak? Somewhere, somewhere maybe deep down in your mind, you know *something!* Think, Danny; think hard!"

He shifted uneasily. A look almost of fear swept into his eyes.

"What do you mean?" he asked sharply. "That I'm holding out on you?"

She ran to him and went down on her knees beside his bench.

"No, no, no. Of course not that. How can you think such a thing? But—Oh, if after all we could only be the ones to find it!"

It was late afternoon, a time of dim dusk among the redwoods. They were in the old moss-green cabin on that bit of wild land which had been Glee Hathaway's mother's, because as a girl she had loved it so, and which was now Glee's own, and for the same reason. Just behind rose the steepening flank of the mountain with the stately brotherhood of giant trees, making their eternal aisles of greenery; and down from the mountain cut a flashing stream, a "crystalline delight." The sturdy log cabin stood where once a great log had fallen across this narrow, steep-banked stream. Fifty years ago that fallen tree had offered itself as a natural bridge; later it had become one of the monster joists supporting the rude plank floor and the thick walls. Straddling the creek bed, a dozen feet above its rocky bottom, it was ever filled with the singing voices of the headlong water. One came up to it either by a flight of steps cut in the steep banks or from the other side by a winding path along the wooded slope.

They had hauled their belongings here in a roundabout way, fording the creek a mile below, following a winding and long-abandoned road through the forest to the cabin. Now the place looked like a bit of home transplanted here, and now for the first time they could sit and talk of what had been uppermost in both their minds all day.

"You keep thinking of what Jet Norcross said; that I was the one who led him to find it," said Jennifer. "That was just venom; his natural viciousness. To try to hurt me, whom he has little reason to like, by making me think that I had served his purposes somehow."

"But he told the truth, Danny! And the truth again when he said that it was six months ago—"

"I thought that over during the night. Six months ago?" Again he shook his head sadly. "I don't remember anything—"

"But I do! Jet Norcross came to see us just about six months ago. It was the dead of winter, and he stayed and stayed even when he knew he wasn't welcome. You remember that, Danny; and how, when at last he must have known that Andrew would have to ask him to go, he had an accident— a sprained ankle—and stayed another week!"

"Ah, of coursc! A sprained ankle!"

"You see! We are going to begin putting one and one together. Why, think, Danny; we've even seen the specimen which Jet Norcross left behind! You, who know every foot of this land, won't be long figuring out just where that came from. It can be done, Danny, and we can do it. We've got to do it."

They looked deep into each other's eyes then, the girl all bright eagerness, the old man looking troubled and uncertain.

"Jet Norcross has kept his mouth tight-shut all this while," she ran on, "because he's careful and crafty and was playing for big stakes. But last night he was so sure of himself, and of having won the game, that he thought his need for caution was over."

"Cautious or not, the man would lie because lying comes natural to him."

"But he wasn't lying when he said it was six months ago, Danny! It was just at that time, don't you remember, just a few days after he left us that he looked Andrew up again and offered to make the loan and took the mortgage. We all wondered how he came by so much money all of a sudden; now we know. He took it from the old lost mine! He only gave Andrew what was already his own."

"Prove that," muttered Jennifer, "and there is no mortgage! Instead, we'd have Norcross over a barrel, shown up for a thief and a swindler."

But she was hurrying on, to make her final point.

"He was telling us the truth, Danny We're sure of that. And so I am just as sure that he told the truth when he said that it was through you that he came to find it. Now wait; you're asking how in the world you could have shown him the way when you did not know it yourself? You must have gone out each morning, prospecting, as you have ever done; he must have followed you. At some time during the day, you must have come very close to making the discovery, Danny; and you just missed. And so, don't you see what we've got to do now? We must remember just what points of the ranch you visited during the couple of weeks that Jet Norcross was with us last winter."

His hands were folded over the head of his curiously carved staff; for a moment he sat with his head bowed upon them, very still and very silent. He sighed and at last looked up.

"I gave up last night—"

"But we're not going to give up ever any more! We've our chance now."

"What chance? With Norcross in the position he holds; with the ranch already sold to Lord Jim Glennister?"

"Mortgaged to Jet Norcross who stole grandfather's gold to make the loan! Bought by Lord Jim Glennister, who counts on finding grandfather's gold and using it to make his payments! They are thieves, Danny, both of them. They have no right."

"Right, my dear," said Jennifer, "doesn't always win."

"It does," she cried passionately. "It must. In the long run it will. Look at it this way, Danny: This man, Glennister, has only six months in which to find the gold, or he forfeits what he has paid Andrew and all claim to the ranch with it. Norcross has only his mortgage, and it is six months before that will mature. Suppose we find the gold, you and I; suppose that we let Lord Jim Glennister forfeit his rights—and they are not rights at all, but wrongs, Danny. Then, before Jet Norcross can make trouble with his mortgage, you and I tell Andrew everything. We buy back the ranch ourselves; we can have the old home, safe for always and always."

The old man sat brooding. Suddenly there came a flash into his sunken eyes.

"That specimen—"

"It was very rich, Danny?"

"Only in my dreams have I ever seen such stuff, my dear. Across the years I've dreamed many and many the time of coming to it; of finding it like that. Rich? Ah, high-grade and no mistake. Drive up a one-ton truck and fill it with that and you'd have—thirty thousand dollars? Or forty or even fifty! And Jet Norcross to say he followed my lead to that!"

"We'll work it out together, Danny. You know how one thing suggests another. We'll talk of last winter; of when Jet Norcross came; of what we did and said; of how we spent our days. We'll find that where we thought we had forgotten, we'd only laid our memory aside a little while. And before we are done you will remember which parts of the ranch you went to."

"And what will Jet Norcross be doing? And Jim Glennister? They will be watching. They're not the kind of men to let a thing like this slip by the ends of their fingers. You and I, a girl and an old man, against men like them."

"But we'll have the right on our side."

"Maybe. Yet, since Glennister has bought and paid down a pretty big first installment, it looks as though on his side he'd have the law."

"The law!" she scoffed. "I don't care a snap about the law, Danny. We're going to have what's ours."

"Norcross would have killed Glennister—"

"They won't dare touch us, Danny. They won't dare!"

Jennifer rose and went to the front door. From here one had broken glimpses down shadowy green lanes through the forest, and heard the water falling, cascading down a rocky spillway, tumbling into a shady, circular pool.

"What was it you told me on our way here?" he asked quietly. "About an understanding you had with Glennister; a bargain, to help him in payment for the things he let you have."

"Oh," she said blankly. "I had forgotten!"

She followed him to the door where they stood side by side.

"The cards are stacked against us," he said dismally, finding speech after a long while. "It's either Lord Jim Glennister to win and bring his wild crowd here to carouse and gamble and turn the whole place into a merry hell; or Jet Norcross to beat him to it, Jet Norcross and his girl, Judy—"

"No! No, I tell you, Danny. Haven't I said all along they are worse than wolves? As to my bargain with that Glennister man—He cheated me!" she said hotly. "For a wagon-load of odds and ends not worth fifty cents to him, he'd have me trade away our chance of everything! That's not fair, and I won't do it!"

"But if you told him you would?"

"I've a right to change my mind, haven't I?" she demanded, righteously indignant.

Glee Hathaway, a far-away look in her eyes, set about getting the scanty evening meal. The homely task—a rather difficult one, too, with things as they were—recalled her thoughts to everyday matters.

"Danny," she said, "we'd better hitch up early in the morning and drive out to the store; we've nothing to eat, and I've plenty of money now."

Jennifer, from where he stooped rummaging among his own litter of personal belongings, said curiously:

"Yes; oh yes. And I—I want to get me a new prospector's pick. Mine doesn't seem to be here— we must have forgotten to put it in—"

She agreed in a manner sufficiently casual to accompany so natural a suggestion. Yet there was an odd look of perplexity in the eyes which, turning swiftly, she hid from him. Dan Jennifer set her wondering, Dan Jennifer and his picks. They had a way of vanishing. During the last half a dozen years he had managed to get rid of an amazing number of them. She recalled that the last had been six months ago—he had vowed that Jet Norcross had stolen it—

"I looked for it at the house before we left," he confessed presently. "Do you suppose Jim Glennister stole it?"

A MAN WHO WANTS TO KNOW
CHAPTER VII

GLENNISTER dashed through the house for his rifle and came racing back into the kitchen. Never was a man more eager for an exchange of hot lead. The game which his erstwhile friend Jet Norcross meant to play with him was sufficiently clear for any man's comprehension and Jim Glennister vowed he was ready to take a hand.

He jerked the back door open, stepping swiftly to one side. Across the kitchen garden he could see the wagon, the old man and the girl upon the high seat. Beyond them was the encircling forest, sun-smitten yet a place of many dark shadowy places in which men might be lurking. The fellow who had fired that shot would be there somewhere; Glennister had but a general idea of just where. At a considerable distance, that much was certain, because the whistling bullet had come across the open fields.

Save for the crawling wagon never was a landscape quieter. A shot had rung out; there had been a mere ripple in the silence; the great stillness returned to brood like the spirit of peace itself.

Glennister left the door and went to a window; then to another. He could hear Dan Jennifer calling out to his horses. A moment later the wagon disappeared up the winding track, lost among the trees. Thereafter only Glennister's quiet footfalls emphasized the silence.

"I'm all wrong," he muttered disgustedly. "That's all for this morning."

He closed the door, dropped its bar into place and returned to the big main room to think it over. He made himself comfortable in an easy-chair by the fireplace, stood his rifle at hand against the rock chimney and indulged in a meditative cigarette.

Essentially this Jim Glennister was a gambler. But then, there is a suspicion abroad in the land that all men are gamblers; that with various individuals it is but a difference in degree. Where one is reckless, another is cautious; where one is skillful another is clumsy; where one is unscrupulous another has his standards and sticks to them, making a godhead of fair play. With some the game is a means to an end, with some a clean-cut side issue, with some it is life. Into this final category fitted Lord Jim Glennister.

A man's inheritance of blood gives him his bent; his environment forces it straight onward or deflects it; his own personality, which draws from each and is superior to both, becomes the final and dominant factor. This man's spirit was akin to that of all pioneers; such, perhaps, had been Dick Hathaway's once upon a time; such, fifty years before, might have been young Dan Jennifer's. Restless, adventurous, most of all venturesome. There was zest in life when it pulsed strongly; one lived most not when the cards were being dealt, not when the game was won and done, but during the supreme moment when the fateful card was being turned face up.

When a boy, when the old order of things obtained in Reno, Glennister had stood in the Palace gambling hall and watched the tall stacks of twenty-dollar gold pieces; had seen them wax lofty, had seen them melt away. Natural phenomena, like sunrise and sunset. One did not weep when the sun went down; he knew it would rise again. He did not go mad with ecstasy when it rose; it would have its setting, and night, after all, had its moon and stars.

As the gleaming stacks of twenties had waxed and waned like little golden moons before his eyes, just so had he seen mining towns boom up from small beginnings, make a merry din through their brief, hectic existences, and vanish from the face of the earth. He had been passingly interested in certain cavernous excavations which other men had moled out in the shell of the earth; had known these burrowings, some of them to cast forth their Pactolian streams, some like hungry mouths to swallow vast fortunes. He had taken his fling among them now and then, like a man playing the races, putting his money on the long shots. Win or lose, sunrise or sunset.

So the game he played now with Norcross was no new game. And yet, like all the old games, it had its novelty. One never knew. And further, he had "sensed" all along that this time he took the supreme hazard; that the stakes were the highest. Life itself; death itself. Everything; nothing. The shot last night; the shot this morning; he meditated upon them. There Norcross tipped his hand. The first attack spelled only blazing, murderous anger, perhaps. The second, after a night to cool a man's wrath, bespoke a set and determined desperation. It said: "I'm here to stay. I'll stop at nothing. I'll balk at no crime in the calendar. I'll run any risk. And I don't care how soon you know it."

"Why did Jet Norcross offer to marry her?" Glennister asked abruptly of the silence and emptiness about him.

Out of the emptiness and silence he had his

answer as he remembered her as she had stood in this room before him only a few minutes ago. He saw her almost as clearly now as he had seen her then. It was as though her eyes again looked straight into his. Honest and frank and fearless, the kind of eyes one liked—and liked to look into. Pleasant and with a sense of grateful coolness, like cool places in her own woodlands. Yet not always cool, come to think of it; hot flashes came their way. Soft gray, but being so full of life, changeful like life itself. One thought of violets and spring-time and all that sort of stuff, mused Glennister. By the way, how they had shone just after he had been playing and singing. Liked music, eh? Loved it, rather. If he had her here now with him, how he would like to look straight into those eyes of hers and sing to her. He'd watch her eyes change; he'd make 'em change! They could be very soft, wistful, tender—

"And Jet Norcross, dirty dog that he is, wants her along with everything else!"

He drew a certain satisfaction from reflecting that Norcross had a man-sized job on his hands in that direction. That girl, now, wasn't to drop into the first man's hands like a ripe peach. Yet it remained that Norcross, as Glennister knew him, was a persistent and resourceful devil; and that women had made much of him. So from grim satisfaction Glennister passed into the frowning uncertainty.

Glennister shrugged. The slight lifting of his shoulder sent a twinge of pain through his side. His thoughts, withdrawn from all minor considerations and side-issues, concentrated upon business. Just now he could consider himself besieged; well, that was all right. He had need of a bit of quiet while his wound healed, and its soreness and stiffness departed. His stronghold was of the sturdiest, walled like a mediaeval fortress, with shutters of thick, ax-hewn planks. Ample provisions for a day or two with more due to arrive to-day; a cask of water in the kitchen and more to be had at the spring at the rear in case of necessity.

All very well, but before an hour had passed he began to grow restless. He got up and went to the old piano, banging out a few chords. In the great hush of the empty house the notes sounded painfully loud. He quitted the piano and made a tour of the rooms, visiting every nook and corner, looking to the fastening at each door and window. What a queer old house it was! Long hallways, dusky, with the shutters closed; a step up from hall to bedroom; a sharp angle here, another step there. From the room he had occupied last night he went through the little ante-room or small hall and on into Dan Jennifer's room. He paused here, pondering. What had the old fellow been poking about for in the dead of night? Just a cup of water? He had been mighty stealthy for that, stepping so quietly in his bare feet, yet going so urgently on his business. Glennister regretted that he had not crept out of bed and followed him.

He came on back to the living room at last, down three short steps from what he termed a "den" and what the Hathaways spoke of as the grizzly room; there was a big bear rug, home-tanned on the plank floor. Here, as in so many parts of the rambling house, were cupboards innumerable; one given over entirely to guns, for the most part looking to be of the days of the spinning wheel. Most of them were filled with books; Glennister took down a number at random, glancing at them curiously. No really up-to-date volumes; many printed in London previous to 1850 and with "Richard Hathaway" written in a copper-plate hand on the fly-leaves. Everything from stock raising in Australia to diamond mines in Africa, and the old poets.

"The girl has a decent ancestry," he judged.

In the late afternoon the creak and rattle of an approaching wagon made music in his ears. Solitude had hung heavy on him; forced inactivity made him feverishly eager to be stirring, to have something, anything, happen. As he went to the door it was expecting to see the old man and the girl returning for a second load. Then he remembered the order for provisions he had placed with the forty-mile distant storekeeper after dealing with Andrew. Here came his supplies: flour, sugar, bread, butter, tinned milk, coffee, bacon, ham, tobacco; matches and ammunition; a jumble of canned goods. Glennister, watching all this come on, grinned his satisfaction. In a state of siege it was a most comfortable thing to have such an addition to one's larder.

The man who brought him this delectable cargo, one Ab Applegate, turned out to be an individual of superlatives: very short, very fat, very red and very talkative. Also, very inquisitive. His eyes were bright and blue and fairly popping with curiosity.

"Pile off and come in," called Glennister. "A word with you before we start unloading."

Ab Applegate left his horses standing with drooping heads and made haste to accept the invitation. His eyes took in every detail of this stranger's appearance, then went roving hastily, prying into corners, probing at closed doors.

"You're Jim Glennister. Well, I've heard a lot of you."

"You're apt to hear a lot more before I move on," said Glennister dryly.

"I better put the horses up first—"

"You'd better listen to a couple of words, my friend. I've got nothing against you that I know. So here's a tip: There's some gent out in the woods taking a pot shot at me every half chance he gets. In case you happened to stop a bullet meant for me I wouldn't have you blaming me for it."

Applegate regarded him with most interested eyes. Yet there was no flicker of surprise in them. He even nodded through the whole explanation.

"I know. Thought I might get here in time to give you the tip. I was to bring you a message, saying you could look out for that."

"A message? To me?" Glennister's brows shot up sharply. "Who sent me any message, and what was it?"

"Jet Norcross sent it," said Applegate. "Know him, don't you?"

"I thought I did," said Glennister eyeing the messenger strangely. "You make me wonder!"

"Saw him out at the store early this morning—"

"Forty miles from here?" Glennister snapped at him. "This morning?"

"That's it. Early. Before I started."

"Look here, Baby Blue-eyes," said Glennister, curt now and plainly suspicious, "I don't want to get you down wrong at the beginning. You may be telling the truth and you may be lying like a horse thief—and I want to know!"

Applegate opened his eyes still wider.

"Lying? Why should I lie about a thing like that?" he demanded.

"Let's have the message."

"Easy. Short and sweet. Norcross was at the store and saw me getting ready to come out here.

'When you see Jim Glennister,' he says, 'tell him I said he better keep his eye peeled. A man we both know and that Jim had trouble with before, out in Nevada, has followed him into this neck of the woods and has sworn to pop him off the first show he gets.' That was the message, Mr. Glennister."

"Anyone else see Norcross out at the store? Or just you?"

"Why sure there was others. Bill Connors, he's the storekeeper you know, was talking with him. So was Mrs. Connors. So was Jet's girl, Judy."

"Just Norcross and his girl, eh? No one else in their party?"

"Two more," said Applegate. "Injuns. I know 'em both, named Starbuck and Modoc."

"And they were forty miles from here this morning—when somebody took a shot at me?" grunted Glennister. "Who did the shooting, then?"

"The guy that Norcross said to look out for, of course," returned Applegate. "That's easy. See anything else likely?"

"I see a nice little alibi for Jet Norcross!—I came pretty close to calling you a liar just now; I'll take it all back. Thinking it over, I'm not even surprised any longer. And I'll bet that Norcross let out what his next plans were? Where he was going?"

"He did. Off to Eureka, the four of 'em. They were arranging to leave their horses there and take Connors' Ford out of the mountains."

"Some more alibi," said Glennister, with a little

grunt of contempt. "There'll be plenty to see them go out, and none to see them come back."

The fat, rosy-faced man was far too alert to miss the point.

"You and Norcross are after the same thing?" he inquired, his head tipped to the side in the frankest curiosity. "The Hathaway gold?"

Glennister laughed at him and gave him for answer:

"If I were you I'd be careful how I went poking around outside, that's all. Whoever is doing the shooting is doing it from a safe distance and he might make a mistake—By the way, is Norcross much of a friend of yours?"

"Not in particular," said Applegate.

"Know much about him?"

"Good deal."

"He has a good many friends among the Indians? Such as Starbuck and Modoc?"

"Sure. Squaw man, once, you know. His kid girl—well, her dam was a full-blooded sister to Modoc and Starbuck, they say."

"The Indians pretty fair shots?"

"Better'n fair, most of 'em. They live on deer and bear meat, in and out of season."

"Ought to be able to bring a man down from the edge of the forest yonder?"

"So that's what you mean? That Norcross left a pet Injun behind to do for you?"

"What I mean is this: It's too far for you to go

back to-day, so we'll bring in the boxes and cook a dinner. Then we'll have a friendly game of cards—"

"Not on your life," exclaimed the other, both hands up. "Not for money, anyways. I've heard of you, Jim Glennister."

Glennister laughed again and went for his rifle. "Come ahead; let's get the wagon unloaded."

"And take a chance, huh? On drawing a shot?"

"Tell me the truth," chuckled Glennister. "You wouldn't mind knowing yourself if he's still out there, would you?"

"And to find out you got to offer him a target? All right; come ahead. Only, this being your party, you go first," and Applegate showed how spry he could be upon his feet by galloping like a playful baby elephant to a place just behind Glennister.

They went out into the yard where the wagon was, partially screened by the wagon itself from the edge of the woods. Applegate appeared brighter-eyed than ever, glancing expectantly in all directions.

"Nobody there," he whispered, not for any fear of being overheard but because some tense quality of the moment commanded. "Quiet as a chur—"

The bullet which corrected his mistake and cut off his words passed with its petty scream of rage between him and Glennister; and since the two men stood scarcely more than a yard apart, it was as close as Ab Applegate had any wish to have it. He went down to his hands and knees behind the wagon so swiftly and silently that at first Glennister thought he had been shot through the head.

This time Glennister saw a little puff of smoke. It rose and idled away upon the quiet afternoon air. He jerked up his rifle and began drilling holes in the ferny undergrowth, firing as fast as he could work the trigger. When he had done, as was told by the little metallic click when the last cartridge was exploded, Applegate reared up and demanded, still in that whispered voice:

"Got him?" And when Glennister did not answer, he insisted: "Got him? Must of; he didn't shoot more'n once, did he?"

"Want to go out and see?"

"I'd like to, honest I would." Applegate scratched his head and then shook it reluctantly. "I'd never rest happy until I knowed if you did get him and who it was. But I guess I'll wait."

Glennister ducked by him, running into the house for fresh ammunition. At his heels came Applegate, slamming the door shut. Like an angry bee pursuing him came a second bullet; its impact was lost in the slamming of the door but they had visible demonstration made by the flying splinters. Applegate dodged, as a man must, after the thing was over. Then slowly a look of satisfaction dawned in his blue eyes. His uncertainty was over; his curiosity satisfied.

"You missed him. Didn't get him at all," he cried out.

"Well? You look tickled to pieces over it," growled Glennister.

"Man! I just wanted to know!"

They heard the wagon creaking; there was a thud of trotting hoofs. Applegate ran to a window, peering out with one eye.

"A runaway," shouted Glennister; "my provisions going all to smash!"

But Applegate turned a contented grin upon him.

"Watch 'em! They been here before, old Jolly and Jingo. They're off to the barn; just scared enough to wake up and hit for the manger. And that's good; one of 'em might have got hit, that gent shooting wild like this. Let 'em be, I say. We'll go out after dark and drag the grub in."

Glennister, though he went to the window, did not concern himself with the cleverness of old Jolly and Jingo. Instead, locating the spot from which the little puff of smoke had risen, he treated himself to the sole possible luxury of pouring another half-a-dozen shots into it.

There came no response from the forest.

"Got him?" Again Applegate was all burning curiosity, like a child. His chubby face actually puckered as he turned it up; it was almost as though he were saying in so many words: "What did you go and do that for? You're the hell of a man. Just as I found out, you went and got me guessing again."

Glennister, frowning down at him abstractedly, could not long be impervious to the appeal of a face like that. His lips twitched, his frown fled, he began to laugh. He put his rifle down and went back to his chair.

In the dusk, their appetites prompting—and perhaps Ab Applegate's lively curiosity having its finger in the pie—they went out to the barn. The wide double doors stood open; horses and wagon were safely inside. While Applegate busied himself with unhitching and then feeding, having brought grain with him, Glennister got the various boxes and bags down. Without adventure they soon transferred the entire load to the house.

Applegate made himself very much at home. Standing among the litter of comestibles, his round eyes darting from package to package, investigating and approving, he rolled up his sleeves.

"I like to cook and I'm good at it," he confided. He got a fire going and began making his selections. "By the way," he demanded, "where's the folks? Andrew's beat it, I know that. But the old man and the girl?"

"Gone," said Glennister.

"Oh," said Applegate. He went to the table with an armful of bundles, set them down and asked: "Where?"

"Away," said Glennister.

"Oh." He scratched his head, sighed, looked reproachfully at his host and sighed again. But there was a look of determination, almost of stubbornness upon his round face. He but postponed the moment; he'd have to come at his quest later on from some new angle.

Meanwhile he was so far from idle that in twenty minutes Glennister was invited to sit down to a sizzling hot and invitingly savory meal. Applegate had spoken truthfully; he was a good cook.

"Want a job, Applegate?" asked Glennister at the end of the meal. "Steady?"

"Doing what, Mr. Glennister? Playing target?"

"Cooking, general housekeeping and chores."

"*And* being shot at? A man would have to charge extra for that."

"*And* finding things out," laughed Glennister. "A lot of things. To a man of your inquiring mind, life out here should afford certain mild interests."

He might laugh, but the chubby face confronting him was very earnest and sober.

"Wonder if you got him that last time? He's been mighty quiet since—"

"You see!" Glennister grinned at him. "You'd be taking chances if you stay on with me, but think of all the things you'd be in line to find out! Where

Norcross went and why, and when he is coming back and where he'll hide himself and who it is left behind to pop me over, and where Dan Jennifer and the girl went and if there really is any Hathaway gold and where it is and who is going to get it and—"

That earnest eager face seemed to brighten with every word Glennister spoke.

"I—I'll stick a day or two, any way," said Applegate, quickly, as though afraid the offer might be withdrawn. "Until we find out for sure if you got him—"

"And who he is and how many he's got with him—"

"I—I don't know, Mr. Glennister. I—" He pulled out his short black pipe and filled it thoughtfully. "It's risky business, I can see that. I've heard of you, you see; and I know a thing or two about Jet Norcross—and I've come pretty close to being shot twice already since I got here!"

His eyes were roving all the while but now stopped suddenly and grew, if possible, more prominent. On the shelf across the kitchen was the bit of quartz which Norcross had left behind. Applegate saw it clearly by the light of their little fire. He got up and went for it; he weighed it in his hand and scratched at it with a cracked finger-nail.

"Holy Moses!" he gasped. "Where'd that come

from? Hathaway gold? There is a mine here then? The old yarn's true? You've found it?"

Glennister burst into rollicking laughter. Applegate actually began to blush.

"As to wages, now," said Glennister.

IN THE NIGHT   *CHAPTER VIII*

A FEW days of this sort of thing—living cooped up within the four walls of a house—went a long way with Jim Glennister. Now, with his wound behaving nicely and giving him less and less annoyance, he meant to be stirring.

"I'm going out to-night," he told Applegate while the latter was washing the evening dishes and whistling one of those ancient, doleful ditties which he so favored at moments of well-fed contentment. "And I don't expect to be back much before daylight."

"Where are you going?" Applegate perked up immediately. "What are you going to do? What's the idea of being out all night?"

"And," continued Glennister, quite as though Applegate had remained silent, "you'd better lock up tight and sleep with the old shot-gun handy. And don't open up to anybody until you've made sure you're opening to me."

Applegate's interest knew no bounds as he watched his employer's preparations. What a pack that was for a man to carry on a one night's jaunt! Ammunition, tobacco and matches, conveniently pocketed; a couple of heavy blankets in a tight roll, and inside provisions to last a good trencherman a week.

"Sure you're ever coming back?" gasped Applegate.

"Not sure but hopeful," laughed Glennister. He had been taciturn and grim all day long, but now his spirits were winging. One knee upon the bundle which he was roping, he glanced up in rich enjoyment of the look he had succeeded in bringing to the eyes glued upon him. "By the way, my dear Abner Applegate, to play square with you I'll tell you a secret. On the mantelpiece in the big room is a stack of books. In the second book from the bottom of the stack there are a couple of bank-notes. In case I shouldn't get back, they're yours. They'll pay you for your strenuous labors since you've been here."

"I'd sort of like to come along, Mr. Glennister. I'd carry the shot-gun; a shot-gun's worth a dozen rifles in the dark. Buck shot, you know."

"Can't be done this trip. You're to hold the fort and be ready to raise the portcullis when I sing out." He took up his pack and rifle and went through the house to a side door, Applegate bearing a candle and following close at his heels. "Shut and bar the door as soon as I'm out. And now—good-night."

He slipped out quietly. There was no moon, but

the night was bright with stars, the sky clear. He heard the bar dropped into place; then after some minutes, Applegate's heavy tread going back to the front of the house. Still Glennister did not move, but stood close to the wall. It was dark here; he had chosen this exit because of the big apple tree shadowing the wall and part of the garden here.

He hitched up his pack so that one shoulder through the rope carried the weight and left both hands free. There was the garden with its few old trees and a sagging trellis or two; his eyes probed into every shadow-filled spot. A dozen men might lurk here, unseen. They'd look for him to come out sooner or later; and at night, too.

So Glennister, when at last he stirred, moved warily, very warily. Where the forlorn garden ended, the orchard proper began. He did not stop again until he stood under the last of the fruit trees. He looked back upon the dark mass of the house; a shower of sparks from the big rock chimney swirled upward, sparks among the stars. He looked forward; yonder, as black as ebony, stretched the forest. But, between him and its shelter, extended the wide clearing. He stood calculating, balancing chance and mischance.

He looked down toward Wild River. The spring which rose at the back of the house and formed a meandering little creek, gurgling down to a junction with the larger stream, was fringed with willows. Glennister could have wished them taller, thicker, with fewer open spaces between their clumps. Yet they invited; they pointed the way he should go. Down to the river, then upstream. So he turned back into the orchard until he came to the creek.

Ten minutes later he was on the bank of Wild River. Its wild uproarious voices were in his ears; its spray showered him with diamonds. Here among tall ferns the fragrance of the rich, damp soil rose about him. The trees stood higher here, broader branched against the glitter of stars. Progress onward from here should be fairly simple and reasonably safe. Even his tread made no sound above the shouting of Wild River.

He held close to the stream until he had traveled a high mile into the hills. He was done with the clearing now, passing like a shadow into the heart of the very domain of shadows. Woodsy fragrances came and went in gentle puffs; there was no wind but the soft air was restless—like himself. He had stepped from a summer night into a night of late spring. Faint, vague perfumes rose from herbs trodden underfoot. Flowers bloomed on here long after their gentle sisters had seeded under the ardent sun. The earth was moist, fruitful. Now and then the thickly leafed branches overhead shut out the stars, only a dim, wan glow lessening while not dissipating the gloom. He slipped deeper into the forest. He went more swiftly now; with less stealth and more assurance. At any moment he might run into one of the Norcross party; he counted all along of having to do with more than one man. Yet he had now what Jim Glennister called an even break. His eyes in the dark of the forest were as good as any other man's; so were his ears. And if it came to half-blind shooting, odds were even. They could know no more of his presence here than he knew of theirs.

Yet he remained tense and watchful; a score of times, hearing a sound not of his own making, he came to a dead halt to peer about and listen, rifle raised. The woods were full of life; there were rustlings in the branches above him, odd scratching sounds against the bark, heavier treads breaking dead sticks, wee noises that were scarcely more than whisperings against the stillness. There were all about him the forest creatures who slept with an open eye; and those who hunted in the dark, all but noiseless on soft pads.

From seeking out the thick of the wood he soon came to turning into the more open places where he not only made better speed but less noise, keeping clear of underbrush all that he could. Even so he could make only a blundering sort of progress, having no such intimate knowledge of the lay of the land as to aid him in this expedition. And he was hard beset to do what he had set out to do; to keep so exactly his sense of direction as to come straight upon his first objective: that spot at the edge of the forest from which some gentleman had fired down upon the house. To have walked straight to the place by daylight would have required perhaps ten or fifteen minutes; to come at it as Glennister attempted now, by going out of his way first, up the river, then turning into the forest and beating back, breaking his trail into a series of angling lines, was the matter of a couple of hours.

But when at last he drew near the spot there was no mistaking it. He had marked it too well for that, before starting. From the thickly timbered mountain slope a low ridge thrust well forward to the open fields, broken down abruptly at the end, blunt-nosed, like a promontory cut off by the wash of old ocean. A grouping of big pines crowned it; there were large bowlders under the pines; a straggling smaller growth ran down the sides of this higher land to a gully on each side. A very logical spot to serve the purposes of a sharpshooter; from here one had a wide view whence he could watch any attempt at approach from in front. So long as he kept his enemy in front it should be for the hidden marksman a rather pleasant and secure occupation. But now Glennister, having gone to considerable pains, came to it cautiously from the rear.

In other words, from the mountain slope back and above, and through the taller timber, he came down toward the blunt nose of the ridge. He rid himself of his roll now, hiding it behind a tree trunk in a patch of brush; there might be no one here to welcome him and yet it remained that there might be the warmest of all possible welcomes awaiting him.

Again he proceeded slowly and with infinite caution. At every quiet step he stopped and listened. He made a zigzag approach, stepping from tree to tree, pausing, peering out in all directions. At the slightest sound—

There, suddenly, was a sound crashing out to make him whip back, leaping to one side, pressed up against a big pine, his rifle at his shoulder, all in one instant. Enough racket for a dozen men, a wild flurry of commotion, a breaking headlong through a thicket—

Glennister lowered his rifle with a grunt, then laughed softly. With the rest of the din had come a low *"woof!"* to tell him a very great deal. He had disturbed a bear, startling the animal into wild flight. From the sounds coming back to him, snapping undergrowth, rolling stones, dead limbs breaking, it was amply clear that Sir Bruin meant to be far from here ten minutes hence.

When Glennister went forward again it was in full confidence that now he had the ridge to himself; the ambush was deserted, as he had supposed it would be; the bear's presence here told him that. He even made himself a cigarette and puffed at it complacently. He could not have asked a better watch-dog.

So in a few steps he came to the spot where his assailant had lain all day in watch for him. There was little difficulty, even at night, in discovering the exact spot where the fellow had made himself comfortable. At the base of the pines, among the bowlders which stood up to a man's height, was a small rudely-circular area thick with its mat of fallen pine needles. Glennister, looking out across the lower lands, saw the dark blot of the old house and its trees, even made out a spark now and then flying skyward from the chimney. Ab Applegate would be sitting up, listening to all the little night noises, waiting and wondering. Chiefly wondering.

Glennister went down on his hands and knees, groping about. He was not long in coming upon an exploded brass cartridge; had he needed assurance that he was at the right spot he had it now. He found further some scraps of food, a bit of meat that had been flung aside as being too fat for the marksman's taste. Doubtless the bear had sniffed these fragments and had been about to satisfy a natural curiosity.

Striking a second match, holding it cupped in his hand and close to the ground, Glennister sought further signs. Finding nothing more to interest him he looked at his watch. He had been out for nearly two hours and a half. He stood up, finished his smoke, pocketed the dead stub and went back for his roll.

He had learned something; not a great deal, yet something. And every little scrap of knowledge might come to be of value. He knew that someone had spent the day here; had come early in the morning prepared and provisioned for a day of it; had gone away again, no doubt as it grew dark. He would have approached this spot as Glennister had done, from the woods, along the crest of the ridge. He would have gone away along the same track, back to the forest. If he returned to-morrow, it would be just before day and over the same ground.

So much for exact knowledge and logical surmise; after these mere speculation. The man might not come back here at all; in all likelihood he would prefer to play safe by shifting his base of operations. In any case, it was no part of Glennister's plan to squat here all night; at least not to-night. With his roll on his back he struck into the woods again. And now he sought out the old wagon track and the trail which he had followed from the redwoods when first he came to the Hathaway home.

Once, at a spot which he marked well, making sure that he would have no difficulty in coming again to it by day or night, he stepped aside into a tangle of dense shrubbery and disposed of his roll. Well-hidden against any casual eyes excepting those of the wild folk, there he meant it to remain until he might have use for it. Then, swinging along the more freely, he struck out in the general direction of a certain well-remembered pool under the redwoods.

He found the pool only after so long a search up and down, back and forth in the dark, that he was beginning to doubt that he could ever come at it by night. It was the gentle splash of the waterfall which finally led him to it. Dark and still, it mirrored a single star whose rays penetrated the lofty screen of branches separating earth and sky; and even as his eyes caught the sparkle and flash, the single reflected star vanished.

The cabin was near; so much and no more he knew. He stood looking in all directions and on every hand saw only the black mass of the forest. He listened, hoping to catch the sound of voices. Unlikely that, he realized. Far more likely that by now both those whom he came to visit were asleep. Yet, listening, he peered all about him, hoping to catch a glint of light. Light? When they had neither candle nor lamp?

Just then a light winked out at him, made a small intense glare and, like the star drowned in the ghostly pool, was gone. He moved slowly forward. He had no doubt glimpsed a light in the cabin, a candle after all, perhaps, carried by an open door or window. It remained possible that here was Norcross or one of his party. So he went silently and watchfully.

He could have put out a hand and touched the

log wall before he made out with his eyes the dark outline of the cabin. All was dark within. He listened; there was not a sound. He groped his way to a door and rapped.

"Who is it?" came a startled voice.

"It's Glennister. I came for the first of our little talks."

"It's so late—"

"I couldn't help that. It seemed healthier for me to do my knocking about after dark."

He had silence for his answer.

"Will you let me in?" he asked impatiently. And, when still an answer was slow in coming, "A bargain is a bargain, you know."

"Wait a minute.—Yes, I'll let you in."

He could hear her moving about now. Presently the faint scratch of a match, a dim glow through a chink, a brighter gleaming light. A heavy bar was lifted; the door opened.

Glennister, from his place at one side the door, entered swiftly and closed the door behind him. His eyes, dark and keen, went flashing about the room. The girl stood before him, a lamp in her hand. The chamber was small with a closed door at the further end. Her tumbled bunk was at one side under a small, open window; there was a similar window which also stood wide open, at the other side of the room.

"By your leave," said Glennister. He dropped the bar back into its place and stepped quickly to one window after the other; there were heavy plank shutters like those at the old home, and he closed both. Then he took time to look at her more particularly. He was ready to smile. She was very grave. He added lightly: "I never did fancy being in the full light inside, giving the other fellow a chance to hang around in the dark and blaze away at me."

Her eyes were not in the least friendly. From being utterly incommunicative they appeared now merely to express a somewhat contemptuous suspicion that he had allowed himself to develop a case of nerves.

"If you are thinking of Mr. Norcross," she said in a voice as aloof as her eyes, "he has gone."

"So you know, I wonder how?"

"We have been outside, Danny and I. We just got back."

"I didn't see or hear you pass."

"We did not go by the house. There is another old road."

"Longer and rougher, maybe? But more to your taste since it did not bring you my way?"

For a little country girl who could not have seen much of the world, thought Glennister, she had a world of poise. She could look at a man as though she were gazing abstractedly into space.

"You came to ask me something?" she said steadily.

"Shall we sit down? Do you mind if I smoke?"

She affected a mild, very natural and indifferent surprise.

"Is it necessary to ask my permission for either? The other day it didn't seem so."

He knew what she meant. He had been willfully rude to her and she had given him not the faintest hint that she even knew rudeness when it was offered her. But she had known and had treasured it up against him.

"Oh, that," he said carelessly. Then he laughed softly. "Circumstances alter cases, Miss Hathaway. We were in my house then; we're in yours now. A man in his own castle has the right to be as great a roughneck as he has the hankering for. You'll note that here, with you my hostess, I even call you Miss Hathaway."

He stepped by her and dragged a bench forward. And then he made her his profound, mocking bow.

"Will you be seated?"

There was but the one bench in the room. So she drew back and sat on the edge of her bunk. Glennister sat on the bench.

"I assure you I'll not smoke without your permission."

"Oh, do as you please! I—What do you wish with me, Mr. Glennister?"

"Thanks." He rolled his cigarette swiftly; his head was down for an instant and when he lifted it his eyes twinkled into hers. "I came, as I have already intimated, to ask you a question or two."

"Yes. What are they?"

Before answering he again took stock of the little room and its contents. There were parcels everywhere.

"Evidently you intend to continue a neighbor," he offered lightly. "I see you've been laying in a stock of provisions. So have I. Also, I note that you've been buying pretty dresses. I'll bet you've been trying them all on!"

The little dress she wore now, very simple yet very gay, and most becoming, was clearly as new a possession as her silk stockings and black pumps. Had her mood been different, could he have coaxed the flash and sparkle into her sober eyes, she would have been most adorably alluring; one knew that she was stubbornly drawing a sheath over a natural vivacity.

"Your questions, Mr. Glennister?"

"Why the haste? I've been consumed with boredom. Won't you be—just neighborly?"

"We'd never be that, I think. And it is late—"

"Oh, all right. Question number one: Where did you buy the gowns? Hardly at Bill Connors' dinky store!"

He could not know how tense she was inwardly all the while; how she had been expecting and dreading his call; how, to her, his very coming was an adventure; how hard it was for her to match his cool assurance. Now, at last he struck a spark which she could not keep hidden; her cheeks flushed up hotly.

"I'll answer any question that—"

"That I ask! Even though you don't see its immediate bearing. First off, still on the trail of a pretty lady's personal purchases, you've been as far as Eureka, haven't you?"

"Yes! But—"

"Just to buy clothes? Or to see good brother Andrew?"

She bit her lip which, when she slowly relinquished it, was scarlet.

"I didn't sell you my soul—nor all my own thoughts—nor the right to interfere—"

"Granted. But remember that we agreed on our price, and at a time when I might have charged you your whole five hundred dollars. What thanks am I getting for my generosity?"

"Generosity! I'd rather it had been the five hundred—"

"All right." He put out his hand. "Give me the five hundred and we'll call it square."

"You—you know it's impossible now. I'll give you all I have left; gladly. And—"

He laughed in the rarest good humor.

"The original bargain has to stand then. I go on with my questions. By the way, where's Jennifer?"

She glanced toward the closed door at the end of the room.

"Asleep. We've had a hard day, getting home late."

"Fair enough. I can talk with you to-night, with him at a later date."

"It was understood between us, I think," she reminded him, "that whatever help you thought you could have from me was to be given during one week. That was four days ago—"

A sudden frown gathered his brows and made his eyes night black.

"You're against me!" he said sharply. "You'd keep to the letter of the contract and the devil take any spirit of fair play. What have I done to make you want to see me lose out? Teased you a bit, maybe; but that's your fault; you inspire it somehow. What's happened? You haven't thrown in with Norcross, have you?"

"I told you that Mr. Norcross has gone."

"You saw him outside?"

"Yes." There was a hint of defiance in the curt answer.

"In Eureka?"

"Yes."

"And both of you saw Andrew there?"

"Yes."

"Well, what about it all? What's up? What sort of conspiracy have you three entered into? Have I got to dig it out of you word by word?"

"I've not refused to answer your questions," she shot back at him.

"Yes, you've answered grudgingly. Precious little help I am to get, eh, unless I force you to it?"

"Force?" She saw that she had angered him and experienced an odd thrill of satisfaction. It was always he who piqued her, himself remaining cool and—masterful. It was that sense of mastery which all along heated her blood. She found it positively delicious now to have matters reversed. So she half smiled and appeared only amused. Again he might not know of her inner tenseness—with a flicker of fear in it.

"Yes. Force." She actually heard the click of his teeth as he angrily bit the word short off.

She shrugged.

"Is there anything else, Mr. Glennister?" she queried.

"A whole lot more. First off, are you the sort to go back on a deal? To break your word to follow an advantage? I suppose so; I am inclined to think that most women are."

"I'm not surprised; I'd think that the kind of women you would know—"

"What kind are you? The sort to keep faith, or the double-crossing variety—like the others I know?"

"I'll keep my promise. To the letter, as you said."

He sat back, clasped his hands about a lifted knee and drilled at her with the steadiest, keenest eyes she had ever seen.

"You saw Andrew. Merely socially or upon any kind of business in any way, even remotely, connected with the place here?"

What little advantage she had felt to have was gone in a flash. She hesitated before answering and in her hesitation, brief though it was, saw how the hint of a sneer touched his lips.

"I did have a business understanding with Andrew," she blurted out. "It was that in case you failed to make your payments, I arranged with my brother to have an option myself!"

"Whew!" He stared; first incredulous, then vastly puzzled. "You? Then, by glory," he burst out, "you and old Jennifer have already put things together? You already think you know where the gold is?"

"No. I have no more idea where it is now that I ever had."

"You think you can find it though?"

"I hope that I can. I am going to try."

"And should you succeed, you'd hardly come rushing to me with the glad tidings!"

"I shall hardly hope to find it within the next three days," she told him.

"And after that, you're free! Free to make it a three-cornered scrap!"

He settled back to stare at her again.

"Let me see. This determination on your part to get in the game came late—and then with a rush. It took you all the way out to Eureka. I wonder what caused it? It began, didn't it, with the break Norcross made? When he showed you his gold?"

The question was too direct to allow of evasion. So she said: "Yes."

"You naturally talked the whole thing out with Jennifer?"

"Yes."

"You went into the fact that Norcross stated definitely when he made his find?"

"Yes."

"Confound it!" cried Glennister. "You'd evade if you could and as you can't, you must just say yes and no. A lot of help I am getting."

"I promised only to answer. I didn't promise to help beyond that."

"Did you see Norcross in Eureka?"

"No."

"How do you know that he was there?"

"Andrew told me."

"What did Norcross want with Andrew? To make sure he got the place if I defaulted?"

"Yes."

She nettled him with that cool "yes" of hers. And she knew it and took joy from the fact.

"You were to be decent to me; that was in the bargain. Is this what you call being decent to a fellow?" he demanded.

"Yes."

He was on his feet in a flash now. She, too, sprang up, terrified. For, from the look blazing in his eyes, she thought that in another second she was going to experience the feel of his hands on her.

"Am I to have all my plans knocked into a cocked hat just because you've got some crazy idea that you can cut in on this thing? You, a little goose of a country kid, buying chips in a game where two men like Jet Norcross and me have got our knives out for each other! You'd make me laugh—if you didn't make me so confounded mad that I'd like to shake you."

She made no reply, for simple enough reasons. First, he took her breath away and she could think of nothing to say. And when she did begin to breathe again and marked how he stared at her and waited for her to say something, she understood instinctively that silence was the most cutting weapon she could use with him.

"I've a notion," he resumed when it was clear that she had nothing to say, "that I can come at what I want to know through you. Maybe you don't know where the gold is; but something has stirred you up over it. If I had a bit more time to corkscrew away at what you're thinking and have been thinking, I'd get at it. . . . You're working on what Norcross blabbed; that Jennifer showed the way and that it was six months ago. I'm right there, eh?" he concluded triumphantly.

As before she said merely "Yes."

But then, when he kept on staring at her as though he would drive the penetration of those dark eyes of his down to the bottom of her knowledge and speculation, she added emphatically:

"And after three days I shall answer no questions of any kind."

Glennister sat down, stretched his legs out in front of him, a gesture she remembered—and resented—and made his second cigarette. She flashed a sidelong look at him; seeing that he appeared deeply interested in the floor, she studied him curiously. He looked cool again, very thoughtful and very determined.

"I sat into this game," he said without looking up, almost like a man communing with himself alone, "to beat Jet Norcross to a big stake. I'm going to do it. You're going to help me. Somehow, between you and Jennifer, you've found a stimulus to go ahead. Given time you hope to come at what we all want to know. You and Jennifer—you and Jennifer—"

He looked up at her at last; not in the least as a man should look at a girl but as one may regard some sort of a puzzle.

"You two talked over what Norcross said and all that it implied. Six months ago—Jennifer showing the way. Then you would have said, 'Let's think; let's remember all that happened six months ago.' Am I right?"

She could only answer "Yes."

He nodded and labored away on his puzzle.

"Of course you two put your heads together. You said that if Norcross followed Jennifer's lead to the gold, why then you had but to remember between you just what Jennifer was about at that time. That would be the logical thing. Yet girls are never logical, they say! Well, let's find out, feeling our way along. How about it. Am I right again?"

"Yes," she cried out. "Yes. Go on. What else?"

"You recalled seeing Norcross six months ago?"

"Yes."

"A few moments only? A whole day?"

"Several days. Ten days or two weeks. He was our house guest."

"Fine. Now, to remember backward over half a year and recall each day over a period of a couple of weeks, every remark and every step taken and every look—quite a job, eh? Still you and Jennifer have gone into all that?"

"We reasoned as you do," she said. "We started to go into all that, as you say. But—we stopped. We haven't mentioned it in four days. And—"

"And—?"

"And," she flung at him in full defiance now, "we'll not mention it again in another three days; you may be sure of that, Mr. Glennister! Not until after the week of our bargain is up."

"I've always remarked that the feminine brain is mechanically beautifully adapted to splitting hairs," observed Glennister. "At this juncture I'd like very much to talk with a man. Sorry as I am to disturb Jennifer's slumbers, I must have a word with him. For, despite your assurance that friend Norcross has gone, you may take it from me that he's back and making somewhat difficult just at present such little trips out as I am making this evening. I can't be dropping in on you every hour of the day, so while I'm here we'll learn what we can."

"Danny is tired out," she expostulated. "It was a long hard trip, we got back very late and—"

"I'm sorry," he said dryly, and rapped at the closed door. When there came no answer he impatiently flung the door open, calling, "Jennifer!"

Still no answer. The lamplight flooded this other small room. A bench, a table; a bunk against the far wall—empty. The covers were thrown back; perhaps Jennifer had gone to bed, but if so he was up again and gone.

Glennister closed the door again and turned a pair of very suspicious eyes upon his unwilling hostess.

"I—I didn't know," she said, the picture of confusion, and confusion may be most readily associated with guilt. "He—he said good-night more than an hour ago. He must have gone out—"

"He must have gone out," Glennister jeered at her.

"But he did not come this way! I did not know. There is the other door, from his room outside—"

"You did not know? You would not have heard him? Or you did not want me to know that you were alone? Afraid of me? Afraid to deny me entrance for fear I'd come in anyway? Afraid, once I was in, to have me know you were defenseless?"

"I did not know," she repeated.

He took up his rifle and clapped on his hat.

"I'm going. And I'm not coming again."

Sudden relief shone in her eyes. He smiled grimly.

"But you're coming to see me. Both you and Dan Jennifer. Come down to the house—my house—tomorrow, prepared not to stay three days only but thirty. A full month. You are to be my most welcome guests for a full, solid month!"

"Good-night, Mr. Glennister," she said angrily.

"Be sure you come. Why? Because your heart, all the heart God gave you, is in that old home. Because if you fail to show up before noon I swear I'll carve my mark on everything in the place. I'll show you, my little miss, just what vandalism can be. Try to play fast and loose with me, would you? Try to beat me out at my own game, eh? Try to cook up a lot of silly schemes with old Jennifer, would you?"

"I won't come. Nothing on earth could make me."

"You'll show up before noon—to visit me a full month. I'll force you to it—remember we spoke of force, Miss Dryad? I'll force you to it, working on your love for your home and your fear of what I might do. I'll force you, by offering you a proposition you can't find any way to refuse: At the end of the month—here's the bribe part," he sneered, "I'll give you my interest in the house and every cursed thing in it. Stay away—and to hell with the house! What do I care for the crazy old barn, anyway? Stay away, and I'll make a fine mess of all the Hathaway junk I can hammer out of shape and get going in the fireplaces. I don't care the snap of my fingers for the house or its furnishings and heirlooms; I don't care a snap for the whole damned ranch! I'm after the gold—and Jet Norcross' scalp—and there's no pretty little girl this side the stars who's going to head me off. No matter how sweet she makes herself in her nice new dresses and silk stockings!"

"I—I'd never come—"

"You'll come; you'll stay thirty days; you'll wash dishes and sweep and make beds. You'll cry first, say ten minutes, when I'm gone. You'll swear to go help Norcross break me. You'll storm about. Then you'll remember my double proposition, half bribe and half threat—and before noon you and Dan Jennifer—who it would seem has the interesting way of poking about when he's supposed to be in bed!—will be knocking at my door, saying: 'Please let us come in, Mr. Glennister.'"

With a sudden gesture he caught up the lamp and puffed out the flame. She cried out in terror—but he had only stepped to the door, opened it with a savage jerk and gone.

GLENNISTER, making his way swiftly through the forest, felt the sudden change in the night. A wind had risen and began piling great clouds above the southern horizon. A ghostly whispering was all about him; tree tops, unseen so were they massed high above him, shook from the impact of the strange air current and shivered as it swept on. A thousand strange noises drove out the serene silence of a moment ago; the creaking of limbs, the snapping of dead branches, a flurry of dry leaves whispering down the wind; sounds not so easily catalogued in the ever-thickening dark. Were one high-strung nervously, prone to uneasiness and apprehension, these were ominous sounds; like moaning voices. In the dance of the trees, objects appeared and disappeared; with the scudding clouds boiling up and racing as though fleeing some fury which drove them, wiping out the stars among which they scurried, what little light there was was full of tricks.

"The devil has decided to make a night of it," muttered Glennister, and hurried on.

There had been no slightest advance warning of any storm; but the mad storm king reserves to himself the right to burst into gusty passion, dispensing with preliminaries. Nor was this the storm season. It was only an unreasonable violence of wind raging with all the relentless fury of midwinter. Where patches of clear sky were left in which the stars still shone the surrounding clouds became somber, grotesquely distorted monsters from which the stars were fleeing. From afar came a low rumble; these monsters were growling. Glennister's coat flapped wildly about him; he buttoned it and bent his head against the wind and pressed on. He was in a little open glade now; it was only in such spots that the wind really reached him. But at every step, even when the thicker forest groupings sheltered the man below, his ears were filled with the voices of the wilderness; voices that whispered and whimpered; that moaned, that menaced and mocked and jeered.

It was well after midnight when he came again to the house. He followed the creek up from the river; the line of willows bent and twisted, writhing into many forms, tossing wild arms. Presently the full force of the storm reached him; he broke into a run, dashing headlong into the orchard. Here he stood for a little while, peering about him. Never a star now; the darkness was so great that it was unlikely that any should see him, even were the orchard thick with men.

He turned toward the house. It was as dark as the rest of the world. He drew nearer, seeking the side door through which he had left. Applegate, no doubt, was long ago asleep; that eager, inquisitive brain of his would be busy with dreams. And, of course, he would have locked every door and window; Glennister hoped the man might prove to be a light sleeper.

He tried the door only casually and with little hope of finding it unfastened, meaning to creep along the wall until he came to Applegate's window. But not only had the door been left unbarred, it even stood ajar. He pushed it wide open, entered swiftly, closed and barred the door after him—and stood listening.

The dark here could have been no greater had a thick black hood been pulled over his head. He was puzzled; why had Applegate left the door open? Further, he experienced a twinge of suspicion; one must ever be on guard against traps and pitfalls when engaged in controversy with Jet Norcross. There had been a faint complaint of old hinges, the slight sound of the door being closed and barred. If trap it were, if there were those within who awaited his return, they knew by now of his entrance. So Glennister stood very still. In this dark all chances were equal. He was in no haste to strike a match.

How the wind raged outside! The heavy log walls resisted it with all the calm of iron cliffs halting old ocean, but the shutters rattled and creaked and clicked in lively din. And, inclosed securely as were the rooms within the sturdy walls, they were unquiet places. In all old empty houses strange sounds make themselves heard; at this hour and upon such a night it was as though floorboards and ancient presses and wardrobes talked among themselves. Once Glennister thought that he heard steps, quick cautious steps, approaching. They resolved themselves, he judged, into the tappings of a loose shutter at the far end of the building. As in the forest there were whisperings, almost uncanny here. There are those who contend that all old houses are haunted houses. It was easy, standing here in the pitch dark, tense and watchful, every sense strained, to imagine all sorts of things.

But Glennister just now did more thinking than imagining. If Norcross or any of his hirelings were here, meaning to ambush him, the great likelihood was that his audible passage through the door would have been the signal for a shot. And it was certain that he could not stand like a statue all night; equally certain that he was of no mind to retreat and make a night of it outside. So he began moving. He felt his way along the wall, nosing the darkness with the end of his rifle. If the muzzle at any moment came in contact with a man's body, Glennister was ready to fire and have his explanations later.

Finding his way thus, even in a smaller and far more familiar house, would have presented diffi-culties. With things as they were, when he had passed through two or three doors, he was fairly lost. He did not know the way to the kitchen, to the living room, to his own bedroom.

"Applegate!" he shouted loudly. And when he had no answer after waiting some seconds, he called again, and louder: "Applegate!"

Still no answer. A heavy sleeper, that man. Or— or perhaps Applegate was not here? The door had stood ajar; it was possible that Applegate had gone out. Where? And why? To strive to satisfy that insatiable curiosity of his? Likely.

At any rate Glennister's calling had brought no attack upon him. He struck a match, holding it at arm's length in his left hand while his right kept his rifle lifted. In the little light there were restless shadows all about him, shadows which like rats seemed to him to scurry to their corners. He was in a bedroom; it was empty save for himself and its furnishings. Glee Hathaway's room, he knew at a glance. Some essence of herself seemed to pervade the place.

The match burned down; he dropped the red ember to the floor, trod it out and went on in the dark. He had his bearings now. When presently he struck the second match he was in the living room. A hasty glance told him that he was alone here. He went to the mantel, lighted a candle; found a box of candles and lighted several. He could do very well just now with a good deal of light. One by one, pausing at each door to listen a moment, he closed them all. And then, carrying a light, he went to find Applegate.

What he found was that Applegate had not even gone to bed and evidently was nowhere in the house. Once more Glennister shouted his name, knowing well enough that he'd have no answer. And again, with his candle this time, he made a tour of the house, looking into every room. In the kitchen he helped himself to bread and cheese; again in the living room, in a big chair drawn into a corner by the fireplace, he sat down. This was growing to be a favorite spot in the house; one could so readily reach out for a rifle standing against the rock chimney; one, while he had his pipe or his sandwich, could keep an eye upon each one of the doors—there were five—leading into the room.

It would seem that he had demonstrated with rather insistent positiveness that, saving for himself, the old house was empty. Yet, sitting there in his corner, his black eyes were bright with watchfulness; they sped from door to door restlessly. And at every sound he cocked his head to listen with frowning concentration. When a floor board creaked or an old table emitted its sharp little "crick-crack" or some far shutter made its moan, gibbeted upon its rusty hinges, or the wind shrilled down a chimney or whistled around a corner, Glennister had the air of a man who analyzed each sound suspiciously. . . . He had not poked into every closet, and the house of so many turns and angles had many a closet; he had not gone up into the attic which extended over the rear of the house, where the bedrooms had ceilings between them and the rooftree; he had not gone down into the cellar under the kitchen. And his expression now said clearly:

"There's someone here. I'm not the only one in this house."

Applegate? Confound Applegate, anyway; he'd have to do a bit of explaining when Glennister got his hands on him. Norcross? Or one of Norcross' Indians?

"Unless the old place is haunted," meditated Glennister, half in earnest. "Never likelier hour or place for the ghost-folk to do their stunts! A shriek, now; a slowly spreading stain under a door; even a jangle of chains—any of the regular clap-trap would fit the moment like a key in its lock—"

He sat bolt upright, rigid and alert to the final degree. Surely that was not "just the wind and nothing more"; not the mere creaking of old furniture full of complaint like an old man of rheumatism. In the "Grizzly Room"; that small den adjoining the living room, three broad low steps up from the main floor. Someone in there, moving cautiously!

Certainty came with a flash, and in its reaction was like a spark in a powder barrel. He went up the three steps at a bound, sent the door crashing back against the wall, and catapulted himself headlong into the little room, into a region of half light and shadow. Be it Norcross with all the Indians of his pack at his back, be it the devil himself, Glennister raging and slinging his rifle was ready for him. And not at all ready for that which he fell upon. He had his "shriek" now, a wild shrill scream, as he hurled himself toward the dimly seen figure.

"You!" he muttered, astounded.

"Yes, it's me," came the rejoinder, sullen and defiant. "Get your paws off, will you?"

"Oh!" said Glennister. And then "Oho!" For when he had said "You!" he had thought it was the Hathaway girl; and when he had his answer he knew it was the Norcross girl.

"Get your paws off, I tell you." She struck at him, striving to draw back; then began scratching viciously at his hand.

She seemed to be alone; at least he could neither see nor hear anyone else. Well, questions later. Now he shifted his grip from her shoulder to her wrist and drew her after him to the door, down the steps and into the big room.

During the moment before either spoke again they eyed each other sharply.

"You're a dirty spy!" shrilled Judy. "You ought to have been asleep an hour ago. Sneak!"

The strange part of it was that she seemed to

mean every word of it. He could have laughed at her had he not been so perplexed. Her being here mystified him.

His keen gaze took her in from head to foot; from the bright red bandanna handkerchief she had made into a sort of turban, to her black boots. Hence there was no chance of his not observing so obvious a display as that dangling from the strap about her waist: at one side a revolver in its holster, at the other a sheathed hunting knife. He judged that, in a fit of temper, she might use either and so, giving her no warning of his intent, was upon her and had whipped the revolver out of its holster before she well knew what he was about. Again she struck at him and scratched, but now he was prepared for her style of warfare and fended her off with one arm while, at last, he did laugh at her. He glanced at the weapon before dropping it into his own pocket.

"Thanks for the hardware," he taunted her. "It begins to look as though I needed to add to my arsenal. An old Colt, thirty-eight—a bit big for a lady, isn't it?"

"You thought I was that Hathaway kid!"

He merely lifted his brows at her, smiling tolerantly.

"You know you did! She's a little fool."

"How old are you?" asked Glennister. "About twelve? Or thirteen? You're no business running around."

"I'm sixteen and over," she cried sharply. "I'm a grown woman. Oh, I know what I'm about. You can tie to that, Lord Jim."

"What are you here for to-night?" he demanded. She tossed her head.

"Don't you wish you knew, though!"

"I mean to know. You were here when I came in, weren't you?"

"Was I?" she countered impertinently.

"What did you want? To pop a bullet into my back? Or try a knife act?"

She appeared to reflect. Suddenly she burst into her sharp laughter. She had looked first frightened, then confused and now appeared to have herself in hand. She sat down, clasped her hands behind her head and looked straight into his eyes, her own insolent.

"What if I came just to see you? Being lonesome, just for a visit with you?"

"Then why hesitate so long to come in? I've been sitting here a full hour; two, maybe."

"What if all of sudden, being a girl, I lost my nerve? Coming right slam-jam to it, I might be afraid!"

"I'd like an answer to my question," said Glennister sternly, clearly of no mood for Judy's playful evasions. "No, you were not afraid of me. You knew I wouldn't hurt you. Why did you come here to-night?"

Judy made an impudent face to his frowning one.

"You won't ever get any place trying to bulldoze me," she said airily.

"I don't believe you had the wild idea of shooting me," Glennister went on, watching her like a hawk, hoping that despite her heritage of Jet Norcross' craft her youth and inexperience might betray her with some gleam of eye or twitch of lip. "What then? The specimen he had left behind? I'll get it for you—"

"Hang the specimen," said Judy. "Say, give me a smoke, will you?"

He gave her papers and tobacco; she made her cigarette deftly and flung the makings back to him.

"That specimen?" she repeated through smoke. "Keep it. I'm not a nickel-shooter, Glennister, and what's more I don't need that lump of rock."

"There's something else, then, in the house that you did want? Something you left here? You or Norcross?"

"I know how to keep my trap shut, mister. That's one thing Jet taught me."

"Where were you hiding when I went looking through the house when I first came in?"

Impishly, she started to answer:

"If you knew that—" and then broke off, glaring at him and adding: "I'll tell you nothing. Find out for yourself."

"I will. By the way, where is Applegate?"

Too young yet, Miss Judy, to have achieved such perfection in what is known as a poker-face as to deceive a man like Jim Glennister. He saw and read the look in her eyes, quickly though she dropped her lids. She did not even know who or what Applegate was.

"Find out for yourself," she snapped sullenly.

"Oh, all right. You're a foxy little brat, it strikes me. Know about all that there is to be known, huh? And know also the rare little trick of keeping what you know to yourself? Where's Jet? Why does he send his women-folk to do his dirty work for him?"

He got a real, honest flash from her now.

"Jet's a big fool!" she cried out passionately. "I hate him. I almost wish you'd make a monkey out of him. He won't listen to me, or—Look here, man: What if I did come to see you? And to make you a sporting proposition?"

"You've quarreled with Jet?"

"Oh, we're always scrapping. But this time I'd double cross him to a finish, with half a chance to grab something for myself. What's he ever done for me? He lied when he told the Hathaway kid he'd married my mother; he never did. He made her think so, but he can't fool me. And what did he have to go and pick a squaw for my mother for, anyway? A dirty trick and he's a dirty dog."

Glennister had his choice to believe her sincere in her outburst or playing some part of her own in some hair-brained scheme to come deviously to her hidden desire.

"You speak of making me a sporting proposition. I wonder just what you have in mind?"

"And I wonder how far I could trust you?"

He shrugged at that.

"You have to judge there. But I'd scarcely expect to be interested in what you might have to offer anyway. Norcross never was the fool to let you or anybody else in on his business to such an extent as to give you a handle on him."

"I know every bit as much as Jet Norcross does. Now, sink your teeth in that and chaw on it, smarty."

"So?" Glennister appeared incredulous while watching sharply for signs. "You know where the Hathaway gold is?" He laughed at her.

"You bet I know—That's why I came to-night. I'd make a deal with you; fifty-fifty, you know. You'll never come at it if I don't put you wise. How could you?" She began to sneer at him. "Poking around at night, trying to work over twenty square miles up and down, in the dark? For by this time even a fool would know that you'll do precious little prospecting by daylight. They'll knock you over like a rabbit."

"You came to-night to tell me? To split on your father? To chip in with me on a fifty-fifty play?"

She nodded eagerly. Her eyes were like a bird's; she was tense as a violin string, leaning toward him. And yet, for the life of him, he could not tell if she were being honest with him now or playing a part.

"Did you ever tell a lie in your sweet little life, Miss Judy?" he asked abruptly.

"You know I did! I'm nobody's milksop, Jim Glennister. But I'm not lying now."

"Odd, though, that having come to tell me this you hid out until I had to go drag you in for a chat."

"Maybe that does look phony; and maybe I'm not tipping you my whole hand yet, either. Look here; I'll tell you this: There's something that I know—and Jet doesn't know I know it—and if you knew what it was and that I knew it—"

"You're getting all tangled up," laughed Glennister, though the very vagueness of what she was saying—or not saying—had him more keenly interested than anything she had yet said. "This great secret that you know and Jet doesn't know you know—"

"Oh, shut up!" she snapped angrily. "You wouldn't be so smug if you guessed. I could bust you and Jet both like that!" And she tore her dead cigarette end to bits with a vicious twist, managing somehow to suggest that the thing she destroyed was a living, sentient thing, and that she delighted in torturing and annihilating it. A new look of cruelty shaped her mouth; he caught a glimpse of her teeth and marked how small and white—and wickedly sharp they were. Indian mother, primitive savagery—and Jet Norcross' blood; burning product, Judy Norcross.

"A baby rattlesnake doesn't look bad," said Glennister idly, "yet is as deadly as an old fellow."

Judy laughed. She understood and appeared to sense a compliment.

"Where's your father?" asked Glennister. "Waiting for you outside?"

"He's a good long ways from here. Waiting for me? Not likely; he isn't wise that I'm up and around tonight."

"Do you know, I was asking myself if Jet wasn't afraid that I'd find the gold with very little trouble. He gave a couple of pretty broad hints, you remember, when he thought he had the deal cold. So he tries to do me in and, failing that, sends you to make me your little fifty-fifty proposition, thinking to horn in on half since he can't hog the whole—"

"You mean I'm working for Jet to-night? You're crazy!"

He sat staring at her, drumming on the arm of his chair the while, endeavoring to fathom her; building up many quick, shifting theories. It would be quite in character for this girl—grown woman that she boasted she was—to betray Norcross or any other for mere whim or greed. Treachery? She was full of treachery. It was rife in her mixed blood; she was bred of treachery, swaddled in it, raised in its murk. Frankly treacherous! That was Judy Norcross. A rather odd thing, come to think of it. One usually masked, took refuge in flimsy veilings. Not Judy.

Here, with a great rush, came the wind again, battering at the doors, rattling the shutters, trumpeting down the chimneys. A dull booming roar, faint but ominous, came from the distance; far-off thunder or just the storm wind in the forests?

"A nice night to be abroad in," remarked Glennister. "I wonder how far from home you are?"

"Why don't you ask me where our hang-out is, and be done with it?" said Judy scornfully. "You don't trap me with that kind of talk. Now that you've—now that I'm here, I'm going to stay until after daylight."

"What if I agreed to your proposition? To let you in on a fair share if you could show me the way to the old mine?"

"A fair share would be half. How'd I know if I could trust you? I don't trust anybody! I'd make you come first with me to some big town, out to Eureka, I guess; I'd go see a lawyer and have a talk with him; I'd get the law trapped all around you 'til you couldn't wiggle your ears. Then I'd—"

"You'd keep me away as long as you could? A week, two weeks, a month? And let Jet Norcross have his way here meanwhile? Nothing doing, little Judy! Maybe you have quarreled with Jet; maybe you're afraid of him and his Indian braves—"

146

"Afraid? Pooh!" scoffed Judy. "Me afraid of those birds? It's the other way 'round, man. Yes; I mean it!"

He laughed at her as he rose and took up a candle.

Judy sprang to her feet and stamped angrily, her cheeks red, her eyes snapping.

"And you better be afraid, I tell you! Know who my mother was, don't you? But you don't know who her father was! He was a medicine man; Starbuck and Modoc know all right. They're his brothers but they were scared stiff of him. And I've got the powers he had; I can send bad wishes, man, and they come true! Jet knows that. You better know it, too!"

"Bad wishes?" His eyes glowed with his genuine amusement; his laugh became a deep, mellow rumble. "You've the evil eye, eh? You can make men's bodies dwindle, their bones turn to wax, their brains to water?"

"Oh, laugh!" shrilled Judy. "Laugh, you poor fool! I tell you I can send bad wishes; I'm always doing it and they're always working. Jet knows and is scared of me; so's Starbuck and so's Modoc. I've sent bad wishes to that baby-faced Hathaway kid; you just watch and see what happens to her! You get me on your side—if you can—or I'll do you in!"

"Ever try sending good wishes?" asked Glennister, grinning at her.

"No!" said Judy shortly. "Who'll I send good wishes to? Who ever did anything for me?"

"Suppose you excuse me for a moment? Make yourself at home; you're free to go or to stay until morning. I'm going to have a little look around in the next room."

"You want to find out what I was up to? Go look, and much good it'll do you."

She flung herself down into the big chair he had vacated and brooded, moody and petulant. With a glance back at her Glennister went out, closing the door after him, mounting the three steps into the little den.

Yonder Judy had stood when he had rushed in on her, across the room, close to the wall. One of the great paws of the grizzly rug seemed to be extended toward the spot as though to point it out to him. There she had stood. Had she come from the door to the right, leading to the room where the piano was? Or through the door at the left? Or had she been in this room all the while, listening for his tread?

Idly he noticed a corner of white paper against the wall near where Judy had stood. It flashed over him that it was something she had dropped there. He went swiftly to it, stooping to pick it up. It was caught and refused to come away, so firmly was it held; it seemed to have slipped half-way into a crack where wall and floor met. Tug as he would he could not withdraw it without tearing it across.

"How the deuce could it get jammed in like that?"

It looked exactly as though the paper had been built into the house; caught between the redwood planking of the partition wall and the floor-boards. Nonsense, of course; yet that was how it looked.

Of a sudden it dawned on Glennister. That innocent-looking old wall had a hidden closet behind its deceptive face. Judy had been in there; that was where she had been hiding. She had dropped a paper as she came out; the hidden door to the closet had closed on it.

He thought that he heard her move. Hastily he drew the bear skin a few inches nearer the wall, so that the paw hid the paper. It would require time to work this little puzzle out; he'd do that after Judy left. No use letting her know that he was near any discovery, great or small. What a secretive old fellow the first Hathaway must have been!

When presently he returned to the living room he saw that Judy had dropped off to sleep in her big chair, curled up like a kitten.

THE HOLLOW TREE   *CHAPTER X*

"WHERE'S that man Applegate?" Glennister demanded of the coffee-pot. And, of the frying-pan, he asked frowningly; "Where did he go? What's happened to him?"

About this time Judy, under the quilt which Glennister had tossed over her, began to stir in her chair. Daylight put long slender threads of light through cracks in the shutters. She started wide awake, stared all about her wonderingly, and then sprang to her feet. From the kitchen came the little homely sounds and fragrances foretelling breakfast. She sniffed the air approvingly.

But, already on her way to the kitchen, she bethought herself of other matters. Her hands went up to her hair; straight and black, it hung now in what Judy Norcross knew to be unbecoming wisps and straggles. She began seeking a looking-glass. When she found one in a bedroom she lingered at it several minutes. She was wide awake and fresh looking when she looked in at the kitchen door.

"Hello," said Glennister, hearing the creak of hinges and half-turning from his pan of sizzling bacon. "You're just in time."

"The coffee's going to boil over," said Judy, coming in. "Look out! Your toast is burning!"

"Confound that toast," said Glennister. "Suppose you watch it? There's butter in that box over there and there's strawberry jam around somewhere—and I wish to high heaven Applegate would come back. I'd forgive him anything—"

"Your bacon, you lummox," cried Judy. "Can't you see it's burning? And who is this Applegate, anyhow?"

"He's the king of cooks. He's a nosy fat man; he numbers both Paul Pry and Peeping Tom among his forebears; he taught all its tricks to the Cat that Curiosity killed—but how the man can cook! He'd juggle seven boiling, bubbling pots all the same time, like a circus juggler with oranges, and never miss a thing that was going on in the next room, out the back door or down cellar. He—"

"Got any eggs?" asked Judy.

"Not so many now; a few left. Here, you tend stove and I'll see where Applegate put them. Oh, Applegate, Applegate, where art thou, Applegate?"

"You're a funny guy," said Judy. She retrieved the bacon, turned the toast and put it farther back on the stove and lifted the coffee from the direct flames. And, having something of that same skill which Glennister praised in the vanished Applegate, she managed to watch her host out of the corner of her eyes all the while. While he was not looking at her, her face was not so hard, not quite so sullen. A softer and a brighter light came into her usually smoldering eyes.

"How many eggs?" asked Glennister.

"Two," said Judy. "You don't get eggs every day out in the woods. What if we rigged up that I was to come and cook for you? We might get together on that proposition of mine, fifty-fifty on the yellow stuff, and I'd throw in the cooking—"

"Oh, Applegate will come back." Suddenly, to mystify her, his grin flashed out upon her: "I've got another cook coming, too. Due here to-day!"

"Hmf! How many cooks does one man need, anyhow?"

They were in the midst of their breakfasting, seated at the kitchen table, when a light rap came at the outer door. Glennister sprang up.

"That's Ab Applegate now—"

But it was a laughing voice that could never under any circumstances be mistaken for Applegate's calling gayly:

"Please let the come in, Mr. Glennister—"

"Oho!" sniffed Judy, her face flaming hot all of a sudden. "You and that Hathaway kid carrying on, are you?"

Glennister, no little taken aback since he had looked for no such early arrival, jerked the door open, meaning to assure himself with his eyes that his ears had not tricked him. There before him, smiling gayly, tricked out in the prettiest new dress of her whole lot, a bright sunshade spinning over her shoulder and all unnecessary at this early hour, stood Wee Glee Hathaway. She had a dimple and she was not the least concerned with hiding the fact. She had taken long hours to come to a decision and, having made up her mind what was to be done, she lost no time in deciding just how it was to be done. She had put her hand to the plow, so to speak, and meant to make a shining furrow and to sing back to the birds while she did it.

"I have come to report for work," she laughed up into his still grave face. "I expected to be here on time to get breakfast; I'm sorry but—"

Last night Glennister had vowed that after his departure she would weep and wail; that she would say a hundred "I won'ts," before she came to the one "I will." But if she had wept, no sign of it remained in the clear laughing eyes. Here was one who, as he would have put it, was a "dead game sport"; one who would play out her string rather prettily.

"You told me I was to knock and say, 'Please let me in, Mr. Glennister.' And now you don't seem—"

"Oh," said Glennister hastily, "come in. Please do," and he stepped aside for her.

When she saw Judy Norcross, sitting at Glennister's table and glaring at her with open hostility, Judy making herself very much at home here and broadcasting a bristling, resentful, "What right have you got here?" Glee Hathaway came to a dead halt. Her eyes opened wide; her lips parted to a half-smothered gasp; her hand flew quickly to her mouth as though to stop that one brief exclamation; she looked all at once surprised, uncertain and distressed.

The humor of the situation appeared first of all to dawn on Lord Jim Glennister—if, indeed, there was any humor in it at all. At any rate he began to chuckle; what he read in the faces of the two girls put the flickering lights into his eyes.

Glee Hathaway, coming prepared for all that she could foresee, was not in the least prepared for just what she had found. Glennister waited for her to speak; not for anything in the world would he have come to the rescue just then.

"I—I didn't know—" she began lamely. "I thought—"

Still he was rarely content to let her flounder. Judy, however, had held silent as long as she could.

"She didn't know—she thought—" mocked Judy, and then laughed shrilly. Glee had flushed but her heightened color was slowly subsiding, leaving her cheeks fresh and cool; in Judy's face still burned two hot, red spots. Judy had made her toilet in the greatest haste this morning and had achieved no resplendent results; Glee wore her prettiest dress and shoes and stockings—she might have been going to a party. Judy's hair, stiff and black and rebellious, was in marked and unlovely contrast to Glee's which was fluffy and curly and bronzy. And of all this the very astute Judy was conscious—blazingly conscious.

"She didn't know!" she repeated with her jeering laughter. "Oh no; of course not." And she added meaningly and as nastily as Miss Judy could remark: "She wouldn't have come if she'd known anyone was with you." And, not satisfied with that, she threw out in the manner which is known as catty, her final word to Glennister: "Look out, Jim; she's after you all by yourself!"

Had Judy understood the meaning and usages of finesse, the situation might have had further amusement possibilities for Glennister. As it was he ignored her coolly and at last spoke, saying courteously:

"Won't you sit down, Miss Hathaway? There's hot coffee—"

"No, thank you," she returned, become by now as stiff as the most unbending of all proverbial pikestaffs. "I had breakfast before starting. I'll just go outside again, and wait for Danny; he's coming with the wagon."

"Oh, don't mind me," cried Judy, jumping up and managing to upset her cup in so doing, spilling the dark brown liquid across the table top. "I'm on my way in two shakes."

"Oh, I don't mind you in the least," said Glee, and smiled sweetly. So sweetly that Judy's sharp little teeth came together with a click. And from the door, came the pleasantly added: "Don't let my coming hasten you."

Judy flew into a rage at that. She had risen with a knife in one hand, a fork in the other, and now hurled both from her; they made a lively rattle among the dishes, scattering some glistening chips of crockery. That smile maddened her.

"You'd treat me like dirt under your feet, would you?" she burst out. "You better look out. I—I— I'll send you a string of bad wishes that'll make you feel like thirty cents. I'll—I wish you a spoiled face, that's what I wish you—a scar across it—a sore—a—"

"I think that I hear Danny coming now," said Glee Hathaway.

Judy shot by her, almost at a run, and darted out into the orchard. It was a ghostly morning after so wild a night, wan and still, with layers of white mist across the meadows, wisps and plumes of white mist here and there above the forest and the mountains. Judy, half-way across the meadow, was swallowed up in the fog, a dark little figure vanishing in that white, opaque sea.

While the two stood looking after her the morning stillness was broken by a growing creak and jingle and rattle announcing the coming of Dan Jennifer with the wagon. The blurred form of horses and wagon broke free from the dark wall of the woods and began gradually taking shape. Glee Hathaway kept her eyes fixed upon it, her face averted from Glennister at her side. But she was conscious of his presence; she felt his eyes upon her; she knew when he stepped away, going into the kitchen. Still she did not turn. . . . She had plunged into this adventure; there had even been some strange, utterly unreasonable and illogical zest in it. Now, all of a sudden the zest was gone; she shivered; the morning was so white and still and sunless and—unhappy—She was sorry she had come.

She heard him returning swiftly. He did not stop when he came to her side but called out curtly:

"You and Jennifer run the house until I get back."

Only when he had passed did she look at him. He had gone for his rifle; he was hastening, breaking into a run as he struck into the orchard. She watched him rushing out across the meadow, a tall, dark form wreathed in the strata of white—hastening after Judy. As the fog had swallowed her and at the same place, it wiped him out of the picture. Yet she stood for a long while, in fact until Jennifer drew up his horses at the door, looking out in the direction which he had taken—to follow Judy Norcross—Just what he could see in that girl—

Lord Jim Glennister saw a very great deal in Judy Norcross: venom, deceit, ambition, greed, jealousy, crafty shrewdness. Yet saw them dimly and vaguely, just as he had seen her a minute ago, dimming in the fog. He saw her motives only as they had pictured themselves to him, in broken distorted bits. When she offered to "double cross" her own father, for instance, she had shown him a flash of what might have been genuine fire. She had her own secrets; he began to believe that here was a girl who could defy tradition and keep them. Well, he meant to have one of them; he held it more than an even break that right now she was returning in all haste to Jet Norcross, and Glennister was of a mind to learn where the two met. If she led the way on to whatever spot Norcross and his men were camped on, so much the better.

"He's got a snug hang-out of some kind handy," was Glennister's way of regarding it. And it would do no harm to look in on this Norcross hang-out—especially if Norcross himself had no inkling of the fact that his own territory was being invaded.

Judy had left in a rage; he counted that in the scales against the likelihood of her so much as looking over her shoulder. He wondered if she had got what she came for last night; he was so dead sure that she had come for something, had been rummaging when he returned, had hoped to steal away when he caught her. And, certainly, she had known the secret of that closet in the grizzly bear room. But had she got what she wanted there?

He made a straight line from the edge of the orchard across the meadow and into the forest. For Judy herself, as long as he had been able to follow her with his eyes, had made a bee-line. Like a bee, exactly, come to think of it; a bee with a sting which it was in all hot haste to use. Somewhere, directly in front of him, she was speeding along; he could not see her, therefore she could not see him. He could hear no sound of her progress, and therefore—unless she had stopped, which he did not think likely—she would not hear his hurrying steps.

And just then, having come to the ragged edge of the wooded slope, he caught the sound of a dead branch snapping noisily; he swerved a little to the side, came into a dim trail and was just in time to see the shadowy blur of a shape vanishing farther along the trail. Judy was hastening through the forest, but no longer straight ahead; the trail angled through the woods to Wild River.

Glennister followed on now without the least difficulty. True, she was forever appearing only to vanish, found but to be lost immediately about a bend in the trail or in some spot where the white mist swathed her about like so much cotton. But she was always pressing on, never tarrying to rest or to glance back; and when he could not see her he could hear her flying footsteps. All unsuspecting of eyes upon her went Judy, a prey to her own unbridled, passionate emotions. How should she dream that Lord Jim Glennister, with Glee Hathaway just arrived and all tricked out in her pretty finery, would quit her so unceremoniously?—She pictured the two together and as she scurried along Judy Norcross kept up a constant muttering; "bad wishes" like birds of evil omen rose in dark flocks from her hard red lips.

Had Glennister not been fairly close he must have lost her entirely at the river. But he was near enough to see when she forsook the trail, burst through a ferny copse and swung up into a tree. The branches were low, the trunk itself leaning out over the water at such a fearful angle that it seemed as if the roots, under so severe a strain, must part with mother earth and let the tree crash down. Up this rugged incline went Judy, as agile as a squirrel; she vanished briefly among thick leaves; she was glimpsed again—and Glennister caught his breath, thinking that she was falling. But she was only swinging by her arms, swinging outward from one branch to another, catching, drawing herself over and up, vanishing again somewhere along her hazardous bridge. Glennister, handicapped by his rifle, went up the leaning tree. He saw the water, a dark, troubled expanse under a bank of white fog, rushing along under him, and heard its roar and splash and once felt its spray in his face; below were black jagged rocks standing like sinister armored giants in the pathway of this swashbuckling roisterer of a river. If a man fell here—

His boots began slipping, a limb gave under his hand, there was a wrench and a stab of pain in his wound, he clutched wildly at his rifle and for a moment cast about blindly to save himself from falling. He must have made no end of noise, threshing about among the leaves and snapping twigs; and when again he could wriggle forward was more than half expectant of seeing Judy just ahead, watching him. But when he dropped safely to earth again, there were the signs of her passing, a narrow way beaten down among the ferns, leading him on to another trail. And ten minutes later, far ahead, glimpsed only to be lost again, he saw her hurrying on.

It was perhaps half-an-hour later and they had penetrated the depths of one of the magnificent redwood groves when Glennister noted a swift change in Judy. She went warily; she began looking back, stopping frequently; she was listening. She hastened more swiftly through the little open glades; she slipped around the enormous boles; twice he saw her peering out from such shelter. His first thought was that she had heard or glimpsed him; or had she only "sensed" pursuit? Or, again, was it that her emotional fires had burned down and her natural craft but asserted itself? Or—and now he was sure he had it!—was it that she was close to her destination, the camp where Jet Norcross and the others had their headquarters, a place to be approached at all times circuitously and with all possible caution?

Being the hunted turned hunter, Glennister matched her furtive caution. He hid, he crept along under what cover he could find; he crawled more than once on hands and knees; he watched all about him, not satisfied with what lay in front, from many a great redwood trunk against which he stood reconnoitering. So many things were possible; among them stood out always the grim possibility that Judy may have known all along that he would follow her; that that was the reason she had not looked back; that she meant to lead him into a spot where all without warning he was to find himself ringed about by half a dozen gun barrels.

Here might lie the very simple explanation of Judy's visit to him; a lure and an ambush.

He saw her climb up over a monster log, one of those slowly disintegrating old giants from whose sides ferns and young feathery trees grew up so lusty and green. She paused a moment at the top, crouching behind the screen of greenery; had he not seen her slip into hiding he would have failed altogether to discover her so long as she remained still. But his watchful eyes had served him well, and he too grew rigid where he was, on hands and knees among the ferns.

She jumped down upon the farther side of the log. She might have sped on; she might be standing there, very still, listening and watching. If the former, and he hesitated, he might lose her and this time, so warily did she go, there would be no finding her again. So he rose and hurried forward; peeping over the log he caught just a glimpse of her. She was running like a deer and disappeared the instant after he saw her.

He hesitated a moment. The forest was very still; high, high above there was the whispering of the tree tops, hidden in the white fog; here about him no wind entered, no breeze blew, scarcely did the air stir at all; wisps and wreaths of vapor seemed unchanging in their ghostly shapes, unmoving. The incredibly big tree trunks loomed all about him and commanded silence. How could that be? Yet one felt that silent command. They, august and brooding, had stood steeped in silence through the days and nights—through the years—through the centuries. Under their thick bark life flowed in them, quiet, unhasting, infinitely serene. Only their high tops stirred and rustled and whispered; youth was up there, high above this ground mist, aspiring to the blue skies by day, the golden glitter of stars by night; youth whispering mysteriously. But here—silence and emptiness—aloofness—

Yet how be sure even of that? Behind the nearest tree-giant looming upward and not a dozen feet from him, Norcross and his whole crowd of hangers-on might crouch well hidden at this very moment; here was a region in which an army might lie concealed. Glennister muttered and shrugged and gripped his rifle—and went on over the log.

He did not see Judy again and did not hear her. But he found that he could track her almost at every step; had it been a clearer, brighter daylight he could have followed her trail at a run. For he saw that everywhere here under the redwoods there grew a little ground-loving plant like the familiar garden clover, but more beautiful with its soft green leaves—and far more tell-tale. For the under sides of the trifoliate leaves were not green, but a deep, almost purple-violet color, and where one walked there were always leaves broken, trampled, tipped so that there resulted a purple-violet trail.

From a clump of young trees Glennister looked out across a hollow threaded by a narrow creek; the creek, in a fold of the wooded hills, must turn this way and that, winding toward the lower lands, glimpsed in broken bits of swift water and dark pools. That way had Judy gone, upward along the stream's bank, toward a natural spillway down which, through a vista of trees, Glennister could see the silvery splash of falling waters. The half veiled cascades fell into a rocky basin ringed with great green, mossy bowlders; musical murmurs echoing eternally, soft-voiced, harmoniously insistent against the surrounding silence, filled the deep-cleft ravine which here gave the creek its bed. Very steep were the walls of the ravine at this spot, become sheer cliffs masked with occasional ferns and broad-leafed plants where the water fell, almost as sheer to right and left. Yet there must be a way up; Judy had come this way and unless she were hidden there by the pool she must have climbed upward.

"Unless here's a land," said Glennister to himself, remembering, "where maids vanish at the edges of enchanted pools!"

He waited some minutes before he moved forward again; he went more slowly than ever, stopping at each step to quest not only Judy but some sign of the trail which she must have taken. Her he did not find; her tracks in a bit of wet gravel by the creek's edge, he did. Just here she had crossed; on the other side, directly opposite, he found the tracks again; then a broken fern frond; then a narrow trail through the ferns which arched overhead, tall and thick. Thus was the way pointed out, if one were sharp-eyed for details and set on finding it; and thus did he come to discover just where Judy had climbed up out of the ravine.

Here and there redwoods grew on the steep flanks of the mountain. One of the largest, no doubt one of the oldest, stood high up from the ravine, looked to be precariously rooted at the base a lofty cliff, was in the midst of a thicket of smaller growth and was hollow at the base. Even from so far below and despite the young trees about the ancient monarch, Glennister saw that the big tree was hollow, made out the inky black, fire-darkened opening like a big door; the top of this opening was clear to see from where he stood, the bottom guessed at through the foliage of the lesser growths. That was the way Judy had gone; straight up the steep pitch of the mountain to the old hollow tree. And into it? There would be a space there like an ordinary room—

He knew she had gone that way because on so steep a slope it had been impossible to hide a trail often traveled. There were broken ferns and grasses where one had slipped and caught at them; there were furrows and grooves plowed by slipping boots, pointing out the way.

Judy, he was sure then, had gone into the cavernous hollow of the big redwood. To rejoin her father and his men? What else? There would be adequate, perhaps ample room there for all. And not a bad shelter in any weather and never an unlikely hiding-place. But, then Glennister should hear voices. If Judy had entered upon last night's adventure upon her own initiative, taking none into her confidence, there would be a sharp challenge from Norcross demanding explanations. If, on the other hand, it was a part of some game the two played with mutual understanding, there would be none the less quick questions and Judy's sharp voice in staccato replies. Instead of this there was only silence.

"Here goes, to find out," decided Glennister, and with a last sharp glance all about set to work to clamber and crawl up the steep path.

It was slow work, since he sought to hold himself in readiness for anything and to make no noise, but in time he pulled himself up the final difficult stage and stood among the delicately slender saplings upon the ledge where stood the hollow redwood. Before him was the yawning opening; three or four men abreast might have stepped into the tree's black interior. A well-trodden way led into it through the smaller growth and Glennister moved stealthily forward. Still no voices, no sound of anyone stirring. Where then was Judy? She was not the one to brood in silence;

rather, though alone, to storm about, hurling things out of her way, talking to herself.

With his rifle thrust before him he stepped through the wide opening. Dim and dusky in here, with light enough for him to see that the place was empty but had known human occupancy. There was an old quilt thrown upon a pile of recently-cut boughs. There was an end of rope dangling from above. He looked up. Light filtered in from a hole in the side of the tree some twenty feet higher up. The rope, tied into a series of knots, dangled from this hole.

Here was perplexity! Why on earth should anyone want to climb up inside a hollow tree just to get out through a hole so high up? There was the rope stoutly proclaiming itself a rough-and-ready ladder of sorts; there was the lofty opening to which it led—

With his belt he managed to sling his rifle at his back; Judy could have gone nowhere else except up the rope and where she led he meant to follow. The hardest part of the job was getting started; and that would have caused him no trouble were it not for the fact that so recent a wound as his grew irksome at this form of exercise. Once, however, that he had pulled himself up high enough to allow him to clamp his feet about the lowest of the knots, it was easier. Hand over hand, head back to watch above, he went up.

When his head was on a level with the hole in

the tree's side he had all the explanation he could ask. He looked straight out into a little open space atop a cliff; on both sides and at the back rose the mountains steeply, thickly-wooded, forming a small amphitheater set in mossy rock and flourishing verdure. He smelled woodsmoke; he saw the camp-fire; he caught the fragrant steam of coffee; and now at last he heard voices. Judy's ejaculations, strident and shrill and bitter; the heavier tones of Jet Norcross; now another voice—

Whose voice was that? It was strangely familiar yet for a moment Glennister was at a loss. He pulled himself some inches higher, got head and shoulders into the hole and not only heard better but saw the group of three standing some few paces from the fire: Jet Norcross and Judy—and one who seemed fairly popping out of his skin with the most eager and inquisitive interest. None other than Ab Applegate.

PEACE—WITH WAR
TRUMPETS BLOWING!   CHAPTER XI

HERE was Glee Hathaway, the very picture of the little house maid on whom the curtain has arisen for some thousands of Act I. Spick and span in a fresh-made white apron and saucy white cap; very neat and very authoritative with the ancient feather duster, renovated. And very gay, as might be known at a distance from bright snatches of song with a sprinkling of whistling notes interspersed; as might be better realized from near-by, by the sparkle of her eyes and her lively color. Making a game of it all, was Glee Hathaway, having had time to think and to plan and to plot. For a game it was—if one but elected to regard it as such. Just like everything, or very nearly everything else in life.

The situation did stimulate her. Confront youth with novelty and you get the spark of exhilaration. Here was zest, if one had a merry heart and a dash of spirit. She was not afraid of Jim Glennister; why should she be? He wouldn't harm her—physically; and how else could he threaten her? And she was going to have at the end of thirty days a golden crown to set upon the smiling brow of accomplishment. There would be an agreement drawn up and signed; Dan Jennifer would witness it. Already she had her option from Andrew. Who knew what might come of all this? She was launched upon big business. She was ready to rush along with the sweep of its tides, buoyed up by hope, and with good luck for the fairest of all trade winds.

Glennister came charging in upon her, like a lusty wind himself. She heard his steps; heard his voice calling. At the first sight of his face at the door she saw that she had to do with a Glennister like him of the morning when he sang at the piano.

Some triumphant satisfaction had his eyes dancing; the sting of the wet air outside put a ruddy healthful glow into his face; his mood stood on tiptoe.

He stood his rifle in the first corner, spun his broad hat across the long living room and fairly beamed upon her.

"You're a brick! Just a downright, God-blessed brick!" was what he had to say to her.

She smiled back at him. That was what she had planned to do all along, come Glennister; whatever happened, whatever he said, was her cue to smile; she was going through with what was to be done, and going through with it smilingly. Hence there would appear to have been the grave danger of that smile, since it might be called a made-to-order one, being also what one might call cut-and-dried. One taken out of stock from many others, handed carelessly down to the customer, with nothing really fresh and spontaneous about it. Yet, it may be because she had been smiling to her own thoughts for so long, or it may be because something in him, tingling and eager and gay, found something of the very same order in her, at any rate, Lord Jim Glennister could find no fault in the world with her smile but, rather, judged it about the sunniest smile he had ever seen.

"Thank you, sir." She made him her best parlor maid curtsey.

He grinned in high appreciation; not only could she play the game, but could play it playfully.

"Look here, Miss Hathaway, why do we always fight like a fool terrier pup and a pretty Persian kitten? Just because we—I—got off wrong at the jump? We do just naturally seem to strike fire, but I wonder if we couldn't be friends—remaining perfectly good enemies for the sake of buiness all the while, if you like! I'll go you trying it; what say? It'll pass the time a lot more agreeably."

She was all dimpling acquiescence; radiant acquiescence. Zest in everything; in friendship with a spice of hostility; peace with the war trumpets blowing. And, after all, what was it to her that he had entertained Judy here? That they had breakfasted together? That he had rushed off to overtake the flying Judy and had been gone upwards of two hours?—Really he and she were strangers; hence each was a mystery to the other. A closed door here confronting a closed door set companionably close; an ardent spirit behind each barrier peeping forth, curious of the other, inspiring an ever-quickening interest. A man and a maid to all intents and purposes upon a little desert isle just now. Two of that order playing at friendship! Dallying, daring, tempting—risking everything.

"I've had a morning!" said Glennister, and again she glimpsed triumph. "I'd like to tell you all about it."

A morning with Judy—and he'd like to tell her all about it!

"Will you?" She allowed herself to be—or seem—naturally eager. "We who live out in places like this are always so avid for news."

"'Avid' is quite a word for the maid to get hold of," he laughed at her.

She curtsied again; she dimpled again. She retorted quickly.

"I got it out of a book, sir. And you will tell me—"

"I'd like to, my new friend—I'd better not, my ancient enemy! Look here: Will you do me a favor?"

"I am under contract for thirty days—at very satisfactory wages," she told him lightly. "I might be persuaded to toss in a favor or two. Who knows?"

"Don't tell anyone—not a soul—that I went out this morning!"

"I've told Danny already." She saw his brows pucker and her own gayety appeared but to increase as she added: "You see, I've told everyone I had a chance to tell!"

"I wish you hadn't. Well, that's done. But no one else; will you promise?"

"Aren't you starting out rather late to make a secret of it? With four people already sharing your secret—"

"Three. You, myself, and Jennifer."

"Why don't you count Judy? Hasn't she a tongue like the rest of us?"

"She doesn't know, and that's the great thing about it all! I followed her and—I'll tell you one thing, if you'll just swear by all that's good and holy not to tell anyone, not even your precious old rascal of a Danny."

But she shook her head now.

"Danny and I mustn't have any secrets between us—"

He cut in swiftly with a question meant to challenge that:

"Where was he last night when I called at your cabin? Did he tell you?"

In spite of her she flushed. She was on the verge of informing him that this was none of his affair when she remembered that he did have the right, granted by herself, to put pertinent questions. So she answered as carelessly as she could:

"No. He didn't—and I didn't ask him."

"What? You don't mean that you made no reference at all to my being at the cabin? For if you did that, he'd be pretty sure to offer some explanation for his absence."

"Of course I told him you had come and that it was your wish that he and I spend a month here with you."

"And what did he say?"

"He said—he asked why I didn't wake him—"

"Hmf. Old Mr. Sly Boots. And you said what to that?"

She didn't want to answer and hesitated. Yet in

173

the end she replied as briefly as she could.

"I only told him that I knew he had had a hard day—"

"You wanted to see if he wouldn't come clean with an explanation without being forced to it, eh? And he didn't?"

"No." The look she flashed at him now was dark with trouble. For Dan Jennifer had appeared to understand that they had not noted his absence and to be satisfied that they had not done so.

"And you go on saying there must be no secrets between you and Jennifer!" exclaimed Glennister. "That old man is as full of guile as any fox."

"No!" she said again, vehemently now. "Nothing on earth could make me distrust Danny. He has his reasons—good reasons—"

"Golden reasons?" demanded Glennister, very close to a sneer. Of a sudden, however, he flashed back to his brighter mood. "Well, maybe we don't need to worry about keeping things from him; a hint of knowledge of what's on the way may bring him to his senses. This far I'll go with you and if you like to pass it on, do so: I'm pretty sure that I could lead you as straight as a string to the old mine! And what do you say to that?"

"I'd say that you mean that you followed Judy, thinking that she might lead you to it? And that you were successful?"

"Put it rather that I've what's known as a hunch."

"Then you don't need to go on with our arrangement? To keep me and Danny where you can watch us a month would no longer be worth the price you were to pay?"

"To keep you a whole month where I could see you daily would be worth anything; I am ashamed to purchase so much for so little! As I have told you, the home here means nothing to me. Once I've got the mine, think I'd go on living here? And I still have my questions to ask during the three days of the former understanding which are left to us."

"I'll answer them."

"Shall we sit down?" He handed her a chair and when she had thanked him and seated herself, he went to a place on the settle. "First off, what do you know about Ab Applegate?"

"Nothing at all. I never heard of him."

He jerked up his brows at that. He meditated that she had lived here all her life and, though she might not have known the man herself, how was it that she had never heard his name? Gossip flourishes in the far-out regions.

"Never heard of him? Now that's strange. He's the man who brought my supplies; teamed in from Bill Connors' store. Tells me he came that way from over in the Hay Fork country."

"I've never been there. I do know some of the Hay Fork people; very few whom I've met at other places. I know the names of others. But I never heard of any Applegates among them."

"Would Jennifer know?"

"I should think he would."

"Where is he, by the way?"

"Outside, somewhere. I think he was going to get some wood for the kitchen."

"Here are some things I've been thinking over. For one thing, how did it happen that Oliver Hathaway, your father, never told, not even just before his death, where the mine was?"

"He did not know that—He was killed in a runaway, Mr. Glennister."

"Oh!—I'm sorry I had to ask that. But there's one other point; you'll forgive me, since we've already touched on this, if I ask you to tell me just what sort of man Oliver Hathaway was?"

"My father? He was fine! You needn't ask me that; ask anyone within a hundred miles. He—"

"Was he what you might term erratic?"

"No! Impulsive, yes. Always ready to do a kindness, no matter the cost or danger to himself. A man full of life, of fire—"

"Quick to anger? Impulsive, you say?—Well, I'm glad he was; that's the kind of people I like. His little daughter is like him. Now, just a little more of my impertinence, Miss Hathaway, and I'm done. In your immediate family at the time of your father's death, there were just how many?"

"Four." She answered quietly yet looked at him wonderingly. What reason could he have for such questionings? Yet he did not appear merely idly

176

inquisitive; one would have said that he was decidedly in earnest. She rounded out her answer: "There were my two brothers, Andrew and Bud. There is my sister, Lavinia."

"May I know about them? I know something of Andrew; we'll leave him until the end and then come back to him. Bud, now? How old?"

"Only seventeen."

"Wild?"

She flushed and retorted defensively:

"Not wild. Just young and—and a boy who is full of life and wants to live his own life in his own way—"

"Something like your father may have been at Bud's age? Where is he, by the way?"

"He went to Eureka six months ago. He is working there, and studying. He comes sometimes to spend a day or two here. Bud wants to be a mining engineer."

"And your sister?"

"She is in Eureka, too. She is the oldest of our four and has not lived at home here for several years. She doesn't like the country."

"Back we come to brother Andrew: Erratic? Or just impulsive like your father? There is a vein of fiery temper in the Hathaway stock, isn't there? Andrew has it?"

"Y-es. Andrew is sometimes—hasty."

"Now the final bit of impertinence for this time: How do you explain the fact that your father, having four children, left everything in his will to Andrew?"

"It was what his own father did—Grandfather Dick Hathaway. It was what had been done before in our family in England. There is with us the love of home and a pride in our home; a hope to keep it home always. My father must have hoped that Andrew would some day marry and have a son and pass everything along to him. And he knew that any one of us, Andrew or another, would be fair with the others, sharing with them."

"Yet, you being your father's favorite—"

She looked at him in surprise.

"How do you know—What makes you think that?" she asked quickly.

He laughed.

"You would be any man's favorite," he told her.

She laughed back at him. The subject was closed and they were reestablished upon the lightly inconsequential footing of the beginning of their parley.

"It's my lucky day," Glennister announced. "I've learned a thing or two; I've gone out and returned without drawing a shot; best of all, I've had you smile! You've been fine! Here you've got every good reason to hate me, here I come pulling the world down about your ears, making no end of trouble—a regular wolf charging upon the lamb!—and you—"

"And I," she laughed, "say to you: 'I'll keep

your house for you, Mr. Wolf, for a full thirty days, that being in our agreement.' And—"

"I was just trying to drop business, and here you start talking like a lawyer. Our agreement! Well, let's get *that* out of the way, too. 'For services rendered' or 'For value received' I am to give you—deed, deliver and assign, or something of that kind—all my right, title and interest as it may appear in this house and lot with the goods and chattels thereunto appertaining!—And how's that for legal phraseology? Come! Paper and ink and let the deed be done."

She brought paper and ink from her room. With these in her hands she stood looking at him curiously.

"You really mean to do it—just for Danny and me staying here a month?"

"I really mean every word of it. I was honest about it too, last night! To-day there may be a bit of trickery up my sleeve. I won't say." He did flash his smile like silent laughter at her. "But when I told you that I didn't care a rap for the home I told you the truth. It means nothing to me; why should it? It's certainly no commercial property for me to bother with. I don't want to acquire it; you do want to keep it. Come; it's yours."

"Not mine," she reminded him. "But you are giving me a chance to get it. And that is generous of you, Mr. Glennister."

"See what comes of playing friends! Now, I'm

179

no lawyer, but I think we can make the purpose of this document clear enough to have it stand—if you ever need it." Again he baffled her with his broad, highly amused smile.

He wrote swiftly and briefly. He signed and gave her the paper.

"There has to be trust somewhere between us," he told her gayly. "You'd have to trust me to make good at the end of the thirty days; or I'd have to trust you to stick by your bargain with the deed signed and handed over to you. Here, Glee Hathaway, is a house and lot done up in a scrap of paper. May you live in it to be a sweet little old lady and may you always be happy in it."

They were both laughing. Then suddenly he saw that her eyes were wet with tears.

"Don't!" cried Glennister, and so did his voice ring out that it seemed whipped from him by anger. "No gratitude, mind you! Business is business and, for full measure, I tell you I am tricking you."

She dashed her tears away and again she smiled. Glennister jumped to his feet.

"Come along," he said. "The devil take business from now on. Let's have a visit with the old piano. I feel like singing."

THE two were at the piano when Applegate
returned. Glennister, touching the keys very softly,
was singing an old love song; his eyes, giving no
inkling of his thoughts, held hers, made prisoners
of them, played hawk and dove with them; with
his singing, as before, he cast a spell over her. He,
the music maker, made music in her soul; almost it
was as though she were the tremulous instrument
upon which he played. He sang, softly yet with
quiet, strong, strangely compelling forcefulness:

"When I was King in Babylon."

Yet, singing, it was Glennister who heard
Applegate's quiet step in the living-room. Glee
Hathaway, so was she held by him, heard nothing.
Glennister jumped up, breaking off upon an unfin-
ished note; she started like one rudely awakened.
He laughed and his laughter jarred on her. Off he
strode for a talk with Applegate.

Glennister counted himself ready for Applegate;
ready and waiting. There was much that he meant
to know and as he came into the larger room his
lips were shaping to the first of a volley of sharp
questionings. Yet it was the tremendously eager
Applegate who fired the first gun. Never had he
looked so alive with curiosity, his bright blue eyes

181

shining, wide-opened, frankly predatory for all facts, large and small, that they might pounce upon, his rosy face tipped a little upward and to the side as though to thrust the more alert ear forward to catch the faintest whisper.

"You're back, Mr. Glennister?" he cried excitedly. "Where'd you go? See anybody? What did you do? Find out anything? Who's the girl in there? What's she doing here? Didn't get shot at, did you? Didn't find out who it was doing the shooting, did you—"

Glennister, despite the determination which had brought him into the room, remained silent, his eyes grown hard and suspicious trying to make what they could of the other man's eyes. Applegate peered at him, beyond him, at him again.

"Look here, Mr. Glennister—"

"I'm looking," said Glennister coolly.

"You bet you're looking! Drilling holes through me, too. What's up? What makes you look like that? Something's happened; what is it?"

"I was just thinking—"

"Sure you were! Anybody can see that Thinking—*what?*"

Suddenly that swift grin of Glennister's drove the sternness from his look.

"—that things are not always what they seem."

Applegate, mouth open, stared at him; he was waiting, hoping for more. Here was only another cue for yet other questions. His brow wrinkled, his rosy face grew perplexed. Glennister laughed outright.

Over his shoulder he saw Glee Hathaway at the threshold. He called to her, saying lightly:

"Come, Miss Hathaway; let me give you the treat of your life. May I present my little friend and playfellow, Ab Applegate from Hay Fork? He has, I think, a question or two he'd like to ask you!"

Glee Hathaway and Applegate regarded each other with interest.

"I'm pleased to meet you, Miss," said Applegate, and came forward, his chubby hand extended.

She gave him her hand and, after it, a quick, rare smile. He pleased her, he looked so ingenuous and downright likable. His own smile, puckering his face into dimples, beamed back at her.

"I thought you'd gone away," he said, as reluctantly he let her hand slip out of his. "My friend, Jim Glennister here, gave me that idea. Back, are you? Here to stay? Going to help Glennister to find the lost mine? Think you can? Think you've got a hunch about it?"

She burst into laughter as Glennister grunted:

"There you are! There he goes! Why don't you answer the man? Do you want to see him explode?"

"I am here to help Mr. Glennister, as you suggest, Mr. Applegate," said Glee, "but only, I am afraid, in keeping house for him. I am under a thirty-day contract and, being paid very nice wages, I am afraid that I should be harder at work!"

She nodded brightly at the two men, caught up her little duster and vanished, going toward the kitchen. A gay snatch of song floated back to them, a door slammed, and in the silence Applegate turned the battery of his intense eyes upon Glennister.

"Say, she's a little peach, that girl! Working for you, huh?"

Glennister had his chance now, alone with his man. Yet he decided swiftly that what he had to say could wait upon an even more propitious moment. He wanted no interruption and Glee might return or old Jennifer might come in.

"Yes, working for me," he said briefly. "I fancy she may even take the cooking off your hands, Applegate. Bereft of that occupation, I don't know that you'll care to stay on here in this hum-drum atmosphere!"

"Oh, I'll stay—Let her tidy the house up and that sort of thing; no sense she should have to do the cooking too; she's too pretty to muss around with dirty pots and pans and tinker with hot stoves. You ought to know that's well as I do, Jim." And with a mildly reproving backward look he trotted off to the kitchen.

"There's more in this little man than meets the eye," muttered Glennister.

Pleasant voices came to him from the kitchen. Jennifer had come in with an armful of wood; Glee made him and Applegate acquainted; the three appeared to get along together swimmingly.

"Three innocents!" Glennister growled and made it his business to keep all three within sight or hearing.

"They tell me you're from Hay Fork Valley, Mr. Applegate," Jennifer was saying in his calm, quiet voice. "I don't recollect ever seeing you out that way—or even hearing of you—"

"Haven't been there long," said Applegate. "Less'n six months. Heard there were good chances there for farm lands; been looking around a bit; took to teaming—and here I am. But look here, I'm of no consequence. It's you folks that are! Consequence—I'd say! Whew! With all the excitement running on—What do you two know about it, anyway? Chipping in with Glennister, I guess? Well, he's a good scout; I like him fine. But the question is, How much do you *know?* Have you got a pretty close idea where the gold is? You, Mr. Jennifer; could you make a pretty shrewd guess, now?"

Jennifer's sunken old eyes regarded the eager man gravely and for a long while.

"Would I have let the place be sold over our heads if I knew?" he challenged quietly.

Applegate was scratching his head violently.

"How do you stand with Norcross, now? Not stringing your bets along with his play, are you? What's he up to, anyway? What's he stand to make sticking around when Jim Glennister has bought over his head?"

"I'm thinking," said Jennifer thoughtfully, "that somewhere I've heard the name, Applegate; and I can't quite place it."

"Oh," came the hasty response, "the world's full of Applegates; common name, Mr. Jennifer; common as dirt. Why, there's a foothill town of that name, down towards Auburn—But it's Norcross we're talking about. What do you suppose—"

Glennister, like Jennifer, began to grope after the vague memories of some acquaintance with that name: Applegate. He, too, had heard it; where? For the life of him he could not recall at the moment; he was certain, however, that it would return to him; he felt that it had its own peculiar significance, that when he could make his memory stand and deliver he would have at least a hint worth while. For, as he had pondered before, there was more in this little man than met the eye.

Glee Hathaway started in to prepare lunch. Applegate waved a stick of stove wood wildly and maintained that she would have to walk over his dead body before she should smirch her hands with toil of this type in which he reveled.

"Why, I've been missing my cooking lately, Miss, eating stuff already cooked for me. I wasn't raised that way; I've cooked since I was big enough to swap a milk bottle for a bottle of hootch, and that swapping process came early out in—out where I grew up. You're hired to keep house, ain't you? That means to flip your feather duster; to go pick posies and put all around in the house; to tidy in general. Men folks can't seem to get the hang of tidying; but when it comes to cooking, that's a man's job. You just watch old Ab Applegate."

He made himself a long apron of a dish towel, rolled his sleeves high upon a pair of round, chubby and yet oddly muscular and ruddy arms, and even in contagious hilarity achieved a cook's cap out of a bit of paper from one of the parcels in the cupboard.

"There was a song I used to sing, being cook—" His voice trailed off wistfully. "Can't do it, though; there's some bad words in it, Miss."

"You might put in some blanks," laughed Glee.

"I could now, couldn't I?" Applegate sounded innocently grateful for the suggestion. He began to hum tentatively. Suddenly, in a particularly tuneless and unmelodious voice he burst out:

"I'm the Cook of this blankety, blankety camp,
   I'm the blankety king of the dump,
Where the guys I don't like gets
     as skinny as snakes,

And my pals grow blank-blankety plump;
For it's pies and cakes with blank-blankety cream
For each man the Cookie calls friend;
And it's pizen for sugar and pizen for salt
For the rest—and a violent end."

Glee appeared delighted with Applegate's rendition and cheered him on to more. Soon they were laughing and talking like life-long friends; he insisted upon doing the heavier, grimier work, but allowed her to assist at what he termed "the lady-like end of the business." And Glennister, meditating profoundly while he listened to them, seemed never tired of muttering over and over to himself:

"More than meets the eye, my friend. A whole lot more."

It was Glee who set the table and announced luncheon. The three men sat down; she insisted on serving, faithfully playing out her role. Jennifer looked at her curiously but said nothing; Applegate pleaded and expostulated and threatened; Glennister made no reference to her but ate in silence and was the first to leave the table.

"Our friend is working something out," whispered Applegate. "He's got something up his sleeve, you'll see."

They saw nothing of Glennister's plan until bedtime; and then only Applegate was fully enlightened. All day each one of them had been aware of

Glennister's watchful regard, keen and suspicious, following every step. After supper he had his smoke by the fireplace, aloof from the others, reserved and silent. When Jennifer had bestirred himself, announcing that he was going to bed, Glennister turned his head toward the girl and said, briefly, about his pipe-stem:

"You'll be sleepy, too, no doubt, Miss Hathaway."

"Sleepy!" cried Applegate. "This time of night? Why, man alive, it's hardly good and dark yet—"

"I'm not suggesting bed for you yet, Applegate," said Glennister curtly. "I was thinking you and I might have a bit of a chat—alone."

The remark was pointed enough and Glee, with a bright good-night which she, for her part, made a point of directing exclusively to Applegate, left the room. Glennister got up, watched her go, closed the door after her and returned to his chair by the fire.

"Pull up, close by," he said, and Applegate, already manifesting all the usual indications of curiosity highly stimulated, hastened to obey. "I want a word with you, and don't care to be overheard. And I want to show you something."

Applegate started forward, all expectant eagerness.

"What is it? What is it? You've found where the mine is? You've got another specimen to show me? You—"

"It's just—this!"

Glennister drew it from his pocket. It was the revolver which had once been Judy's. And now Ab Applegate sat staring straight down into its muzzle. His mouth fell open; he stared wildly, became a picture of mingled incredulity and consternation.

"Make one crooked move now, my little friend," said Glennister sternly, "and I'll drill you."

"What's eating you, man—"

"Suspicion, mostly. You're just a bit too damned innocent to suit me. What's the game, my friend?"

"Game?" said Applegate indignantly. "What's your game? What are you throwing a gun on me for? What makes you think I've got any game? Who told you—"

"First of all, I've been thinking all day about that name of yours: Applegate. Like Jennifer, I knew I'd heard it. Seems to me there was an Applegate out in Nevada; wherever there was a boom, there was that Applegate. Whenever word of a new strike got out, there was word of Applegate mixed up in it. Nevada Applegate they called him, didn't they. Know anything about this Nevada Applegate?"

Applegate cleared his throat. Then he scratched his head.

"Well? How about it?" snapped Glennister.

"Same family," muttered Applegate. "But I wish to goodness you'd turn that gun another way."

"Same family, eh? Suppose you tell me all you know about them?"

"I—I'd rather not talk about the—the Nevada Applegates, Mr. Glennister. Honestly—"

"Why not talk about them? They've cut the mustard. Old Nevada Applegate rates high in mining circles—in any circles. Well, for the moment we'll side-step him to come at something else. You say that you first came into this country about six months ago?"

"Into Hay Fork Valley, sure. They said farm lands—"

"About six months ago? *Just after Norcross found the old mine?*"

Applegate's eyebrows shot up sharply, came down heavily.

"How do I know? What makes you think—"

"Stand up!" commanded Glennister, and rose to his own feet as he spoke. "I may be able to come at a thing or two the direct way. Now, don't quiver a muscle unless you want to stop a bullet. I'm going through you."

"This is a nice way to treat a—"

"It does seem little short of unholy, you being such an innocent old duck. But I'm just beginning to wonder . . ." He slapped Applegate's pockets. "No hardware, eh? Well, I hardly expected it but—"

Glennister broke off to whistle softly.

"Under your shirt, old timer? In a holster, close

191

up under the left armpit. A forty-five Colt, I'll bet a man. You'll do, Applegate; you'll certainly do! Let's get at that gun now, and we'll talk all the more quietly. But what you want it buttoned up inside your shirt for—"

Applegate was actually blushing, turning fiery red.

"It's a sign I didn't expect to use it—like a man having a gun at the bottom of a trunk—"

Glennister jerked the shirt open and drew out the weapon.

"Big enough to shoot elephants with," he observed and tossed it behind him to a corner. His eyes grew more and more speculative. "Of the same family as Nevada Applegate? Hm. Yes; I expect so. Well, let's get forward. Will you turn out your pockets or shall I?"

Expostulating, Applegate, turned out his pockets. Odds and ends; keys, two knives, quantities of tobacco for smoking and other purposes; a pipe, matches, a handful of forty-five cartridges.

"Pull off your boots!"

"I'll see you in—"

Click! That was Judy's weapon speaking with a voice oddly like Judy's own, the hammer coming back under Glennister's thumb.

As red as a rose Applegate jerked off his boots. Something fell out of one and he strove wildly to kick it under his chair with his stockinged foot. Glennister saw and caught it up.

It was a tight little wad of bank notes, Glennister counted them. There were ten in all—and each was for ten thousand dollars! One hundred thousand dollars, in cash, in Ab Applegate's boot!

"Ab Applegate—teamster!" cried Glennister, and of a sudden began to laugh. "Ab Applegate—looking for cheap farm lands in Hay Fork! And would prefer not to discuss the family—"

Applegate grew redder and redder. With shame, one would have said; filled with that brand of mortification which is not unknown to childhood when detected at many a forbidden game.

"Welcome to our friendly midst," laughed Glennister. "Thrice welcome—Nevada Applegate!"

"WHAT A NIGHT! WHAT A NIGHT!" CHAPTER XIII

WHEN a man laughed as Glennister did now, there was far less of mirth in his laughter than of some savage satisfaction known only to himself. Applegate stared at him uneasily.

"I say, Mr. Glennister—"

"Shut up, you damned little snake," Glennister snapped, an ominous flicker in his black eyes. Grim and hard-mouthed, dominant and arrogant, he towered over the other; he was suddenly become steel against which any circumstance like a flint might strike sudden, blasting fire. All that there was of fierce passion in the man seethed to the top; he saw himself surrounded by enemies and tricksters who, though they might contend among themselves, were united in the wish to see him pulled down. The girl and the old man, pursuing their vain silly hopes, strove to set all his efforts at naught; this scheming Applegate, millionaire many times over, thought to rake in the pot while fools battled for it. Enemies within the house and without—And Jim Glennister growing at every second more set in his sinister determination to heap confusion confounded upon the whole crowd of them.

Applegate stirred restlessly, rubbing his stocking feet together, puckering his face and all the while watching Glennister curiously.

"I've sat in a good many little games, my friend—"

Glennister glared at him.

"You'll sit just exactly where you are for a spell," he commanded. He caught up the weapon he had tossed aside and pocketed both it and Applegate's roll of banknotes. "Don't you stir until I come back unless you want trouble to open wide up on you—and, by the Lord, I half hope you'll invite it! I'm fed up on you, my fat friend, and would just as lieve blow you to glory for the side-stepping, nosy weasel that you are, as light a cigarette."

"What's up?" Here was Applegate surging up, taking that intense interest of his again, demanding as fast as he could fire off the words: "Where you going? What're you going to do?"

Glennister grunted disgustedly and turned on his heel, merely calling back warningly:

"Sit exactly where you are until I come back."

He left the room, making sure that the door stood wide open behind him and hurried to his own room. The thought kept ticking away in his head that he had them all against him and that every mother's son—and daughter—of them would bear watching. Jennifer, most of all. Now that he had that ancient mariner under his roof he meant to take no chances with him indulging in any of his nocturnal jaunts. Jennifer ought to be asleep by now and Glennister, first of all, meant to assure himself that he was.

He went up the three steps to the Grizzly Room; a backward glance showed him Ab Applegate fairly goggling after him, but sitting as still as a mouse. Glennister hurried on, passing very near a certain spot behind which the plain, deceitful wall hid a closet in which he was keenly interested; on and into his own room; through it, across the narrow hallway and to the door of Jennifer's room.

Here he paused, listening. Jennifer's light was out and but a dim glow came in through the windows from the starlit night. Listening, he heard the old man's steady breathing; it seemed that old Dan Jennifer was sound asleep. But already Glennister had told himself enough times to-day that it would not do to risk all on appearances. He went quietly into the room.

When, a moment later, he came back to the living-room, it was to find Nevada Applegate sitting in the same position—and now all of a sudden more goggle-eyed than ever. For, swift to notice what Glennister brought back in his hands, he came up, surging to his feet, exclaiming:

"What on earth, man? You've got the old man's shoes—and coat and pants! What have you been up to? Murdering him or what?"

Glennister dropped Jennifer's clothing to the floor and went to his chair.

"I've fastened his far door and left the near one open," he took the trouble to explain. "I don't think he'll go rampsing around without me hearing him. And if he goes at all, it will be in his nightie."

"But where would he go? What would he want to run around this time of night for? What makes you think—"

"Oh, dry up!" cried Glennister impatiently. "If there are any questions asked, I'm asking them. First off—"

"What are you pocketing my roll for?" Applegate began clamoring at him. "Think I'll let you walk off with a wad like that? And what do you think you're going to do with my gat? That gun, I'd have you understand—"

"Be still!" Glennister roared out at him, and

caught him by the shoulder, fairly hurling him backward into his chair. "Keep still for once in your life or I'll hammer your head off for you. Haven't you the brain of an overfed goose? Can't you get the idea into that skull of yours that I'm the one to ask questions which you're going to answer without any of your own?"

"Go ahead then," growled Applegate, red and fidgety. "Ask your darn' questions and don't keep me on edge all night wondering what they're about. Snap into it, Jim Glennister; what do you want to know? What are you going to ask me? What's the idea of pouncing on me to get your information out of? Who told you that I—"

"Good heaven!" groaned Glennister. "Can't the fool hold his gab a single second?—No funny business now, my friend; answer me this first of all and shoot straight with me. If you lie I'll know it and you'll pay for lying to me. *Do you know where the lost mine is?*"

Applegate, who had been wriggling and squirming while he held his silence, now suddenly popped up out of his chair as though jerked upward by some invisible string, shouting:

"No—Do you? Have you got any hunch? Do you think old Jennifer knows? Or that Miss Hathaway—"

Glennister, glaring at him, thought within himself: "The slick old customer! Playing his part to a farethee-well finish."

But, still watching Applegate, he began revising that thought. Just what part was the man playing? Making pretense at exactly what? Why, this amazing individual needed play no part at all; all along he had but to be his own natural self and what risk had he run of being suspected as identical with the somewhat renowned Nevada Applegate of recent years? He struck the outstanding keynote of childlike curiosity, but struck it sincerely and with no slightest need of counterfeit. With Applegate curiosity was and ever had been the driving, compelling force. To find out, to go and see for himself, to pry underneath—just this seething characteristic had led him in his time to his share of the gold under the grass roots. He rushed in among men, he demanded to be told this and that, everything; he left laughter behind him while he sped along to his discoveries.

"He told me no lies," conceded Glennister to himself.

No; not even in the joy of doing little homely duties, cooking and serving meals, had Nevada Applegate made any false pretenses. In the city he lived as did other city-dwellers of means; he had servants and costly apartments and the rest of it. In that environment, if anywhere, one might conceive of him masquerading, and growing restive at it, too. Here he was himself. A man who was forever chattering, as loquacious an individual as you could hope to come upon, yet one who was eternally busied at absorbing information, and—one scarcely noted this—giving nothing out!

How had he, to begin with, gotten wind of happenings here? He had been interested for some six months; and that meant since Norcross made his discovery. Had Norcross gone to him, soliciting financial backing? No; else there would have been cash paid Andrew and the deal closed long ago. How then? What more likely than that Norcross, managing to get some of the richest ore, had conveyed it to San Francisco to turn it into cash? And that, having raw gold to sell, he had taken it to Applegate's bank? And then that Nevada Applegate, "smelling it out," had begun firing his questions at his clerks, learning this and that after his fashion, and thus had been led into this northern California county?

Certainly he was no other man's emissary, no spy of the Norcross interests. He was too big a man for that. Rather he had jumped it "on his own," a small fortune in his boot, to snap up the whole morsel at the first opportunity.

"Why didn't you hop to it ahead of Norcross and buy Andrew out?" Glennister demanded abruptly.

A look of shame dawned on Applegate's face.

"I was a chump; Norcross had me fooled from the getaway," he conceded unhappily. "I thought he hung around this particular ranch because he was sweet on Miss Hathaway, and that the stuff was a good twenty mile from here."

"And now?" Glennister asked sharply.

"Now, knowing what I do know, which ain't much, Mr. Glennister, there's a question or two—"

But Glennister wasn't listening. Had he required any assurance that gold was here or hereabouts and in big, paying quantities—high-grade—he had it from recognizing who Applegate was. Where bees gather, look for honey; where Nevada Applegate elected to prowl, look for gold. Here, in this ingenuous looking little man, he saw one who twenty years ago had made his own bright page of mining history in a virgin district; owner now of the Western Consolidated Midas Mining Corporation, president of the Western Miners' and Assayers' National Bank—one of the very few men on the western coast who really "sat in" where big mining interests framed their deals. A man to toss flap-jacks, with a hundred thousand dollars in his boot!

Glennister, from a long period of frowning at the floor, jerked his head up suddenly, a little crooked, sinister smile on his lips, a mere shadow of a smile sharing in the mirthless qualities of the short laugh with which he had greeted recognition of his guest.

"I'm rather inclined to believe, Mr. Nevada Applegate, that I've got you dead to rights for once in your slippery life!"

Applegate's eyebrows shot up, his mouth rounded, and altogether he looked the picture of gasping astonishment. Perhaps he had managed somehow to catch the thought which Glennister swiftly put into words.

"Your hundred thousand is a sizable stake—and I've got it!"

What a face Applegate had for the display of emotions! It seemed that every muscle, every tiny wrinkle, must get into play to take a hand in limning his every shade of thought so that any but a blind fool could read to the bottom of his mind. Big bold letters chalked on a blackboard could have scarcely been more clear. That first flash—astonishment—came, registered, and went. His face was a blank. The slate was wiped clean. Then appeared stupefaction. Then incredulity. And then again, that utter astonishment.

"That would be highway robbery!" he gasped.

"No uncommon thing, after all, is it?" demanded Glennister.

Applegate's two big toes rubbed together violently. His face, for a moment marvelously screwed up, cleared and he began to chuckle.

"You won't do it," he announced positively.

"No?" Glennister's brows shot up. "You're so sure? May I ask why I shouldn't do as I please?"

"Two good reasons, Jim," and Applegate was all affability again. "You're not that kind of a guy. You're hard as nails and keen as steel, but you're no dirty thief."

"Thanks. The other reason?"

"Those ain't copper pennies you've lifted off me, young fellow. Ten thousand dollar bank-notes, that's what they are, and the woods ain't thick with 'em. Meaning, so to speak, you can't toss 'em recklessly over a counter here and a table there, asking for your change like they were ten spots. Get me?"

"Hardly."

"You would, if you knew what a cautious sort of man I am. Bills that size are easy kept track of. They came out of my own bank and the numbers are jotted down by my cashier. Same as marked money, Jim, my boy."

"You crafty old cuss!"

"Not crafty, just cautious, Jim." Applegate was beaming genially. "Better toss 'em back to me."

Glennister drew the roll from his pocket and looked at it thoughtfully.

"I owe you something, old boy," he said, sternly. "What if I take and drop the whole works into the fire?"

"Burn a hundred thousand of my money! You wouldn't dare!"

"Wouldn't dare?" Glennister made a sudden swift gesture toward the small blaze in the fire-place. Applegate sprang forward, clutching him by the arm.

"I'll take it back!" he shouted. "Darn you, you'd dare most anything. But that would be a fool thing—and a low down, mean one."

Glennister shook him off and again put the money in his pocket.

"I'll think it over," he said curtly. "Anyway, you don't get it back to-night. I'll talk with you in the morning. Meanwhile I keep the wad, and by the same token I keep your claws pruned for you, Mr. Nevada Applegate. You'll do no crooked work against me with this little pile."

"I've got a notion," cried Applegate, "to bash you over the head with a poker! I've got a notion to chip in with Norcross after all and skin you proper. And, when I'm done with you, to hand you over to those Injuns to stick full of pitch splinters and roast. I tell you—"

"You're off to bed," snapped Glennister. "And in a hurry. I'll keep your boots here; and, giving you five minutes to get undressed, I'll serve you like old Jennifer and take care of your clothes."

Applegate's full face went from fiery red to congested purple. For a moment he was absolutely speechless. Thereafter short and furious was the argument which followed, at the end of which Applegate marched off to his bed with his own forty-five jammed between his shoulder-blades. Within less than five minutes Jim Glennister, with a sour smile, had made a bundle of Applegate's clothes with Jennifer's. From Applegate's room came at last an explosive volley:

"Look here, Jim Glennister, you're all right in your way but you're too darn high-handed! I got a right to know a thing or two, I guess! You got my gun and you got my wad and you got my duds—but you ain't got my goat yet! What are you going to do next? I'm not to be satisfied lying here all night, wondering, am I? You got to tell me one thing: What I want to know is—"

Glennister slammed the door shut on him.

Back before the fireplace in the silent house he fell to pondering. Of the secret of the closet near which he had discovered Judy, he knew more than he had told—he had hinted to Glee herself—but not all that he wanted to know. The bear paw in the Grizzly Room still hid that portion of the paper which had been caught in the hidden door. Last night, while Judy slept before the fireplace, he had gone silently to it and had read that incomplete fragment of writing which the triangle of paper, hardly more than a corner, had let be revealed. He could recall it almost word for word; he had it in mind when, making Glee her deed, he had laughed at her, saying that he was tricking her. The words had run:

> you, my youngest
> afraid sometimes that
> if ever Andrew should be
> day, in justice to you, so have
> deed of the house itself and the
> st will this date.
> "Your loving father,
> "Oliver Hathaway."

"A note from Oliver to his little daughter," Glennister had been swift to declare, "in which he tells her something of his doubts of brother Andrew and that in his latest will he is giving her the house itself. She has never seen it, else she would not have fallen for my offer to give her that which is or should be already hers."

But he had had no opportunity to get the whole paper free and had not wanted to tear it. While Judy slept in the next room he had searched very briefly for the secret of the hidden door and had found nothing. A more exhaustive search at the time he had been unwilling to make. Judy was just the one to lie awake, "playing possum," and he had had no wish for her to suspect that he had received any hint pointing in the direction of her interest here, suggesting any reason for her visit. Even yet he could not know if she had come for that paper, or if there were something else in the secret closet which had drawn her.

Now, with the house silent and a moment to himself, he meant to know all that was to be known. For ten minutes he stood idly before the fireplace. All remained quiet; there was no further outcry from Applegate; no creak of ancient floor boards came to him to betray anyone who might be astir; even Glee must be asleep by now. He went quietly up the three steps into the Grizzly Room.

The walls here were finished in large redwood panels, left unpainted or stained, mellowed with time. He held his candle close; knowing just which panel it was that must serve as door, he should have little difficulty in coming upon the catch and getting it open. The panel was framed in with a broad batten at each side, and molding above, the baseboard at the foot, and as he studied he had to admit that never had he seen a more blank, non-committal and innocent-looking wall. Were it not for that scrap of paper thrusting forth its tell-tale corner under the baseboard he would never have thought to search here.

But so narrowed was his field of investigation it would have been hard for the cunningest secret to have escaped him long. There was a thin film of dust upon everything; moving his candle slowly back and forth he saw at last a spot where fingers—Judy's, no doubt—had left an almost invisible trace; there were thumb and finger-prints at the top of one of the battens and on each side. He placed his own thumb and finger upon them and began exerting pressure this way and that; trying to force the strip of wood to move inward, to one side, to the other—out toward himself. A soft exclamation of satisfaction broke from him. He had it. The batten, cleverly hinged at the bottom and kept in place by a long flat steel spring, yielded as he pulled on it; slowly he pried it outward at its top from the wall. Behind was a little catch; a moment's work with it and he was able to swing the panel itself inward. He thrust his candle forward and peered into a small closet lined with shelves; he looked upon a clutter of old account books, some tumbled to the floor and hastily thrust into a corner; packets of letters, yellow with age; other papers which could have been any sort of legal documents; a couple of tin boxes with their lids thrown back and bespattered with candle grease. The place looked as though it had been rummaged in the greatest wild haste. By Judy, no doubt. He wondered if she had found what she sought?

Then he remembered the paper which he had come seeking and stooped for it. Not finding it where he had thought to find it he supposed that the thing had slipped under the bear rug. He tossed this aside and found nothing.

It was possible, since the door opened inward, that the panel had dragged the paper inside. He began looking for it. It was not under the door; not in the space back of it when it folded in against the wall. But it was in the closet and Glennister, having found it, stared as though he could not and would not believe his eyes. It lay, folded neatly, upon an empty space on a shelf just in front of him.

"Since when have letters learned to get up off the floor and put themselves away!" he demanded of his thoroughly amazed self.

He looked closely to make certain that it was the same. A glance gave him the entire contents; as he had guessed, Oliver Hathaway wrote this to Glee, informing her that the house was hers—

A scream, ringing wildly through the still house, affected him like a powerful electric current poured through him from head to foot. For an instant he stood transfixed. The scream, ringing out the once only, had come from the far part of the rambling old house—where Glee Hathaway's rooms were.

His moment of rigidity was of the briefest. Tossing the paper pack into the closet, sweeping the door shut with a bang, he caught up his rifle—he had brought it here as a precaution against it falling by any chance into Applegate's hands—and dashed across the room, down the steps and into the living room. Here he crashed headlong, full tilt into Applegate himself. For the moment in the uncertain light Glennister did not know him, so was he, for modesty's sake, bundled from head to foot in a blanket from his bed. But Applegate's voice, lifted vigorously, was unmistakable.

"What's up?" he clamored. "Who yelled like bloody murder? Was it Miss Hathaway? You haven't been putting your dirty paws on her, have you? What's happened? What's the matter? Who—"

Glennister shook him off and raced through the long room and jerked the door open. He heard a patter of bare feet flying along and Glee herself in a hastily-donned dressing-gown rushed fairly into his arms. He drew her swiftly into the room, demanding as earnestly as even Applegate could have done:

"What is it? You screamed—"

She was white and trembling.

"I was asleep," she whispered. "Something woke me. There was someone at my window— trying to get in, I think. I just saw a figure and screamed—"

"Stay here with Applegate," Glennister commanded, and ran out into the hall.

It was ten minutes before he returned to them to find them talking excitedly before the replenished fire. They fell silent at his approach. Perhaps it was only to hear what word he brought them, but again, within reason or without it, Glennister sensed union of all other forces against him.

"No use," he said shortly. "If there was anyone prowling about he's had ample time in the dark to get clear."

She shivered and turned frightened eyes from him to Applegate who, clutching his impromptu toga about him with one hand, patted her shoulder gently with the other.

"Don't you be scared, Miss Hathaway; there's nothing and nobody going to hurt you."

"But why would anyone try to get in at my window?"

"Why?" echoed Applegate. "That's what I want to know? And who was it and—"

"Off to bed with you, Applegate," commanded Glennister so savagely that both wondered at him. Just what whipped up his anger he would not have admitted to himself. But there was a steely menace in his eyes, and it had been there from the moment when he entered and found them whispering together. He concluded dryly: "You're in no proper costume to entertain a lady—" His smoldering eyes drifted to her. She hastily clutched her dressing gown tight about her. "You, too, were better in bed," snapped Glennister.

"I'm afraid! I'll not go to sleep again. I'll go get dressed and sit up here by the fire—"

He shrugged.

"As you like. But, for reasons known to Applegate and myself he'll not dress just yet. Off to bed, my fat friend."

And Applegate, though he expostulated and at the end looked as if he were going to cry, trotted off to bed. Glennister slammed the door on him and, candle in hand, stalked off to his own room.

A moment he stood listening for Jennifer's breathing, meditating that the old man slept soundly not to be awakened by all this racket. All of a sudden, a black frown gathering his brows, he hurried into Jennifer's room.

The bed was empty. A glance showed him that the room was empty. And, though for an hour he searched high and low through the house, storming about in towering rage, no Jennifer and no sign of Jennifer was to be found.

"What a night, what a night!" wailed Applegate from his room into which for the third time Glennister had driven him. "All I want to know is—"

Glennister had slammed more than one door that night but never in all his life did he slam any door with greater vehemence than now.

INTO THE NET   *CHAPTER XIV*

ONCE open the door to suspicion, its whole ferret-eyed progeny comes slinking in; microscopic detail is at once magnified and distorted; doubt and mistrust peer crookedly. Glennister was in the proper mood to suspect everyone of any evil up to murder, grouping old Dan Jennifer, the girl and Nevada Applegate into an infernal trio who would balk at nothing. Of Glee Hathaway, hastily dressed and looking nervous and frightened, he demanded with a bluntness that reeked of plain brutality:

"Let's have the truth now, young lady, if it's in you: Was that scream of yours part of the game just to pull me away while the night-prowling Jennifer sneaked out?"

As hostile as his own was her mood by now.

"You brought his clothes in here—even his shoes. Why? What have you done with him?"

"Did you see anyone at your window? Or were you just plain lying?"

She flushed and her head jerked up. About to retort, she thought better of it and remained maddeningly silent.

"Confound it!" cried out Glennister. "You've got to answer me. If you did see anyone outside, was it Jennifer himself?"

"Of course not!"

"Where is he then? Where could he have gone—and why?"

Pure terror was in her eyes now.

"I don't know. I can't understand. I am afraid!"

"Of what?"

"Of—of everything—"

"Of me?" he half sneered.

"Yes!" she cried wildly. "Of you most of all! What have you done with Danny?"

"Listen to me," he said sternly. "You have admitted to me that you and Jennifer, working together, hope to beat me to the thing I'm here to get. His absence from the cabin when I visited you goes still unexplained. His vanishing to-night, just before or just after your most thoroughly convincing scream—"

"I saw someone! If you have had nothing to do with Danny being missing—Then it was Jet Norcross or one of his men!"

How he jeered at her then!

"They came into the house, I suppose, with the

212

rest of us almost next door to Jennifer! They gathered the sleeping gentleman up so softly in their arms as not even to awaken him! Then, the powers of darkness being thoroughly in accord with their plots, they rode off on a broomstick or some such sensible affair!"

"That's not any more absurd than your accusing me of spiriting him off," she reminded him coldly. And turned away from him to drop down on the settle, her hands caught up tight in her lap, her shoulders drooping dismally.

Glennister watched her narrowly. Her very attitude threatened to disarm suspicion. What reason, after all, had he to think the things he certainly did think? With an effort of will, stiffening physically, he drew his eyes and thoughts away from her. In a corner were Applegate's clothes. He went to them, gathered them up and left the room. At Applegate's bedside, holding up his candle, Glennister said sharply:

"Snap out of it, little playmate. Here's your raiment."

"You're a good guy," exclaimed Applegate with enthusiasm. "I knew you'd cut out the funny business pretty soon."

He flung back the covers, scrambled out and began pulling op his trousers.

"I'll sleep in 'em, after this, bozo," he announced as though he meant what he said.

"You'll do no sleeping of any kind to-night,"

Glennister was quick to inform him. "I'm leaving you to run the house—"

All of Applegate's burning inquisitiveness came flooding back.

"Hey? What's that? Off somewhere? Where are you going, Jim? What have you found out?"

"I left you once before and you sneaked off the minute I did," ran on Glennister sternly. "To-night I've a hostage. Just exactly one hundred thousand dollars of yours. Maybe you'll get it back or some of it, if you behave yourself; I swear by all that's good and holy to do you out of the whole of it if you don't do as you're told this time."

"Oh, I'll be good dog," grunted Applegate, still busy getting into his clothes. "Just want me to ride herd on the house while you're gone?"

"No one but myself is to go out; neither you nor the girl," Glenniser explained emphatically. "Got that, Applegate?"

"I got it. But I'd like to know—"

"And no one but myself is to come in! If there's anyone outside, as she said, he's to stay out—"

"How about the old man?"

"He seems to do pretty much as he pleases, that crafty old Jennifer. Yes; I'd want him in and I'd want him to stay in, if he did show up."

"You're meaning my job is to keep Norcross and his Injuns out?"

"Exactly. In case they should come asking for a night's lodging."

"All right. I'll see your game through this trip." And Applegate thrust out his hand. "Slip me my old forty-five—"

"Don't be a plumb fool! I've got enough on my hands without taking you on, handing you your young cannon and asking you to try to stage a come-back for your little wad."

"How'm I going to keep out a gang like Norcross and his Apaches?" queried Applegate irritably.

"See that your doors and windows are locked; have the lights out; meet anyone who wants to come in with a poker."

"Gee, I love you!" said Applegate. And then, as he saw Glennister about to leave the room, he darted forward, asking somewhat meekly: "But I say, Jim, let me know what's doing! I ought to know where you're going and—"

"You confounded quiz-box—Yet—" Glennister paused and seemed to hesitate. "I've got a notion—"

"Yes," exclaimed Applegate. "That's right, Jim. I got to know."

"If I told you—"

"Go ahead, man!"

"I'll do it—on one consideration." Glennister was eyeing him strangely; Applegate could make nothing of him. "And that is that you promise me not to ask me another question of any kind for a full twenty-four hours!"

Applegate looked both shocked and hurt; also, perhaps, doubtful. Yet he was constrained to answer:

"I'll promise. Go ahead. Tell me. Where are you going now?"

"I'm going," said Glennister slowly, "where I think the old mine is!"

"But—what—where—"

"Look out!" Glennister sang out to him. "Your promise! Not another question for a full day and night."

Applegate turned red.

"You darned Judas—"

But Glennister, armed as they used to say "to the teeth" since he carried not only his own rifle, but two requisitioned revolvers as well, tarried no longer. He took his momentary grim satisfaction in stirring the mining adventurer to the very bubbling ultimate degree of curiosity and then, out of doors and on his way, swept him from his mind for other considerations.

First of all, his suspicions still rife, he was interested in the rather inexplicable Jennifer. What earthly reason could the old man have for slipping away in this, his own, peculiar fashion? And where could he have gone? As Glennister chose to regard him, he was a devious individual playing some underhanded game of his own. That he had sought to depart so secretly more than once hinted that he went to see someone; a man could hardly be looked to be sneaking about at night just for the sake of the pastime in itself. He would meet someone. Whom, if not Norcross?

Glennister went a bit further in his speculations. There may have been a man at Glee Hathaway's window; that man, Norcross or another, might have been the person Jennifer crept out to meet. On the other hand, Jennifer may have had no knowledge of this man's presence and may have gone further afield for his assignation. Where, then? Where, save to the Norcross "hangout"?

Once outside, Glennister went quietly, all ears and eyes. He stepped silently into the blackest pools of darkness; he stood without moving many a long minute; he was fully half-an-hour in circling the old house. In that time he had assured himself that no one lurked in the gardens; Jennifer, he judged, had betaken himself straight off to whatever rendezvous he meant to keep to-night.

So Glennister turned his own steps toward that hidden place beyond the big redwood to which he had followed Judy in the white mists of early morning. He went hurriedly and with little fear of being seen. Arrived in the narrow ravine below the walls of rock, he grew somewhat more cautious. The big hollow tree rose like a solid tower of ebony. He went up the steep slope to the clump of smaller trees about the big fellow's base; all was quiet and dark. Noiseless and watchful, he came to the opening like a door in the mighty bole; only silence and dark. He stood listening. No one here; he could swear to it. When the moments passed with neither challenge nor bullet, he congratulated himself on finding the approach clear, entered the tree-room and struck a match.

The steady little yellow flame gave sufficient illumination for his purpose. He saw the blankets on the ground; no one sleeping there as had been a possibility until the last minute. He saw the knotted rope dangling from the upper dark. He blew out his match, slipped a shoulder through the strap of his rifle, and went up hand over hand.

As once before he had come to the orifice high above, so now and with readier ease did he reach the point whence he might look out, his eyes level with the upland plateau. But this time he saw no one, no gleam of firelight; and though he listened intently, caught no sound of human voice above the gentle murmur of the tree-tops.

"Which is just as well," he consoled himself by deciding, "until I can have negotiated the way from the tree to the cliff edge."

He drew himself a trifle higher up and squeezed through the hole in the redwood's trunk, clinging with one hand and one leg. He discovered that thus, leaning outward, he could easily reach the rock-crest of the cliff; it was simplicity itself, disengaging the other hand now, to secure a firm hold with both and so pull himself up.

Once on the edge of the precipice, he crouched

and sought to make himself somewhat conversant with the bolder features of this lofty table-land. Off to the left rose the hills, thick with flourishing timber; lesser hills, standing farther back, rimmed the place about on all other sides saving that one by which his trail had brought him here. The plateau itself, of some ten or twelve acres in extent, was threaded down its middle by a gurgling brook overhung with red-boled madrones; here and there, making for bold irregularity, huge bowlders lay where they had in their time come bounding down from the higher hills. Otherwise the place was of gentle aspect given over to grassy slopes.

"Norcross would establish his camp handy to the creek," judged Glennister, "nor far from this place and yet hidden by a grove."

Already his eyes were upon a clump of trees, madrones for the most part, in whose shadows the purling brook lost itself. He went forward toward it, his rifle in his hands again, moving more cautiously than at any time since he had left the house, but in caution welded to haste. His eager impatience rode him as it had done from the start, spurring him on. Almost immediately he knew that he was close to the camp; voices reached him and, at the same instant, he saw a shower of sparks swirling skyward above the little grove.

Since no gleam of the fire itself reached him he concluded that Norcross had a cabin of sorts here, walls to conceal the fire flicker. All the better; if those whom he sought were housed it was all the simpler for him to come close to them without them suspecting his presence.

The cabin, which he finally made out in the middle of the grove, was the crudest imaginable habitation, obviously the work of Starbuck and Modoc and their fellows, a thing of cut saplings interwoven with lesser poles, thatched with the branches of evergreens and the broad leaves of ferns. Through a hole in the flimsy roof smoke and sparks went up; as he came close, he saw the fire-gleam shining through the walls at a score of places.

He had drawn so close now that no longer were the voices an indistinguishable blur of sound. He made out Norcross' deep, sullen tones. Then another man speaking serenely, placidly—old Dan Jennifer!

"The infernal old hypocrite!" Glennister cried within himself, and not without a certain savage satisfaction. For it was something to have gambled and won tonight on the probability of Jennifer slipping out of the house to come here for word with Norcross. "Last time," thought Glennister, "it was Applegate and Norcross. Jennifer and Norcross now. And next time, Norcross and the Hathaway girl! They're all standing together somehow. Just how, I'd give a lot to know!"

Though he had caught a word or two from Norcross, not more from Jennifer, the words meant nothing to him; contending with the difficulty which is ever a man's who comes upon two others talking and in the midst of their conversation, he felt the necessity of missing not so much as a monosyllable. So he crept on, like a shadow for patient silence.

Between steps he looked all about him; there were others of this outfit remaining unaccounted for, Judy, Starbuck and Modoc, and perhaps other Indians, and Glennister meditated that when you don't know exactly where any certain person is, he may be anywhere at all. He scrutinized every shadow, harkened to every thin whisper of sound—and crept on. So close did he approach the flimsy shelter that at last he could peer through the many cracks and holes, seeing everything within.

There was a small fire ringed about by rocks and affording all the light there was. Norcross stood with his hands in his pockets, his hat far back, smiling the old Norcross smile which Glennister remembered so well, a twisting of the features in his silent, devilish mirth. On a box, with thin old hands extended toward the blaze, sat old Jennifer, looking as usual unmoved, unconcerned. He was barefooted and clothed in ragged shirt and dirty overalls far too big for him. With these two was one other and him Glennister came near overlooking; the Indian Starbuck squatting in a corner, a rifle leaning against his leg, his beady black eyes watchful.

Glennister stirred again; he stood within a yard of a great, low-branched madrone, and meant to come even nearer; it would be a comfortable thing to have at his back and its thick trunk should hide him effectively. But just as he lifted his foot to move, the silence about him was shattered, torn to quivering shreds, by the frenzied, staccato barking of dogs. The deep-lunged, booming notes of a hound, the sharp quick yelping of at least one other dog. And with a rush here came the dogs, leaping up from among the shadows within the cabin, darting out under the blanket over the doorway, headed straight and with mighty clamor toward him.

As quick as a flash Glennister went up among the branches of the madrone. He'd have the camp against him in another moment, but up there above them, in the dark cast by the leafy branches and with his rifle trained upon Norcross, he swore he'd give an account of himself that would make all odds of no avail to them.

The dogs, baying with all the frenzy of their kind with a quarry just out of their reach, leaped wildly about the base of the tree, then settled back on their haunches and with lifted muzzles poured out their furious barking. And just then, when Glennister saw no possible earthly hope of escaping that detection which he had been for once at such pains to avoid, the incredible happened. Judy, from somewhere down among the shadows, called out sharply and of a sudden appeared below him, storming at the dogs, striking and kicking viciously.

"You big fool varmint-dogs," she railed, "I'll teach you to bark at me. Shut up! Shut up, I tell you," and she rained blows right and left.

Barks turned to yelps and howls of pain; with a frightened yip-yip-yipping the mongrels turned tail and fled, followed by Judy's missiles and vituperation.

There came a shout from Norcross:

"What's going on out there? What's wrong? Judy, what the devil are you doing?"

"Those two whelps of Starbuck's started barking their fool heads off the minute they heard me coming," snapped Judy. "I'll show 'em a thing or two if I have to break their heads in for them—"

"Leave them alone, I tell you," Norcross called angrily. "What do you think we've got them around for? Want to spoil a good pair of watch-dogs?"

"You needn't yell at me," Judy informed him, turning away from the tree. "I'm coming in. And I know what I'm doing, don't I? Spoil those two?" She cackled at him derisively.

Glennister could hardly credit his senses. Yet the dogs were gone, fleeing from Judy's flaming attack as for their lives, and Judy herself flinging a last stone after them, flipped aside the blanket at the door and presented her impertinent self before her father. Glennister, leaning forward through the leaves, watched her like a hawk; on a night like this, when the very soul within him rankled with ready suspicion, he was ready to weigh every act, word and gesture of such as Judy.

"The Lord gave me a fool for a daughter," muttered Norcross.

"Oh, dry up, will you?" Judy spat back at him, as sharp and quarrelsome as a blue jay. She broke off to sniff contemptuously. "Still ragging this poor old goat? Why don't you ease up on him?"

From Glennister, relaxing for the first time, a sigh of relief; narrow as had been his escape, he began to thank his stars for Judy's coming. From Norcross she drew a look of pure amazement.

"Oh, I'm just sorry for the poor old boob," was Judy's answer to his look. "You just lay off and let him be."

"Getting soft-hearted?" jeered Norcross.

Glennister, too, wondered.

"Oh, you make me sick!" she flared out. Glennister, watching her face which was clearly revealed in the red fire-light, had never seen so downright baffling an expression. "With the big stake to be raked in, you play pussy-wants-a-corner with old Jenny here. He's a harmless old fish and I'm for him. You leave him go!"

Norcross, for answer, caught her by the shoulder and whirled her aside. "The girl's gone stark mad," he grunted.

"It's you that's plain nuts," Judy shrilled at him.

"Why don't you break into the game like a man and quit your side-stepping? Why don't you tie into things man-style? That's what Jim Glennister would do, if he had half your chance. It's what I'd do myself, if I was let free to do anything. If it had been me, I'd been out of this and wearing diamonds long ago. If you'd only listen to me—"

"You'll be out of this shack in two shakes—wearing stripes from a quirt," snapped Norcross. "Beat it, I tell you."

"You go chase yourself, you big stiff—"

He leaped at her and caught her by the shoulder again, this time to hold her squirming.

"Here, Starbuck," he called. "Take her back to her own shanty and keep her there."

Starbuck rose expressionlessly. Judy, writhing in her father's iron grip, spat out over her shoulder:

"Don't you dare touch me, Starbuck! I'll send a whole raft of bad wishes after you if you do. Twisted foot and blind eye and swelling tongue—"

Starbuck cringed. Judy cackled with laughter.

"The stupid fool," scoffed Norcross.

"Oh, no, he's not," laughed Judy, breaking free with a sudden jerk. "Look what happened to Modoc—"

"Slipped and sprained an ankle—what's that amount to?"

"Ask him! Ask him if he'll cross me again. Or Starbuck, either."

"No can do," muttered the Indian gutturally. "Bad wish', him all same debbil wish."

"Now," said Judy, "I'm going to tell you something, Jet Norcross: I'm through. I'm done with you and your piffling ways. And I hope Glennister gets your scalp. What's more, I'll help him do it. You're a nickel-shooting hold-back and he's a sport. I'd help you get your gold and you'd hand me ten dollars maybe—maybe not. Jim would square me with ten thousand. That's the difference in the breed of dogs."

"So you'd sell me out to Glennister!"

"You bet I would! I'm not half the crook you are, anyway. And—"

"Damn you," cried Norcross, suddenly in a flaming rage, and caught up a thick stick lying at his feet.

Judy screamed wildly. Dan Jennifer, electrified, sprang forward, trying to thrust between father and daughter. And at that moment Jim Glennister having rushed about the corner of the shelter, burst in on them like a storm wind.

"The girl has double-crossed me!" roared Norcross.

Starbuck, in Glennister's headlong path, jerked up his rifle. But Glennister, his own gun clubbed for close quarters, was just that all essential second too quick for him, striking savagely. Starbuck, smitten by the rifle barrel which struck him a terrible blow on the side of the head, crumpled in his tracks.

Of them all Judy seemed least spellbound by any shock of surprise. Like a young tigress she was upon Jet Norcross, her strong lithe arms about him, screaming shrilly:

"Quick, Glennister! Quick, before he pulls a gun—He'll kill me!"

Glennister stepped swiftly by the astonished Jennifer and rammed his rifle barrel into Norcross' side.

"Up with your hands, Jet, old boy," he commanded, "And make it snappy!"

"Damn you—"

"Certainly—but up with them!"

Norcross, his hands lifted high, glared at him only briefly. From Glennister the stabbing eyes in which sulphurous flames seemed to flicker, traveled to Judy.

"You she-Judas—I'll get you for this if I have to hang high the next minute!"

"Tie him up," called Judy, dancing about excitedly. "He'd do me in if he got the half show. There's a rope in the corner. Tie him and Starbuck together. Quick, before the rest of 'em pile in on us."

Norcross, with locked lips, made no slightest resistance. Only his eyes were unsurrendering, only they promised that the game was not yet played out.

Judy ran to Jennifer, catching his hand.

"Come; hurry! Gee, we're in high luck to have Jim Glennister pop up out of the ground in front of us. Come ahead, Jennifer; run if you ever did."

Leaving Norcross bound hand and foot, Glennister hurried after them. Starbuck lay on his back where he had fallen, his face looking in the uncertain light as though death had set its seal there.

"Dead, ain't he?" whispered Judy.

"Stunned, more likely," retorted Glennister. "Come, Jennifer."

"Me, too," cried Judy. "I wouldn't last any longer here than a rabbit among coyotes."

"It looks as though you were just as well with us," he conceded. "This way—"

"No, no," she exclaimed. "Not the way you came. You climbed up through the old redwood, didn't you? Not that way; we'd run into Modoc and the others; there are six of them. But another way I know; through a pass in the hills right over yonder. The horses are there, too."

"She's right," said Jennifer. "We came that way and on horseback."

Glennister agreed curtly and they struck across the little creek and toward the timbered, steeper hills. They had gone scarcely a hundred yards when, with a sudden exclamation, Judy whirled and started running back.

"Wait for me a minute—"

"Here!" said Glennister sharply. "Where are you going?"

But, fleeing like a shadow among shadows, she was gone and with never another word.

"A night of puzzles," Glennister said. "What's the girl up to?"

"My suggestion," said old Dan Jennifer quietly, "is that we step along. There's something downright queer about that young miss."

"She stuck up for you bravely enough," Glennister reminded him. "Queer or not, we'll give her her minute."

Almost immediately Judy came flying back.

"I'd forgot my wad," she explained, panting the words out. She flourished a tight-shut hand. "I've got a hundred bucks in that and maybe I'm going to need 'em. It ain't going to be healthy in the same part of the world with Jet Norcross after this. Come ahead; let's shove along."

Glennister, though he stared hard, could make nothing of her face in the dark. His thoughts were scarcely less than chaotic. All that he could do was watch her, shrug and follow. She led straight on, almost at a run, toward the hills.

"There's a trail here. It leads through the pass."

"I know," said Jennifer. "By the old dugout—"

Judy treated them to her strange, cackling laughter.

"You've been blind as any old fool bat, Jennifer," she told him. "You prowled around these hills so much, you led Jet here straight as a string, you even kept your grub in the old dugout—and never guessed!"

Jennifer, with an alacrity not to be looked for in

a man of his years, sprang forward and caught her arm.

"Never guessed?" he repeated excitedly. "Never guessed what? You don't mean—"

"Don't I?" laughed Judy. "Ouch! You pinch me, you old crab!"

"What's all this?" asked Glennister, catching up with them.

"What are we all here for?" snapped Judy. "Mushrooms or gold?"

He stared at her.

"What has the old dugout to do with it?"

"What's a nest got to do with eggs?" she flung back at him. "But come ahead, you two. I'll tip you the story when we get safe inside four walls. What's in the dugout can wait a little longer, I guess."

"But," remonstrated Jennifer. "Norcross said I had my feet in the stuff to-night! What did he mean by that? I wasn't there—"

"Oh, Jet is a slick one all right," she conceded airily. "But so is Judy. Just as slick and a darn sight slicker—I'll show him."

They hastened along, found the trail, entered a dark depression at the base of the hill and began a winding way up toward the pass.

"I tell you," Jennifer burst out, "there's no mine in the dugout! I've been there a thousand times. It's impossible!"

"Oh, is it? I don't know what I know, don't I?

I'm a blind little fool, am I?" she laughed derisively. "Tomorrow, or as soon as you like, when I'm clean out of this mess, you go see! I'll tell you just where to poke and where you can budge a big rock out of the back end and find the old shaft and a cave in the hill behind it. But all that can wait until Jim here has played square with me and slipped me a nice fat bunch of prize money and got me off to the railroad. For the love of Mike, you two, get a move on."

Jennifer, the old, old fever burning in him, said quickly:

"This trail takes us right by the door—"

"And keeps taking us right along, mister!" said Judy sharply. "We stop just long enough to yank the door open, drag out the saddles and bridles and then hotfoot along. Think I'm going to take any chances on Jet getting loose? Or on Modoc and the rest of the bunch getting back to camp before we're clear of the woods? Not little Judy!"

Again in silence they pressed forward into the hills. Perhaps five minutes later Judy ran ahead, calling:

"Here we are, boys. Wait a minute and I'll slam out a couple of saddles and bridles."

Hinges complained; Glennister coming up with her found her pulling open a sagging door. The dugout itself, an ancient affair of stones piled into low walls of what had once been a squat habitation amounting to a room half of which was a hole in the hillside, loomed up a black, formless mass. Jennifer hastened to join them.

"You two guys stick where you are and keep your eyes peeled," Judy urged. "I know my way about like a cat in the dark. I'll get what we need."

She slipped in at the open door. Glennister, conscious of an eagerness akin to Jennifer's struck a match only to have it hastily dashed from his hand by Judy, who exclaimed:

"Do you want to get us all plugged full of lead?"

"You're getting nerves all of a sudden," he told her lightly.

Jennifer had pressed by him entering the black maw of the place. Glennister struck the second match.

"Drat the fool!" snapped Judy. "If you're bent on having a light, you two gold-diggers, at least get behind the door."

He stepped to one side, holding his match high, Judy stood at his side. The place was foul and close the match spluttered and cast but the most sickly of lights.

"Sh!" whispered Judy. "I think I hear somebody coming!"

And then Glennister and Jennifer heard a sound which explained a very great deal—and left a great deal unexplained—the heavy bang of a door slammed shut. That and a metallic click; the click of a lock.

The light died out. Glennister groping wildly found only Jennifer within the sweep of his arm. He flung himself against the door. From without came from Judy a burst of mocking laughter.

TRAITOR—OR MADMAN?   CHAPTER XV

"JUDY!" shouted Glennister. "Open that door."

"Jet! Jet!" screamed Judy. "Get a move on! I've got the two of 'em locked up in the dugout!"

"Stand aside, you, Jennifer!" commanded Glennister wrathfully. "I'm going to shoot the lock off."

"You girl," came Norcross' voice from some little distance. "What—"

There was a tremendous roar as Glennister fired, rifle muzzle close to the lock. In the narrow confines of the almost air-tight dugout the explosion beat with fearful impact upon eardrums. Glennister fired the second time, hearing Norcross still shouting from closer by. The heavy air was filled with the fumes of burnt powder. Jennifer began to cough.

"Hurry, hurry, hurry!" Judy was screaming, dancing up and down in the stress of her excitement.

"You little fool!" came in booming rage from Norcross. "If you'd let the dogs alone—"

"I knew what I was doing," Judy screamed back into his face. "I knew the big stiff was there all the time. I followed him and would have done for him myself if the dogs hadn't started yelping."

"Why didn't you tell me?"

"Oh, you big jackass!" she shrieked at him. "With him standing right on top of you, covering you with a rifle all the time, ready to drop the whole works of us in our tracks? That's what you'd have done; you would have spilled the beans like any other lummox of a man that can tote only one idea at the time in his wooden head—and look what I've done for you! Got 'em both bottled up tight, yours for the taking."

Glennister rattled fiercely at the door. It stood as sturdily as fresh, heavy timbers could hold. Something clinked at his feet; a case of bottles. He understood now why Norcross would want a place with a lock on it, safe from the thieving fingers of his own Indian hangers-on.

"Now take a hand, Jet Norcross! I've saved your bacon for you," Judy railed on, "by playing a part like a Hollywood actorine—if you'd used what God gave you for brains you'd have twigged I was up to something when I started getting soft. I've done everything, trapping your meat for you and even running back to cut you loose; now suppose you come alive and step up and take a hand. The game is ours, right now."

An overpowering rage gripped Jim Glennister. Fool that he was, fool seven times over, to have been taken in by a girl, to have gone blundering headlong into the first trap she set for him. He hurled himself savagely against the door, recking nothing of the bruise of the impact, set on breaking through heavy timbers and into the open—and to Norcoss.

"No use," he growled deep down in his throat. "It's like a jail door. Well, by the lord, they've got to open up to come at us, and when they do—"

"I say Glennister!" called Norcross.

His tone had changed. Sullenness and bitterness had departed; his voice rang out mockingly, vibrant with triumph. He even had a kindly thought at last for Judy.

"I'm proud of you, kid," he commended her. "You've played this just as slick as the next one."

"Hmf!" sniffed Judy. "Some day, maybe, you'll realize who's got all the brains in this family."

Norcross laughed. Then again he turned toward the dugout.

"Hey, there, Glennister!" he called.

"Well?" growled Glennister, never in his life more disgruntled than at this moment, holding himself a greater howling jackass than Judy had named her father.

"Do you want to dicker? I've got you where I want you for once, and whatever I say goes. Just the same, to save trouble, I'll deal with you."

"The devil you will!" jeered Glennister. And in a fresh access of rage, began battering at the door.

When Norcross spoke again it was from only a

few feet away—yet safely to one side of the door.

"I'll make you a fair proposition," he said coolly. "I'll pay you back the seven thousand you gave Andrew. On top of that I'll hand you a bonus of ten thousand. For all of which you transfer to me all your equity in this ranch and get out. It's a lot of money; it's easy money for you—and it's a whale of a lot more than you'll get any other way. What's the answer?"

"The answer," Glennister told him hotly, "is this: When you have whiskers as long and white as Dan Jennifer's, I'll talk to you."

"Oho, so that's the way you feel about it, eh? Well, we'll see how you feel about it after you've had a few hours to think things over."

It grew very quiet among the hills about the old dugout. Low voices, the words indistinguishable, filtered in for a while, Judy's sharp tones rising insistently above her father's. Judy, plainly, was making her suggestions and Norcross, for once, was impelled to listen to her. Perhaps he began to realize that he had never, done her full justice before, this daughter of his craft and an Indian mother's cunning, and now stood ready to counsel with her. Presently even their tones fell away into the deep brooding silence.

Glennister struck the third match, found a splinter of wood and improvised a thoroughly wretched torch, its pallid and uncertain flame scarcely supported by the thick, foul air. Little as he liked to exhaust a single breath of oxygen, he was set on seeing what the inside of this trap looked like. And not at all to his liking did he find it. The rock walls, though very old, were as sturdy as the walls of a fortress; crevices were chinked up with clay. He held his torch aloof; it showed him several heavy beams, poles laid crosswise, and what was no doubt a thick sod for thatch; thereupon the flame slowly faded and died, leaving but a red ember in his fingers.

"I can get out," he muttered to himself, for the moment oblivious of Jennifer. "I'll pull down the wall I or go through the roof."

The silence outside was disturbed rather than broken by vague sounds which came and went, died away and came again. Thereafter he made out low voices and it dawned on him that there were several beside those of Norcross and Judy. The Indian contingent of the camp had put in an appearance.

Nor was it long before he made out what they were doing. They had taken a suggestion made by Judy. Gathering much dead wood they built a big fire not ten steps from the dugout door. The flames leaped high and a broad circle of light spread further and further; did Glennister find the way of breaking out now it would be to be shot down at Norcross' will.

By now a change had come over Jim Glennister. To begin with he had lost his temper most thoroughly—and that was less because of the predicament itself in which he found himself than because he saw himself so easily tricked to his undoing by a baby she-devil like Judy. A man in such an insensate rage would set his teeth to steel bars. But the red-hot flash of anger passed swiftly. This was not the first time in his life that he had found the cards stacked against him—and he had always found a way out into the clear. So he ceased struggling like a maddened animal in a net and forced himself to take cool stock of existing conditions.

A faint sound coming to him from near-by in the dark recalled Jennifer whom he had actually forgotten. It was a quiet, regular, entirely business-like sort of sound.

"What are you up to?" he demanded.

"The two of us, left shut up here a few hours, would smother to death," Dan Jennifer told him placidly. "I wouldn't put it beyond Norcross to try the experiment, either. I am scraping the clay out of a chink here and hope to let in a little outside air."

Glennister grunted. Breathing here was almost impossible; Jennifer was quite right. And what was more, Jennifer instead of hurling his old frame against the rocks, was at work to do something worth while.

"Serves you right, if you smother," Glennister said savagely, "for hobnobbing with a crook like Norcross."

There came no answer. Jennifer kept scraping away with a long splinter of wood from the liquor case at his feet, saving his breath. Yet, somehow, his very silence spoke for him. Certain events and words of to-night surged back upon Glennister, bringing mystification and doubts. In what haste old Jennifer, given the opportunity, had fled from the Norcross camp. And Judy's words of a moment ago: "I've got the two of 'em locked up!" and "Got 'em both bottled up tight, yours for the taking."

"Look here, Jennifer," he said, "I'm going to fight clear of this mess somehow. And what about you?"

"Oh, I'll be all right," said Jennifer quietly.

"You will, eh? You stand in with Norcross, do you?"

"No," replied Jennifer. "I do not."

"Then how explain your dickering with him tonight?"

"I don't explain it!"

"Why did you come, then? What brought you?"

"Norcross and his Indian brought me."

"You mean—"

There was a sound that might have passed for a long sigh. The scraping sound had stopped. Glennister realized that the old man, having opened a crevice, was drinking in a great lungful of the fresh, outside air.

"If you'll step here, Mr. Glennister, I'll treat you to something rarer than champagne."

"I'll do nicely a minute or two yet," Glennister

returned shortly. "What I want first is an answer to my question. How came you here? And why?"

"I can't tell you. I don't know. Except that I was surpised—somewhere—knocked over, half-stunned, utterly confused and brought to the camp here on horseback."

"You don't know where you were or what you were doing when Norcross grabbed you?" Glennister asked incredulously.

He received a calm, dispassionate rejoinder:

"I do not."

"Then—What does Norcross want with you?"

"I think," Dan Jennifer surprised him by saying, "that I must know where the mine is and—"

"What! You must know? And don't know you know? Confound it, I've no wish to hear babbling nonsense. How would such a thing be possible?"

"There could be but one explanation. I am growing old, Mr. Glennister." Jennifer sighed, but the calm tones did not falter. "I am afraid that I am a little—mad."

"My God, man!"

"Several things have made me doubtful of myself lately. I have had dreams—or visions— Norcross has said things to me. I have been looking for gold, this gold, all my life. It may be that I have paid the price. I don't know."

Glennister laughed at him But, as laughs go, his was no great success. Perhaps the old man was a little mad—

There came a call from Norcross:

"Are you ready to talk turkey, Jim?"

Glennister made no answer. Norcross continued curtly.

"Then I'll bid you good-night. I don't mind telling you what you are up against. My men will keep a big fire blazing all night so that you'll make a good target if you find any way to get out. Pop up through the roof, break down the door, pull a rock out from the wall or tunnel under, it's all the same. And if you do slip through—Well, you know you will be forcing matters and they'll have to shoot to kill."

Still Glennister held his peace.

"All right," Norcross told him. "It's good-night then. I'm leaving you, but there are half-a-dozen of Modoc's and Starbuck's tribe sticking here. With Captain Judy in command!" he concluded.

It was Jennifer who answered him, calling eagerly:

"Where are you going, Jet Norcross?"

Norcross laughed.

"Where do you suppose? I'll leave you to guess. You can't guess wrong!"

They heard the clatter of hoofs. Norcross was off at a gallop.

DISCOVERY—
AND TERROR

CHAPTER XVI

FOR a long time the two left behind at the old Hathaway home sat in silence before the great living-room fireplace. Finally Applegate jumped to his feet as though he had been suddenly impelled upward by the release of some gigantic spring, and began striding wildly up and down, back and forth, muttering excitedly to himself. Glee Hathaway, already utterly at sea for any explanation of to-night's happenings, watched him in wonderment.

"What is it, Mr. Applegate?" she asked him when in one of his wild orbits he passed close to the settle.

He came to a halt and stood rocking on his heels, looking at her with the most earnest bright blue eyes she had ever seen.

"Ask me!" he groaned. "Old Jennifer pops off in his nightgown, gone like a puff of smoke, and where's he gone to? Up and after him goes Jim Glennister—or has he popped off the other way? My roll in his pocket at that! When will I see him and it again?"

"Your roll?" she asked. "What do you mean?"

He waved both arms.

"Let that go. It's considerably more than a bag of peanuts, but I can stand it if I have to. Serve me right, I guess, for being such a tarnation fool. But what I want to know is, where's Jennifer and what's Jim Glennister up to?"

She could only shake her head wearily and sigh.

"I don't know; I can't think. I am worried about Danny."

When she rose and took a candle down from the mantel, Applegate asked sharply:

"Now what? Where are you going?"

"Into Danny's room again. I keep thinking that there may be something to give a hint, some sign—oh, I know it's foolish to even hope so, but I'm going to look again."

"Better than doing nothing," he agreed. "I'll come along."

He took up the heavy poker from its place against the smoke-blackened rocks, the only weapon which Glennister had seen fit to leave him, and carrying it like a sword went at her heels on her brief journey. Thus they passed through the Grizzly Room, through Glennister's room, across the narrow hallway and in at Jennifer's door. Once before, shortly after Glennister's departure, they had made this pilgrimage, noting the carelessly thrown-back bed covers, the empty room. This time both searched through every inch of the small chamber, hoping to find—something. And this time Glee Hathaway did make a discovery though she could not see how it added to the sum total of their definite knowledge.

"Danny's pick is gone," she said thoughtfully. "The short, prospector's pick, the new one which he bought on our last trip out to the store. It was here yesterday; it's gone now—"

"Well?" demanded Applegate breathlessly. "Well? What's that mean? What does it point to? Gone, eh? Where? Why? What would a man want with a pick, poking around at night?"

"I suppose it doesn't mean anything. But—that's the only thing missing, the only sign here for us."

Since no other concrete focal point for his mental activities offered itself, Applegate strove manfully with the new problem of a missing pick.

"A pick makes a man think of a mine," he argued, staring at her as though for inspiration, "and that's what we're all after; a certain old lost mine. And Jennifer disappears, taking the pick with him. And you told me Norcross told you Jennifer told him—showed him, I mean, where the mine was. Now, then, has old Jennifer gone poking off to the old mine? Jim Glennister thinks he's a crook and is holding out on everybody—"

"No!" she cried emphatically. "Danny would not hold out on me; he would not treat any of the Hathaways like that."

"Well, well," agreed Applegate soothingly, "I guess you are right. You know him better than I do. Come, let's get back to the other room and poke up the fire; I'll get some coffee going. No telling what time Jim Glennister will come back and I want to be on deck when he does show up."

So they returned slowly toward the front of the house. Glee cast a curious look about her as they passed through Glennister's room. What a man he was—strange, to her, unfathomable; the Glennister whose bold eyes, bright with suspicion and hard with determination, had more than once fairly glared into hers; the Glennister who sat at the piano and sang—and started vibrations within the very soul of her. Again she sighed.

They were half-way through the Grizzly Room, she carrying the candle and leading the way, while Applegate, with his poker, followed at her heels, when a small, almost negligible thing happened to catch her eye. It was only a shadow, but upon a wall otherwise shadowless, cast by one of the battens which appeared to have come loose at the top. Carelessly, pausing a moment with her mind but half occupied by this unimportant trifle, she quite naturally and mechanically put out her hand to replace the narrow wooden strip; her thought upon the subject, if she really actually thought of it at all, was that the old nails at the top must have given away. She thrust the batten back into place. There was something oddly smooth in the way it responded; there were no nails to be re-thrust into old nail holes; the batten snapped into place with a faint click.

"That's funny," said Glee, still but half-interested.

"What's funny?" asked Applegate, startled from a reverie. "What are you doing there?"

"Nothing—I suppose," she answered, and they went on, returning to the living-room. Here, grown very thoughtful, she dropped down to her old place on the ancient settle, while Applegate, finding another candle-end, wandered off to the kitchen to make his pot of coffee.

"I suppose it's nothing," she said again to herself. But in fancy she fingered the batten again, felt it respond to her touch as though hinged at the bottom, heard the faint click. She did not stir, however, until she heard the rattling of stove lids in the kitchen; then she sprang up, caught up her candle and ran back to the Grizzly Room.

In front of the secret panel she, like Glennister, stood a long while puzzling. She held her light close, just as he had done and, like him, she saw those tell-tale spots where other fingers had brushed the dust aside. She tugged at the batten and it came away from the wall at the top. It was hinged. It did hide some secret. A strange excitement gripped her.

She found the little catch, tarnished with age, but winking dully in the candlelight. A door—a hidden door. Leading to what?

She was almost frantic in her haste now. She wanted to get this strange, undreamed-of door open and to have at least one peep inside, before Applegate came. Why keep it secret from him?

She did not have time now to analyze motives. She liked him immensely and had from the first look into his eager blue eyes; she had no slightest reason on earth to distrust him. Perhaps it was that the very secrecy of the door bred secrecy in her. To have lived all her life long in this old home, and not to have ferreted out its last, tiniest secret! Another click—the panel giving under the pressure of her eager fingers—the door wide open. She held her candle inside, saw the closet with its shelves and most interesting-looking japanned boxes, its litter of papers; papers curling at the edges, papers yellow with age, papers in bundles tied about with string.

She heard Applegate coming into the living room and called out to him:

"Come here, Mr. Applegate! Look at what I have found!"

The impulse to invite him to her side came suddenly and she acted on it. The rest of the night she would devote to rummaging through all these old documents—who knew what she might not find here? Even the secret of the old mine!

Applegate, poker in hand, came at what amounted to a gallop. His eyes seemed to be popping from his head.

"What is it? A door? What's in there? Not old Jennifer, murdered and stuck away?"

"I don't understand! A closet that I never knew about; full of papers!"

He appeared no less excited than she. A thing like this whipped up the imagination to full speed ahead. She dropped to her knees and began gathering up fallen documents, letters, account books and journals with which the floor was littered. He watched her a moment; gradually the look on his rosy face altered and when he spoke his words were a surprise to her. Instead of asking a score of answerless questions, he said in a suddenly hushed voice:

"Those letters—those papers—they'll be things of your own folks. Your mother's and father's, maybe; even your grandmother's and grandfather's, from the look of them. You'll want to be alone. I'll be in the next room, Miss."

And away he went, grasping his poker as though it were a living serpent which he meant to choke to death—just as, for once in his life, he was throttling his inordinate curiosity.

"I like him more than ever now," thought Glee Hathaway.

She sat down on the floor and for a little while merely drew papers to her, glanced at them, set them in little stacks. A task here for all night? For weeks. She recognized her mother's handwriting; her father's. She came, with a little start, upon a letter from her own baby hand; it was written to her father at one of the times when her mother had taken the children out to Eureka for a vacation trip. There was a leather-bound journal inscribed,

"Richd. Hathaway, his book." It was dated 1850; under Hathaway's name was written: "London, Eng."

The japanned boxes were filled to overflowing; the closet floor was an untidy litter. Many papers were crumpled; they seemed to have been trodden on ruthlessly. She gathered them toward her tenderly, smoothed them out with soft, loving fingers, placing them like the others in little heaps.

All the while she was marveling at the fact that such a repository for so much of interest, old family treasure trove, could have existed all these years without the general family knowledge. Grandfather Dick had known, of course; it must have been at his orders and under his supervision that this place had been so cunningly constructed here. And her own father, Oliver Hathaway, must have known, since these papers for the most part appeared to have been his, placed here for safe keeping. There had ever been a marked vein of secrecy in Grandfather Dick; his keeping the location of his mine to himself, the many anecdotes which Dan Jennifer had told her of him, bore ample testimony to that fact. But he would have told Oliver, bidding him keep the secret. And Oliver had died all without warning.

In making comparative order out of utter chaos, she came upon one paper on the floor which seemed stuck to the boards. She lifted it gingerly, lest she tear it; no doubt an oozing of pitch had glued it down. When it further resisted her gentle efforts, she brushed all dust and litter away from it, making a closer examination. Now she saw what held it; it appeared to have slipped half-way down a crack between two boards and to be held there, tight-wedged. Odd, that a thin sheet of paper could have slipped down into a crack and become so fast there.

And thus, after a puzzled moment, was she led to her second discovery just as Jim Glennister had come upon his first. The paper was caught because there was a trap door in the closet floor. Someone had opened that trap, the paper had slipped half into it, the closing trap had caught and held it.

A trap-door, so painstakingly hidden—unguessed all those years—leading where? She jumped to her feet; new excitement surged upon her; she began the wildest seeking.

With the clue which she had and which indicated for her the edge of the trap-door, she was no great time in coming upon the second secret. Near the wall was a short section of floor-board which had the look of being rather more loosely fitted than its fellows; there were slightly wider cracks about it than elsewhere. She worked with it, thrusting it this way and that and finally, with a little gasp of pleasure, found that one end, when pressed down, sank readily, while the other rose accordingly; the short board pivoted in the middle. In another moment she had one end of it standing straight up, the other disappearing into a box-like opening beneath. Holding her candle close, she saw a handle-like piece of iron bar which offered itself to be tugged at. She grasped it, pulled eagerly—and the trap-door at her side opened with but the faintest complaint of hinges. At her feet now was an opening, large enough for one to pass through readily. Below was yawning blackness with but the first few steps of a steep stairway leading down.

Again, impulsive and obedient to impulse, she called to Applegate. But at the moment he was in the kitchen stoking his stove and did not hear her. About to run to him, a fresh thought—or rather a confused medley of thoughts—stopped her. Secret doors opened before her to-night. Hidden things stood revealed. Who knew but that already she had her foot upon the first step leading to a discovery greater than any other? Someone had come this way before her, as the paper caught by the trap-door indicated. Had that, by any chance, been Danny Jennifer? Did he after all have the one great secret they all sought? She would not call to Nevada Applegate. Not just yet, at least. Not until she knew.

She leaned over the steep stairway, holding her candle low. One step after another, they led down and down into a region of utter dark which the dim ray of the candle failed to penetrate. Breathless, she listened. All was quiet. Quiet and darkness down there—and emptiness. There need be no fear of going down; at the first alarm she could race back, she could call Applegate to her.

Yet, as she began the descent, a strange shiver shook her. It may have come from the cold; it was into a thick and chilly atmosphere that she was descending. What was she going to find down there?

She set foot to the topmost step, testing it warily. This staircase must be very old, as old as the house itself. She recalled tales of the building of the Hathaway home. Grandfather Dick had sent all away, his wife and the two babies, with Dan Jennifer charged with their responsibility, while he set to work to build the home. He had wanted to create something fine for them; he wanted it to come as a surprise. Therefore, while at his command that would brook no argument they grew restive traveling and dwelling in the cities, he with his corps of men had made haste here. What a canny old fellow he was! A young fellow, by the way, when the house was building, but canny even then.

Old as they were, the steps were sturdy and firm, giving out never a complaining creak under her light weight. She took the second step, hesitant, half-afraid of she knew not what, lingeringly because of a strange formless fear, yet stubbornly determined, so urgent and insistent were the commands laid upon her lively interest. It grew chillier at each step; despite her assumption of fortitude she was conscious of a wild flutter of apprehension. Low as she held her candle, it penetrated but a little way into the gloom below; she had the sensation of one going down into a bottomless pit, a place of forbidding and mysterious shadows. She told herself that she was fanciful and childish; yet almost from the first struggled against the obsession that at any moment a cold hand might clasp itself about her ankle, dragging her down.

Never had a dozen steps constituted so long a journey. But at last she was at the bottom. She twisted about swiftly, making sure that no weird menace stood just at her back. And then for the first time she forgot her fears as she saw into what sort of chamber she had entered.

It was like a natural cave for irregularities. The rock and earthen walls were gouged out into what, in this dim light, looked like the mouths of tunnels. How far these excavations, whether man's or nature's, extended, she could have little idea. Great pillars made of the boles of redwoods, supported the heavy beams above, which, in turn, supported the floors. Piles of earth lay about, heaps of broken fragments of rock were everywhere. A sort of pathway seemed to lead windingly among them. She began slowly going forward.

With a startled exclamation she stopped, looking at something which she saw leaning against the wall of rock and soil. It was Jennifer's new pick! The one which had vanished only to-day!

She ran to it to make sure. There was no doubt; Jennifer had been here before her during the last few hours.

Before she had done with the first shock of amazement she came upon the second discovery. There was another of his favored short-handled prospector's picks—and another—and still another! Those picks which Jennifer had "lost" during the many years—they were all here! Then he had known all along; for years and years while the Hathaways sought and while Dan Jennifer pretended to seek, he had known!

"Oh!" she gasped. "I can't believe that of him!"

Yet believe she must. There was something else. On an old bench lay a coat, neatly folded. She recalled the coat. It, too, was Jennifer's; it, too, he had complained two or three years ago of having lost! Why? Why? Why?

There was the testimony of her eyes to tell her why. She must, though it pained her infinitely, though the knowledge came with a positive shock, look upon old Dan Jennifer with new eyes: One who lusted and ever had lusted for gold, for gold only. One who, since he could not claim it as his own, hoarded it away like a miser and came to gloat. One who chose rather to see the Hathaway family destitute than lead them here.

For here, just under their questing feet, was the

old lost mine, and she had known it from the first step on the stairs. And such a mine as she had never dreamed existed; some gigantic pocket, maybe; an end of the great mother lode itself? An out-thrust vein of rock gleamed with the soft rich light of gold in her candlelight; a fragment at her feet was streaked and pitted with gold. What would those tunnels reveal? Gold in pockets, gold in nuggets, free gold to be taken up almost without labor. A place of high-grade ore which had scarcely been scratched. It was more like a mint than a mine!

Found at last—and yet at the moment she felt more like weeping than rejoicing. For to learn that Dan Jennifer, than whom she had ever held there was no more loyal friend on earth, was a traitor, struck at the very roots of her faith in humanity.

"Danny, Danny," she whispered, "how could you! I can't believe it."

There were the many picks, silent but eloquent; there an old coat which she remembered well; she had sewed buttons on it. These things were not to be brushed away. But why had he left them here? Or, leaving them behind him, why had he always gone about pretending to be seeking them, and in the end buying others to replace them? And then bringing the newer ones here to be abandoned, to be replaced yet again in their turn? A new thought flashed into her mind; Dan Jennifer need not in his heart be a traitor—it might be that, upon this one matter alone and only after long years of brooding, he was stark mad!

This thought, like the other, was terrible. Yet she chose to harbor it. Thus, instead of bitter contempt and scorn she could feel only a deep sympathy for him.

Where the winding path led among heaps of debris she followed a little way, hesitant at every step, afraid yet impelled forward to know more of this secret place. There seemed to be the major tunnel, straightening before her as she advanced, and several minor horizontal shafts. How far did the chief tunnel run? Where did it end? It was narrow and low; she crouched a little in walking, yet one might make progress along it without difficulty.

A sudden sound, very faint yet pronounced because of the great stillness about her, brought her to a sudden stop, her heart in her mouth. There was someone down here! Jennifer? Or someone else? The sound she could not catalogue exactly; a footstep? or a stone under which loose soil had given, rolling down some heap of earth and rock? It mattered not; she *felt* that no longer was she alone here.

She whirled and ran back toward the stairway. The sudden movement extinguished her candle. With horrible blackness the dark closed in about her. She ran on, stumbled and fell. Springing to her feet she strove wildly to locate the stairway.

Now again she heard a sound. Footsteps were coming upon her swiftly; relentless, implacable, evil footsteps she sensed them. A scream of pure terror burst from her.

"Mr. Applegate!—Help—!"

A flash of light blinded her. Whoever it was approaching carried an electric torch. It shone brightly and briefly and went out. She sought frantically to escape. Utterly bewildered, all sense of direction lost, she crashed into the rock wall. And, before she could recover herself, she felt hard hands upon her, strong purposeful arms dragging her back. A heavy hand was clapped over her mouth.

Whose hand? That of Norcross? Of Jennifer himself, mad Jennifer? Of Glennister?

She did not know. She knew nothing save that in the utter dark some creature of the dark held her as one is held in a nightmare.

THE TRIUMPH OF JET NORCROSS — CHAPTER XVII

NEVADA APPLEGATE, busied with his ever-seething thoughts, occupied himself no less with his self-appointed kitchen tasks. He pictured "that little girl in there" as he had left her, plunged deep in the suddenly discovered treasury of old family papers. She, too, would sit up the night through, no doubt of it. Further, she'd be glad now for a few minutes alone. So to coffee he added nice hot biscuits; such biscuits as he had taken pride in bringing brown and crispy from the oven in many a mining camp. He found an old serving tray; made an inroad upon Glennister's larder for some jam; and half-an-hour later bore his culinary triumphs to the living room. Table set, fire replenished, he called cheerily:

"Miss Hathaway! What say you join me a minute over a cup of coffee?"

Having no answer he hesitated; perhaps he ought not to interrupt her? But his hesitation was brief. Of course she should have a bit of supper, just the thing for her since there were the long sleepless hours of the night ahead of them. So he called again and more loudly.

"So deep in that bunch of old letters and stuff," he advised himself, "that she wouldn't hear a thunderstorm."

So he went up the steps to the Grizzly Room. She was not there at all! The secret door was closed, concealed; and there was no sign of her!

"This is the darndest household I ever stuck my nose into," he muttered, staring about him into the shadows. He had brought no candle with him, and the room, fitfully revealed by the one candle and the firelight in the adjoining chamber, might hold her somewhere in a dark corner. "One by one they slip away—Oh, Miss Hathaway!" he shouted. "Where have you gone?"

When still he received no answer he hastened back for a candle. Holding it high, peering to right and left, he went through the room and on into the next. At almost every step he paused to call again. He went through room after room; in a few minutes he had made his first circuit of the entire rambling house.

He had been mildly surprised when he had not found her at first. He began gradually to grow puzzled and by the time he had come back to the fireplace and the coffee going cold, he was a most thoroughly mystified man.

"She's hiding somewhere. Now, why? Why should she want to hide unless—Good Lord, she's gone out for some fool reason!"

He began another hurried search, this time for the unbarred door or unfastened window to show him which way she had gone. And, when for a second time he stood beside a tray on which now coffee and biscuits were stone cold, he had arrived at a stage of utter stupefaction. She was gone; clean gone—and every single door and window was fast barred—from within.

"That closet!" gasped Applegate. "She's got herself shut up in there—My God, maybe she's smothered—"

He rushed at the steps and fairly hurled himself against the paneled wall, beating at it with his fist, calling her name over and over and over again. Just where was that infernal door? How did one get it open? Why didn't she answer—unless already, for lack of air, she were dead. Why had he been such a fool as to wait all this time—why hadn't he thought of this first of all? But how on earth was a man to dream that a girl would want to get into a closet and lock herself in?

He was on the verge of rushing out for an ax when one of the battens assaulted with a frenzy of vigor gave under his hand and came away at the top. He found the concealed catch, fumbled with it a moment, and at last, all atingle with excitement and yet cold with dread, he got the door open.

"Thanks," said Jet Norcross, and stepped out into the room.

Step by step Applegate fell away from him, staring wildly as though at an apparition. His jaw sagged, his eyes bulged. He could find never a word to say, never a question to ask. Glee Hathaway had vanished as by magic; as by magic, here stood Jet Norcross in her place!

Norcross laughed.

"Got you guessing, have I, old-timer? Well, you're not the only one," he added grimly. "To-night I've got the world by the tail, if you want to know. By the way, let's make sure of you. Got a gun on you?"

Norcross, bringing his right hand forward, indicated how he himself was armed. But Applegate in his present state of confusion-confounded had no eye for such a commonplace thing as a mere revolver. His jaw began to work; he managed to half whisper:

"Wh—wh—"

"Up with your mitts," Norcross commanded, and Applegate, as in a dream, obeyed. Norcross ran a hand over him, taking due stock of all pockets and all places where a man might carry a weapon.

"Lord Jim cleaned you, first, eh?"

Applegate nodded. And now his teeth came together with a click.

"Damn it," he burst out, "tell me—"

"I'll tell you a lot before I'm done," Norcross cut him short. "But I've got something to do right now beside talk. You—"

"Where is Miss Hathaway?" shouted Applegate.

Norcross' eyes flashed.

"That's all I wanted to know!" he chuckled.

Applegate stared harder than ever.

"What? What did you want to know? What did I tell you, man? I just asked—"

"You just told me that you don't know—anything! Which is exactly as I'd have it for a while."

A change came over Applegate. His face lost something of its smooth roundness, his under jaw shot forward and there was nothing in the least pudgy about two fists suddenly clenched.

"You dare lay a hand on that girl—"

But Norcross was watching every gesture and

261

the weapon in his hand came up with a jerk, its black muzzle taking those imposing proportions which a pistol muzzle ever does when presented close to any pair of eyes. Applegate groaned and shook his head; blue fires of wrath and impotence blazed and flickered in his eyes.

"Into the next room with you," Norcross commanded. "And don't get any fool ideas, Applegate. I don't want to hurt you and I don't want your carcass on my hands. But I mean business to-night."

Applegate, having no alternative did as commanded and in silence. Norcross followed him as far as the steps down into one room from the other. Here he stopped, closing the door at his back enough to shut out any view through it, yet leaving a crack of an inch or two. He put his fingers to his mouth and whistled shrilly. Once, again and a third time. Then he slammed the door and went on after Applegate who by now had dropped down on the settle by the fire.

"You're taking almighty chances, Jet Norcross," he remarked dryly.

"For almighty big stakes," grunted Norcross. "I've done that before."

"You'll never do it again!"

"Perhaps I'll never need to," Norcross shrugged.

Applegate, about to make a further remark, remained silent, listening. Somewhere a door opened; footsteps sounded noisily. Someone in the Grizzly Room or beyond was hurrying; someone who came in answer to the sharp whistle, twice repeated, from Norcross.

It was the Indian, Modoc, limping markedly from the sprained ankle—of Judy's bad-wish sending?—coming down the steps and stopping at the bottom to lean on his rifle and fix a pair of brilliantly black eyes on Norcross. Applegate was quick to note the coil of small, stout rope which Modoc brought with him, and to leap to the correct explanation.

"Put down your gun, Modoc," said Norcross tersely. "I can keep him good. Tie him up for me in such style that the devil himself couldn't get loose."

Modoc set his rifle against the wall and came forward, uncoiling his rope.

"Have a good time—while it's your innings," muttered Applegate, and made not the slightest resistance.

"Hands behind him, Modoc," said Norcross coolly.

Swiftly and skillfully Modoc executed the orders; once Applegate winced as the cords cut into his wrists.

"Legs, too?" asked Modoc.

"In a minute. First, we'll let him use them. To the kitchen, Applegate."

In the kitchen Modoc finished his work. Applegate, with hands bound behind him, with ankles lashed together, was given a chair; the door closed behind his departing captors and in pitch dark he was left to ask and answer his own questions. Where was Miss Hathaway? What had they done with her?—And Jennifer?—And Lord Jim?

Norcross, with the Indian at his heels, returned to the fireplace. He glanced at the tray with its cold dishes. Set for two—and some interruption had spoiled the feast. He shrugged and turned to Modoc.

"Bring the tools, Modoc; hammer, saw and plenty of big nails. And bring the girl along with you."

Modoc departed. Norcross stood frowning down into the bed of glowing coals. But his concentration, deep though it was, was not such as to preclude hearing a light swift step. With the old flash in his eyes, the flash that had been there that night when he had thought himself master and owner of those broad acres, he greeted Glee Hathaway.

"Mr. Norcross! So it was you—"

She stopped just within the room. Something of her recent terror still made her eyes look unusually large; her cheeks were pale with vivid splashes of color like that of fever.

Norcross made cool mockery of her with a somewhat elaborate bow as with his sinister smile.

"I? Just what is it that I have done? I arrived about ten minutes ago."

"Where is Mr. Applegate?" she asked hurriedly.

"Where he will not trouble you to-night, my

dear. As a matter of fact, you and I need fear no interruptions at all."

She shivered and her eyes went to the fire. She saw the tray with its little golden heap of biscuits, its cold coffee cups, plainly the work of Nevada Applegate, who was not to trouble her to-night— She shivered again. Norcross laughed.

"You're not cold; it's not a chilly night," he said. "Just nervous, that's all. But come up by the fire, my dear, and we'll chat."

He flung himself into the big easy-chair without waiting for her and began filling his pipe. Then he saw Modoc at the door.

"Where is Charlie Bear?" he asked.

Modoc answered with his thumb which, to save words, he jerked over his shoulder. Norcross appeared to understand that the man he required was in the next room, and called sharply:

"Charlie Bear! Here!"

He came silently, another of the people of Starbuck and Modoc, but a bigger, squattier and more animal-like looking individual than either.

"What do?" he asked stolidly, his great arms folded about the rifle hugged to his breast.

"This girl," said Norcross, "stays here—in this room—until I come back. Understand? She is not to leave the room."

Charlie Bear grinned.

"She stay alongside me," he promised. And Glee, shivering again, at last drew near the fire—

and thus some few steps farther away from her appointed guard. Norcross, with a nod to Modoc, led the way out of the room.

Glee Hathaway sat down and covered her face with her hands. Thus she could shut out the vision of the flat, brutish face. Still she must hear the whisper of the soft tread as he came closer until at last he stood motionless within arm's reach of her; and it seemed to her overwrought nerves that she could feel those bright evil Indian eyes upon her. She grew rigid, scarcely breathing; ready at the slightest sound to spring up and run from him, yet afraid to move lest she precipate his attack. This was the big silent beast, she was sure, in whose arms she had struggled so wildly down in the dark beneath the house.

Her thoughts were all kaleidoscopic fragments tinged and colored by flashes of emotions. The mine, discovered at last, only for her to be pounced upon and made terrified captive; Dan Jennifer and his "lost" picks; Glennister's long and unexplained absence; the presence of Norcross and these others, here; and now Nevada Applegate's disappearance.

From a distant part of the house came the sound of violent hammering. What could Norcross be doing there? The noise continued for several minutes, both hammer and saw making a thoroughly businesslike racket. Finally here came Norcross, dusting his hands together as he entered.

"I am rather taking liberties with your house, eh?" he said carelessly. "Trust you'll forgive? I am obliged to nail up a few doors and windows, with a board here and there, and all that—but you understand? You, Charlie Bear," he said abruptly, "go help Modoc."

The Indian withdrew. Glee Hathaway, though left to deal with a man she had ever feared, drew a breath of relief.

"Do you know," said Norcross, going back to his easy-chair and his pipe. "I think the best thing you can do is to marry me!"

She bit her lip and, having flashed the one look at him, held her face averted. He had his answer and accepted it in silence.

"Where is Danny?" she asked him.

"I am afraid that I can't answer any questions just yet," he told her angrily. "Here I offer to marry you and you treat me like a dog—"

"No!" she exclaimed, her own anger matching his. "Not like a dog."

He understood and made pretense at laughter that carried a shrug of indifference with it.

"What of—of Mr. Glennister?" she asked presently. "Is he—have you seen him to-night?"

"Oho!" he sneered. "I ask you to marry me—and your sweet maiden thoughts fly like little white pigeons to Lord Jim, eh? You poor little fool!"

Why the blood surged up into her cheeks, she did not in the least know. She only knew that of a

267

sudden she feared for Jim Glennister as much as she did for Dan Jennifer—or herself.

Changing lights came and went in Norcross' eyes. Gradually the expression of his hard features altered; he became, of a sudden, placating. When he spoke it was very gently for Jet Norcross.

"Strong measures become absolutely necessary sometimes, Miss Hathaway. When men are strong men. I am sorry; sorry that I must act as you find me acting now. A man chooses his destiny to begin with, but there come times when it drives him along; there is so much at stake that I cannot pick and choose among possible lines of action. Yet I would make no war against you. Rather I would be your friend; I would lift you up—high up!"

"How?" she asked wonderingly.

"I love you, Glee Hathaway," he said softly, on his feet now, his arms out to her. "You know that, don't you?"

"No! I know anything but that! And I don't want to hear."

Norcross remained outwardly conciliating, yet there was a hint of stress, a suggestion that he held himself in check with an effort.

"Why do you treat me like this, Miss Hathaway?"

"Because I hate you! You know I hate you! You have brought all our trouble upon us; you, did all that you could to lead Andrew into folly; from the beginning you were set on robbery."

268

He stirred restlessly.

"Robbery? Hardly that; I advanced money, I offered to buy and pay a fair price. Had it not been for that infernal crook of a Jim Glennister—"

"He's a better man than you are, and a bigger man!" she flared out then. "You seem to have the advantage just now, to-night; but—"

"Ah!" said Norcross. The old sneer returned making his voice ugly. "You and your precious Lord Jim! He has crooked his finger at you and you've come running!"

"I think I'll go to my room—if I may?" she said coldly.

"You'll do nothing of the sort, until I send you there," he told her angrily. "I come to you in all fairness. I offer to marry you—"

"Offer to marry me!" she gasped. "You—*offer!*"

"Exactly," he said steadily. "I am going to be a millionaire before long; a millionaire many times over, with a half decent run of luck. And I offer to marry you—"

"At least you make me wonder why."

"I love you—"

"Oh, no you don't. You don't love anyone. You couldn't."

There was from the far end of the room a cackle of derision and Judy, as once before, burst in upon her father's strange wooing.

Norcross frowned, then began to stare at Judy. Glee Hathaway, too, forgot other matters for the moment as she looked at this little half savage, Indian-blooded vixen. Judy's eyes were burning bright with some secret conflagration. She gloated; she strove to conceal her gloating and with no better success than if she had tried to hide a blaze with a glass screen. Impish glee? More than that! Just the triumph which had been hers since leading Glennister into the dugout? More than that even. Something had happened to make Judy feel like dancing—and she strove to appear as though there were nothing.

"Judy!" called Norcross harshly. "What is it?"

"What is what?" demanded Judy innocently, but turning as red as a beet under his probing eyes. Her own, for once, she dropped swiftly. "Nothing that I know of—unless," she flung back at him, her head up again, "you count that I've got Glennister and the old sheep outside, asking to be told where to head in."

Glee started.

"They are outside? Mr. Glennister and Danny? You've made them prisoners?"

"Sorry I interrupted, Jet," sneered Judy. "Love stuff again? What do you think you are, a Hollywood sheik? Get on with it; work it out of your system. As for me—"

"You've been up to something on your own," snapped Norcross. "What is it?"

"Mind reader!" scoffed Judy. "Well, if you're so smart, go ahead and pick the secrets out of my gray matter. Oh, you big hulk! Have you always got to be side-stepping when the clear-cut job lies straight ahead? I brought in the meat for you; now what?"

"I didn't look for Glennister to cave in so fast," said Norcross. And added jeeringly, "What's gone with the nerve I thought he had once?"

"Oh, he's got it yet, and don't you fool yourself, Jet," laughed Judy. "He did it I guess, because he's sort of chicken-hearted after all; the old man would have smothered in another hour, and Lord Jim threw up the sponge to save him. Why, he cared," she shrugged, "gets by me!"

All this was but so much mystery to Glee who listened and watched every look and in the end was at a loss to explain what had happened and where. The only thing clear was that somehow they had taken both Dan Jennifer and Lord Jim Glennister prisoners and held them outside awaiting orders from Norcross. And now at last orders came fast enough:

"Judy, Miss Hathaway goes to her room; it's fixed for her so that she'll stay there until I want her! Lock the door and bring me the key. Put Modoc on guard there to make sure. Then come to me here."

Judy laughed, jerked up her hand in mock salute and whirled in her own skirt-billowing fashion upon her new captive.

"Off we go, Little Bo-Peep," she commanded. "No more love making for you to-night."

Glee would have remained to know and see more, but a look from Norcross and her memory of the brutish Charlie Bear, sent her from the room without a word. Straight to her room she went and, when Judy would have followed, slammed and bolted the door on her. Judy shook the latch, paused a moment to rail at her and then went skipping down the hall, calling to Modoc. Leaving that worthy posted in front of the locked door, she went skipping back to her father.

"Something's got into you to-night," he muttered, eyeing her suspiciously.

"You're dead right," she told him impudently. "We're rolling high right now, Mr. Jet Norcross; and if you want to know who greased the wheels, why, it was little Judy!"

"Oh, you're all right," said Norcross, not without a gleam of proud satisfaction, "so long as you don't get the big head and try something of your own. Play close to the table, kid; and we're going to cut the velvet just about now, and cut it wide, large and lovely. Now, go and send old Jennifer to me. I'll take 'em one at the time—and don't mind keeping Lord Jim cooling his hot heels a while."

Judy's shrill laughter gave him high approval.

"You're playing king of the roost to-night, eh, Jet? Lord, how you strut! I didn't know you had it in you. Only, giving orders around, you might keep in mind that I'm nobody's slave, but the king's daughter." She threw herself down on the hearth sprawling, cupping her chin in her hands and advised: "Send Charlie Bear on your errands. Or yell, and the boys outside can hear you."

Norcross went to the door and shouted:

"Bring in the old man. Got Glennister safe? Look out for him. He's shifty."

Starbuck appeared at the door and at his heels old Dan Jennifer. The old man's hands were bound and he seemed on the verge of exhaustion. But the look he directed on Norcross was steady and calm.

For a moment Norcross ignored him, saying to Starbuck:

"Take no chances with the other man. Got him tied?"

"Hobbled, too," grunted Starbuck. "Three men watch."

"Make it four," ordered Norcross. "You keep your eye on him, Starbuck."

"What have you done with Miss Hathaway?" asked the old man, and the first hint of anxiety came into his eyes as he made out that none was here beside Norcross and Judy.

"I'm answering few questions to-night," said Norcross crisply. "I'll ask one: Have you been fool enough to tell Glennister where the mine is?"

"Nor will I answer a single question," said Jennifer with quiet determination, "until I know what you have done with Miss Hathaway."

"Well, then, she's in her room and all right. I'm

273

not going to do her any harm. Now, what have you told Glennister?"

"Nothing. What should I tell him?"

"You might have told him—to spite me, for it could do you no other possible good—where the mine is!"

Jennifer looked at him piercingly. In the end the old eyes looked troubled.

"Why do you insist that I know?" he asked curiously. "I tell you I haven't the vaguest idea—"

Norcross appeared at once satisfied and highly amused.

"You'll go straight to your room," he commanded. "You'll find that it's going to be harder for you to sneak out of it than it has been before. Doors and windows are nailed up and there'll be a man with you or just outside your door."

Jennifer lifted his hands; the rope about them was mercilessly tight, cutting deep into the flesh.

But Norcross only shook his head.

"Off you go, and just as you are. No chances tonight, Jennifer. Judy, you go lock him in. Starbuck!" he called. "Bring Glennister in."

Judy made no move to obey.

"I told you once, Jet," she said, staring up at him from her place on the hearth, "that I'm nobody's errand boy. Send one of your noble redmen."

"You're getting mighty independent all of a sudden," said Norcross. "I'm not sure that I make you out. Don't get too high and mighty."

"I've got reason to," jeered Judy.

"What reason?" he demanded. But she only laughed and hid her bright eyes from him.

He turned his back on her and went to his chair, flinging himself down into it savagely. The devil take the girl! He had other fish to fry; here came Jim Glennister, hands bound at his back, ankles tied so that he could move along only in a series of little hops, and yet with three men guarding him, a man at each side and one at his back and all armed and watchful. Norcross indulged in a mocking smile while into Glennister's cheeks came a dark angry flush.

"Got you, Jim Glennister! Got you right!"

Glennister hopped a few steps farther into the room, dropped down into a chair and thrust his feet out in front of him. To Norcross' gloating remark he made no answer. Even his eyes appeared to have done with his triumphant enemy; they went, with a curious look in them to Judy.

Judy flounced up, stared back at him, fidgeted about and with her cackling laugh dropped back to the hearth. The frown deepened on Norcross' face.

"I'm willing to make you a proposition, Glennister," he said, still frowning.

Glennister awaited in silence. A proposition from Norcross? He had little doubt of its nature. It was to be but a repetition of one already made, outside the dugout door. He glanced about him; all doors were closed. Where were the two whom he

275

had left here? Glee Hathaway, what had they done with her? And Applegate, what of him?

"First off, Glennister," said Norcross, "you ought to have sense enough to admit that you've played out your string—and lost! Things go my way from now on!"

Glennister merely raised his brows—and smiled. Norcross brought a fist crashing down on the arm of his chair.

"Don't be a fool! I've got you where I want you. And I've got the rest. I can do with you as I want—indefinitely. No one ever comes out this way, and did we have a chance visitor I'll know before he gets here, and I've a place to put the crowd of you where you'll never be found."

"A man like Applegate cannot disappear indefinitely without making people wonder—and investigate," said Glennister coolly.

"Applegate," cried Norcross, "is going to write a letter to-night. I'll dictate it; he'll write and sign—and there'll be no investigation on that point." And then, since Glennister made no answer, he added: "Further, I've got two trucks hid away in the hills. I start them to-morrow carting off high-grade. It will disappear from the face of the earth, until I get ready to realize on it. And it is high-grade, I tell you man! I'll haul from twenty-five thousand to seventy-five thousand dollars at every load. Finally, it's just a pocket; give me a few weeks and I'll clean it to bedrock—and leave the hole for you. That's all you get, unless you accept my offer—"

"Which is the same, no doubt, as you made me a while ago? To sell out my equity to you for a song?"

Norcross sprang to his feet, crying out:

"You've got my offer. Take it or leave it!"

"Thanks. I'll leave it."

Norcross turned to Judy.

"Did you have the fool's pockets searched? Are you sure he hasn't a gun on him?"

Again there flared up that strange look in Judy's eyes.

"No chance," she said hastily. And then, "I cleaned him good and proper, Jet, down to the last cigarette paper. Two guns, mine he swiped off me and a forty-five, a handful of trash and a paper signed 'Oliver Hathaway.'"

She produced it from somewhere with a flourish; Norcross snatched it from her, glanced at it swiftly and swung about on his prisoner.

"So you got wise to that, did you?"

"Yes, I got wise to that," retorted Glennister, but all the while his eyes were on Judy. And there came an odd quirk, hardly a smile, to the corners of his mouth. "Your little daughter made a thorough search. Quite a haul, too, eh?" he demanded of Judy.

"You know it!" she laughed back at him.

Glennister sighed and relaxed in his chair. When

at the dugout in order to save an old man from hardship which might have resulted in death, he had accepted Judy's terms of surrender, he had had Applegate's hundred thousand dollars in his pocket. Truth to tell, with other matters on his mind, he had forgotten the banknotes entirely. And they had been quick prey to Judy's questing fingers. And now he knew, what he had more than suspected: Judy had decided to say nothing to her father.

Should Glennister speak where she was silent? The money was not his; yet his was the responsibility. And certainly he would prefer to see Applegate have it back than for it to go to Jet Norcross. Further, with it in Judy's possession, it was safe—oh, quite safe!—for the present. So Glennister, like Judy, was silent. And Judy, who had looked to him for silence, was content.

Norcross all the while was frowning at the scrap of paper he held in his rigid fingers. So Glennister knew. Knew that the home belonged to Glee Hathaway. But Glennister did not know—what was under that home!

With a sudden angry gesture Norcross hurled the crumpled paper into the fire.

WHAT a pair of lungs Nevada Applegate had, when once he set his mind on really using them.

"Ho! Ho, there!" Throughout the silent old house his words surged and boomed with a fine bellowing roar. "Applegate broadcasting! They got me in the kitchen, tied hand and foot. Who else? You, Miss Hathaway? You, Jim Glennister? You, Mr, Jennifer?"

Glennister, locked in his own room, tied hand and foot, heard and understood. Though Applegate could do nothing else, he could make his brave attempt to establish communication among the imprisoned ones and, to some small extent, strive to feed his own curiosity. With all his might Glennister shouted back:

"Tied hand and foot and locked in my room, Applegate. They trapped Jennifer and me. Judy's work. *Judy cleaned out my pockets—*"

Faintly came Glee's voice, answering the call:

"Locked in my room—Danny!"

"Jennifer is all right, but a captive, too," Glennister shouted back to her.

And again came faintly from her:

"Under the house—it is—"

The words ended abruptly. Some heavy hand had been clapped over her mouth. Applegate shouted again; Glennister called. Out of a brief silence rose the deep voice of Jet Norcross, curt in command. There followed the clumping of heavy boots, then silence again. Glennister's door was jerked open and Norcross, bearing a candle, entered.

"What you'll get is a mouthful of dirty rags, if you don't stow your gab," he said angrily. "I'll have no more of this yelling."

Glennister, though he had never felt less like mirth, managed a laugh to taunt his old enemy. And he did experience a certain odd glow of satisfaction; their voices, calling back and forth at Applegate's prompting, had done something for them; Glennister felt, and knew that the others must feel, that they four, Norcross' prisoners, were at last banded together in one common interest. Misfortune visited them all together and from the same source, and though walls and space separated them, they were united for the first time in their common misfortune.

"Poor old Jet," said Glennister. "He's out on such a limb that his nerves grow shaky and any little noise disturbs him."

"You hear me," growled Norcross. "One more squeak out of any one of you calls for a gag of kitchen rags. Now shut up."

Glennister smiled. It was a forced smile, perhaps, yet as Norcross glared and then went out, slamming the door after him, there came a flicker of the old spontaneity to it.

"Down and out, eh, Jet?" muttered Glennister after the departing figure. "Looks that way, I'll be bound—yes, bound," he added grimly. He strained at his bonds, first testing those about his wrists, then those at his ankles. The result was that he gave over with an angry shake of the head; he but forced the ropes to cut the deeper into his flesh; there was no chance there.

"Just the same," he told himself stubbornly, "there's always a way for a man to get out of a bad hole—give him time. And, from the look of things, we're to have time galore!"

He eased himself all that he could in his chair; it was most devilishly uncomfortable sitting thus, his arms cramped behind him, his hands at the middle of his back. Poor old Jennifer; he began to feel sorry for the old man. He couldn't quite explain Jennifer, but whether humbug, villain or madman, he was enduring hardship that must have been crushing at his age, and enduring with a fine show of spirit.

He thought of Applegate; he, too, was paying for his inquisitiveness and quality of inserting himself into the affairs of others.

"I note," mused Glennister, "that Norcross is dead set on keeping us four apart. There'll be a reason. Each of us, perhaps, knows a little; add the four scraps of knowledge—and we know it all! So Norcross sets us in different rooms and commands us to hold our tongues."

Most of all he thought of Glee Hathaway. What a devil of a time she had had of it—ever since the coming into her life of such men as himself and Jet Norcross. To her Glennister and Norcross must seem of the same black breed, ravening wolves. Well, just where was the difference? There was a difference, one as wide as the empty spaces between the stars; Glennister in his soul knew it. Yet what of himself had he shown to her that she might so much as glimpse this truth which he clung to? He fell to straining at his ropes again. Sitting there alone in the dark, he felt the hot blood in his cheeks. He set his teeth hard. Norcross had the upper hand now, but always there came a break in any man's run of luck; that was a gambler's axiom.

"I'm going clear of this," said Glennister, and grew quiet again. "And I am going to set her clear—and make her understand that I—"

That he—what?

He frowned and shunted his thoughts back to Norcross. Norcross thought to keep them locked up, hidden away, indefinitely, did he? Well, the thing was not impossible. With his two trucks, which no doubt he had somewhere in the woods, he meant to start in hauling off the richest of the ore—a few weeks, Norcross had said, and anyone could have the hole he left—and if he took the trouble and a few days' work, there would not even be a sign to show where that hole was. A few weeks? Well, that gave time for anything to happen. Be patient, and the unexpected always turned up. A man's chance always came soon or late, if he but had the eye to see it, the quick wit to grasp it before it shot glimmering by.

There, too, was Judy to think about; never would he overlook Judy again! And Judy had Nevada Applegate's hundred thousand dollars—and meant to say never a word to Jet Norcross about it. What then?

"She's the kind to take the cash and let the credit go," decided Glennister. "She'll skip at the first chance she gets. What does she want with gold in the rocks and dirt, with a roll like that in her hands? Looks to me as though Nevada Applegate for once in his life is about due to have a slice taken off his nose for sticking it into the other man's game!"

Well, he had done what he could there, too, shouting to Applegate the news of Judy having gone through his pockets; trust one as lively of wits as Applegate to know what was meant.

"And here I sit—waiting for a break in the run of luck. It may come in twenty-four hours—or as many days. And meanwhile—"

Meanwhile—his thoughts shifted back to Glee Hathaway. Prisoner to Jet Norcross—Glennister, whenever he thought of that, fell to straining at his bonds. Norcross wanted to marry her; he knew of the deed to the house and, wanting to come at a clear title to the whole ranch, no doubt judged it wise to have the home himself; "all in the family." Norcross had been set on that; and Norcross now had her helpless. Who knew what means the brute might seek to employ?

He heard from a distance the murmurous rumble of Norcross' voice. Distinct words did not reach him; low-toned and quiet, the voice seemed gently argumentative rather than brusque and commanding. Why? Norcross was dictator to-night and tempted toward ruthlessness. To whom, then, was he speaking thus?

"He's gone straight to her!" fumed Glennister. "Why can't the man leave her alone?"

He could hear nothing from Glee Hathaway. Her voice had been too low for that; just a subdued: "No, Mr. Norcross. I'll not open the door to you."

While Glennister, glowering, was asking the darkness about him, "Why can't Norcross treat her like the God-blessed little kid of a girl she is instead of one of his roughneck crowd," Norcross was saying:

"Please, Miss Hathaway. You see, I don't like to be any harsher with you than you make me. I simply want a word with you—"

"You must have it through the locked door, then," she told him defiantly. "I'll not open."

"I think it might work out better," said Norcross stiffly, "if you'd meet me half-way when I offer to be ordinarily decent. If you force me, I've got to remind you that in one minute, with an ax, I can break your door down. Come now, will you open?"

She hesitated. What was left her? With trembling hands she unlocked the door. Norcross flung it open, came in with his candle, and closed it after him.

She drew back and back from him; the width of the room was all too little space. She was afraid; she had been afraid to unlock her door yet more afraid to refuse. She strove with all her might to keep the fear out of her eyes, yet Norcross must have sensed it. He laughed quietly.

"I'm not going to eat you—at least not just now," he told her. "You've lived alone with Glennister; I'm no worse than he is, am I?"

"I did not live alone with him! There was Danny—and Mr. Applegate—"

"Well, they're still on the job, and the most discreet of chaperones, too," he chuckled. "They lend an air of respectability yet do not inflict themselves upon us."

"Just what do you want with me, Mr. Norcross?"

"A two-minute talk; then I'll leave you. I have other matters on my mind, if you want to know," he said curtly. Then he forced a smile, becoming or attempting to become something less implacable than a jailor, assuming the role of a friend forced by stress of circumstances to appear the reverse of friendly. "As a matter of fact, Miss

Hathaway, I am downright sorry to have to coop you up like this; I don't wish you any harm. It's just fortunes of war for you. Everything would have gone off peaceably if Lord Jim Glennister hadn't taken a hand in our affairs; I would have bought from Andrew; would have made a nice piece of change; and, in the end would have seen that you remained unmolested upon your old home."

She said nothing in reply. But she recalled the night to which he referred, and knew that he lied. His attitude then had been that of a man who has an enemy by the throat and means to exert the final, tragic pressure. There was no mercy in Jet Norcross.

"With things as they are," he went on smoothly, "I am forced to a certain line of action. I bartered with Andrew, he promised to sell to me at a specified figure; the papers were drawn. Therefore, I count that in all justice the place is mine. I shall proceed to act as though in law it were. Which means that I shall have to keep certain people, you among the number, shut up for some few days; three or four weeks, even, perhaps. But I offer you personally no hardship and, I trust, but little inconvenience. I came to tell you and to do whatever I could to make you understand this."

Fearing Norcross the more when she did not understand what purposes might lurk behind smooth phrases, she said only:

"Thank you. There is nothing. If I am to be locked up, there is nothing you could do."

He set his lighted candle down on her table.

"You were in the dark here; there is no need of that. I tell you, I have no desire to be unnecessarily brutal!" He put down some matches and went to the door. "Nothing else?"

"Nothing, thank you," she said expressionlessly.

"Oh, all right. I'll see that you don't starve. And you have but to call if you need anything. I'll have men awake and at hand, never fear, every hour and minute and second both day and night. And, since I have no choice, your door will be fastened from the outside."

She made no answer. He went out and was closing the door when a sudden thought engendering a certain wish, flashed on her. She called to him:

"In that secret closet, the one in the Grizzly Room leading—"

"Yes? I know; leading down to a certain place where I have men at work right now!"

"There are old family papers in the closet. Letters, just family letters no one but a Hathaway would care for. Don't let them be destroyed!"

"I left my little daughter Judy rummaging among them—"

"Oh!" She pictured Judy at the task. The thing was sacrilege. Norcross laughed; he understood.

"I'll save them for you," he promised. "More

than that, I'll bring them here to you now. They may help you while away some rather monotonous hours."

As good as his word he returned with a great heap of papers which he had tumbled upon a table cloth and brought in a confused litter. He had taken a moment or two over them himself; the more legal-looking documents he had laid aside, thinking it just as well to make himself at least superfically conversant with their natures before letting them pass through his fingers.

This time when he left her she heard him busying himself for a little while just outside her door. He meant to take no chance on her escape. To the knob of her door, which opened inward, he tied a piece of the same clothes-line which had served already in binding three men; the other end he tied to the knob of a door just across the hall, drawing it as tight as he could. He even explained to her, pretending to apologize. It was with a sigh of relief that she heard him move away. She turned eagerly to her precious papers—and then, sitting there with eyes which stared and saw nothing, she fell to thinking of the others: Dan Jennifer—Nevada Applegate—Jim Glennister—

As for Jim Glennister, at the moment he was telling himself that nothing stood in the way of his freedom—except a silly piece of rope. Should a man and all his plans accept defeat—because of a few feet of clothesline? True, his door was fastened from without; and equally true, a man was, no doubt, on guard just outside or near-by. But let Glennister have the unhampered use of hands and feet and he swore he would sweep over such obstacles like headlong Wild River rushing over submerged rocks. The house for the most part would be dark; there were few candles and Norcross would not be burning them everywhere. In the dark a man armed haphazardly, with a chair or a bed slat or a table leg, might come upon a more satisfactory weapon by charging full tilt and without warning upon him who carried a rifle.

So, slipping from his chair, Glennister lay on his side on the floor. He curved his body backward; he pulled his heels upward toward his bound hands. His fingers—they were terribly swollen and numb and almost useless, so tight were the cords about his wrists—barely brushed the rope about his ankles. But they did touch and he set to work in grim earnest. Just give him a little time, a few minutes—say half-an-hour.

His little time was given him; half-an-hour, a full hour without interruption and at the end he had achieved exactly nothing. Numb fingers brushing back and forth in tiny restricted arcs found the knots they sought and contended futilely with them. Glennister endured agony both mental and physical. To have those knots stand between him and freedom with all which it implied at this moment—and to have his fingers fumble and fall away from very weariness; to force them again and again to the task, and again and again to fail. Never were knots so cunningly made, never drawn so terribly tight. Yet he strove on and still on, while his whole body complained.

It was pitch dark. Had there been a light outside his door he would have seen the glow of it at the bottom. If only they had left him a candle he could so easily have burned the ropes that held him. Trust Norcross to think of that. And trust Norcross for what happened now.

Steps sounded in the hall, coming on swiftly. Glennister rolled over on his face, drew his knees up under him and surged up to his feet just as the door opened. Here at last came visitors; Norcross carrying his rifle, the Indian, Starbuck, at his heels with a candle.

"Look him over, Starbuck," Norcross commanded. "He will have been at work, you can gamble, trying to get loose. See what luck he has had."

Starbuck made a swift and minute examination. He grunted and left the room. In a minute he was back with an old broom. He cut the handle off, cut notches near each end and then, with his first semblance of any facial expression, a broad grin, stepped behind Glennister and lashed one end of the broom stick to the cords about his wrist, the other end to the bonds at his ankles.

"Good now," said Starbuck. "No bend some more like snake; him keep straight and no get loose."

Norcross laughed, comprehending; Glennister had sought to get free and by a very simple expedient the Indian now made it impossible for their captive to bring hands and feet together. And so, laughing, Norcross went out again, Starbuck at his heels. The door was closed and fastened. Glennister had said nothing. For once he was too near choking with rage to admit of speech. He hopped across his room and dropped down on his bed.

"No use," he admitted within a sinking heart. "He's got the whole works dead to rights."

In a little while he must have dropped off to sleep. He awoke with a start; dawn was in the air; pale light was slipping through chinks at the shuttered window. His first act was to strain at his bonds. No use? There was always use! One way or another he'd go free. And once free, let Jet Norcross look out!

Of a sudden he realized what had wakened him. The dawn silence was troubled by the thrum of a motor. What automobile here? The first flash of a thought was: "Visitors!" Perhaps friends of Nevada Applegate.

Then he remembered the trucks of which Norcross had spoken. But why here? Why, unless the gold were near at hand, very near?

No; that was impossible. It was just that Norcross meant to make him think that; just wanted to mislead him.

He heard men going up and down about the house. The smell of coffee floated in to him. They were frying bacon, too. He heard Judy's shrill voice; she was screaming anathema. Nervous, was Judy; quarreling with all and sundry. Anxious to be off and away, thought Glennister; yet, little fox that she was, abiding her time. No doubt she'd find an excuse to go out with the trucks—and once at a safe distance, she'd disappear.

The thrumming motors grew silent, one after the other; he made out that there were two cars. They were close by; not over a hundred yards from the house. He hopped to his window but could see nothing; there was but little light outside and he doubted if he could see much through those heavy shutters even by full day.

He tried to peer behind him, craning his neck and working his hands to the side; only the tips of his fingers were visible and it was hard to know them for his own. The cords cut deeper than ever into his wrists; his fingers felt to be bursting. The pains through his tortured arms and legs were like knives stabbing.

Hours passed before he had a visitor. At last Starbuck entered alone. He had set his rifle down by the door and carried Glennister's breakfast in his hands. A platter with bacon and hot cakes, messy, broken fragments; a cup of black coffee. Never was a man more watchful than Starbuck. He set the dishes down on the table and went out without a word.

Glennister was hungry and ate. The broom-handle lashed behind him made it impossible for him to bend straight forward, but he managed. Twisting sidewise, bending what little was allowed him at the knees, he got his head down to the table. With no hands to help him, he must eat as best he could—like a dog. He lapped at his coffee.

"There'll be a way. My chance will come. I'll go free yet!"

Food enheartened him. After eating he moved about a little, hopping across his room, setting his body to swaying from side to side, trying to get the cramp out of stiff muscles.

The trucks were still near the house; he would have heard their motors had they been moved. Now and then he heard voices from without; the heavy rumble of Norcross' tones, an Indian voice in answer. At times Judy's. What were they up to? What was Norcross doing out there?

Hours passed. The house remained silent except that, infrequently, business-like steps sounded; someone making a tour of the house, looking to locked doors, making sure that no one escaped. The sound of a car being cranked; the motor coughing, settling down to smooth running. And then noise of a car departing; a heavily-loaded truck, one would say.

From his window Glennister could see nothing beyond a very limited space of empty yard. He listened; the second truck was started and lumbered away.

What were the others, imprisoned like himself, doing? Were they, too, bound as he was? Applegate, yes; he had thundered the news through the house. Jennifer? probably. Glee Hathaway? No! If Norcross had dared subject her to that. Then, too, he recalled her own words: "Locked in her room." Well, what of these three? Each and every one would be set on escape; set one free and let that one really get away, out to the first home, the first town, and Norcross was at the end of his tether!

Ah, but Norcross was thinking of that, too. How could anyone help them win free—unless it were Jim Glennister?

The trucks were gone; that meant—what? That men had gone with them. How many? Well, two at least, one man to drive each.

"If only I knew exactly how many men he has here."

Norcross, Starbuck, Modoc; three. There were others; not over six all told, Glennister judged. And Judy.

At least two with the trucks. And if the trucks

were really here for the purpose Norcross had intimated—and what other purpose could have
brought them?—there would in all likelihood be
two men with each truck. Which would leave not
more than two men on guard here. And Judy.
Unless she had gone with the trucks?

Well, then, what of Norcross? If the man was
actually hauling off free gold. By the truckload!
Think of it! Would he remain here while his
Indians carted it away?

"Not for a minute!" Glennister judged. "There
will be risks to run. He would have canvas over his
load; he would not want it seen and pried into; he
would have some place to cache it. And, always
preparing for the unexpected, Norcross would go
with it. Which leaves us here, a couple of Indian
bucks. Hm."

They let him go all day without food. It was a
day of torture. A day of hideous silence. No one of
the imprisoned ones called; there was that threat of
a mouthful of dirty rags to deter anyone who was
sufficintly uncomfortable as matters already stood.
Only once did he hear voices; the voices of a
couple of Indians. He listened eagerly; he felt a
glow of satisfaction. Norcross had gone; pray
heaven Judy, too.

They would return but, it seemed most likely not
for hours; there would be nothing gained in
hauling any such precious freight as he began to
believe they actually did haul, some trifling, brief

distance. They would not get back until late at night or early morning.

"If ever I am to win free of this," Glennister told himself sternly, "the job is for to-night. There's got to be a way——"

In her own room Glee Hathaway, thinking as he thought, had not wasted her time. To win free; somehow to win free! With her, not tied as he was, it seemed a fraction less hopeless. She had thought only of escape from the beginning; a score of wild schemes had offered themselves only to loom up as impossibilities. Oh, if she, instead of Applegate, had been shut up in the kitchen! There was a way there up from the kitchen closet into the attic.

It was silly wishing, but from the wish she had progressed in a flash to inspiration. There was her own ceiling—and the wide attic above. If only she could come upon a loose board in her ceiling and pry it upward; if only she could manage to climb up into the attic! Once that was accomplished, she could creep warily to the rear of the house where a small window looked out upon the gently sloping shed roof; she could slip through—she could be away in the dark, running. Through the still forests, out to the road, hiding at every sound but always pressing on again. Thus through the night and on into the broad day, and to help.

Keeping her door bolted from within against

being surprised at what she meant to attempt, she found that by standing upon her table she could reach the ceiling of heavy broad redwood planks placed across the heavy beams. Beginning at one corner, getting up and down as she was obliged to shift her table, she tried every inch of the ceiling boards. How firmly they were fixed in their places! It would have sufficed to have merely tacked them here and there lest they warp at the edges, but that had not been Grandfather Dick's way; everything must be sturdy. More than once, stifling a little moan of disappointment she sat down listlessly, on the verge of giving up.

But, again like Glennister, she could not stand inactivity, could not surrender hope, could not and would not bring herself to a supine acceptance of an irksome fate. In her, as in him, flowed the blood of those who had extended frontiers, who had trampled on difficulties, rising from them to fresh labors and had ever refused with a fine Napoleonic scorn to accept into their vocabularies the word which adorns the banners of do-nothings, the word "impossible." Thus she gave up but for the moment; she rose again and again worked for her freedom. As Glennister spoke of a rope, so she of those insensate boards which barred her way, vowing they should not hold her here.

He thought of her; she thought of him. She found it hard to think of him as Norcross' prisoner; too dominant and strong and purposeful a man to be prisoner to any. Trickery, trickery only had brought him down. She recalled Judy's words to Norcross, explaining yet failing to explain Glennister's capture: "The old man would have smothered in another hour, and Lord Jim threw up the sponge to save him!" Glee Hathaway felt herself warmed by the thought. With renewed vigor she set to work.

She required a lever, some instrument with which to pry away at the ceiling planks. For the purpose she removed one of the slats from under her mattress. To muffle any sound she wrapped a towel about its end. Then she stood on her table, wedging her lever against the ceiling, working at it with all her strength, yet always in guarded silence. When the house grew silent she must ever be still lest the smallest sound betray her; when the men tramped about or talked and laughed, she worked swiftly. She had found a board which had seemed to give ever so slightly under the pressure she put upon it. She labored at it hour after hour, whenever she dared. And at last, and in silence, she achieved the most glittering success of her life. The plank was loose, and above her head was an open space amply wide enough for her to slip through.

And now. To climb up, to come to the rear window, to flee, in wild desperate haste for help. She sent up mute prayers to God to be with her now. If only she could free the others, if she could liberate one of them! There was the way to get down into the kitchen where Applegate was. But the Indians were there with him; she could hear them jabbering now. And then—

A heavy, oncoming tread, the clatter of crockery. Someone was coming with her supper. In a fury of haste yet making never a whisper of sound, she came down from the table, moved it across the room, hid her bedslat. She was afraid to blow out her candle; they might grow suspicious, wondering why she was in the dark; but she placed it at the far side of the room from the corner where she had labored.

Her heart in her throat, she went to the door; she would accept the tray, ever anxious not to awaken suspicion, but would open her door only enough to allow its being handed in.

It was the villainous-looking Indian, Charlie Bear. He stood leering in at her.

"Norcross, him go 'way. Judy, him go 'way," grinned Charlie Bear. "Me boss now; Starbuck, him other boss."

She snatched at the tray.

"Go away!" she cried.

"Bimeby," grunted Charlie Bear.

She dropped her tray and by a sudden, unexpected quickness, managed to slam and bolt the door. The Indian stood a moment, grumbling and putting his bulky weight against the panels until they whined and cracked. Then, when she was half-fainting with dread, he laughed his guttural laugh and moved off.

He meant to come again! She knew that he meant to come again. He would beat her door down the next time. If she could but come, through the attic, to a spot above Jim Glennister; if only she could break through the ceiling to him. She caught up her pair of scissors, the only thing she had that might cut a rope, stood her chair on the table, climbed up and began pulling herself up in the attic.

A clatter of dishes again and the heavy tread. Charlie Bear was passing her door. He stopped.

"I like talk," he told her. "You good girl, you—"

"No!" she cried out at him. "Go away. I'll tell Mr. Norcross and he'd kill you!"

Futile threat. He laughed and the heavy tread and rattle of dishes went on. He was carrying food to the others. Now, before he came back, was her time.

She was through the opening. Pitch dark up here and she dared have no candle since a single downward ray through any one of a number of broad cracks would betray her. She must feel her way, creeping stealthily lest a board creek under foot. She went in her stocking feet, her shoes in her hand. Her spirits shot upward, the mercury of her courage standing high. She was going to escape; nothing could interfere with that glorious fact. She was going to escape, to flee from this place—to bring confusion upon Norcross and his crowd, to win through to a great, golden victory. And, first of all, she was going to find a way to rescue Jim Glennister. How safe she would feel, once he was free with her!

Below she heard Charlie Bear going through the house with his tray of plates and cups. He was intoning a singsong guttural Indian song. Dodging rafters and cross-beams, she sought to keep behind him; he led the way.

She heard him at Glennister's door. He set down his burden and struck a match. He lighted a candle; she caught a glint of it like a spark through a knot-hole. She stooped and peered down. Glennister was just below her. The door was open; Charlie Bear was taking his supper to him.

Jim Glennister's plans were made. A man always had his chance—provided that he was man enough to make it for himself. He was desperate, yet cool and watchful of details in his desperation. A man who had bet his all more than once on a single card, he was on the verge now of making the supreme wager with destiny itself. Luck was always at a man's elbow; good luck or its dark and evil sister, bad luck. Which, one could only know after the dice fell from the box. In what he meant to do, the odds stood against him. That was nothing. The long shot sometimes won. Odds were not everything.

He stood leaning against the wall. He seemed to stand wearily, stooping a little. One could not tell how the muscles of his body were tensing, how his whole eager soul stood tiptoe within him. As tense as a taut-strung violin string. Ready!

Ready but waiting the exact moment for the desperate chance. Charlie Bear came into the room. He sat down the tray on the table; he turned toward Glennister, holding his candle up, grinning.

"You make big fool mistake," he chuckled. "Me heap—"

It was as if a thousand tight-coiled springs within the body of Jim Glennister released at the same instant. From being an idle, half-stooping, lax-looking form he was altered in a split second to a human catapult. He launched himself forward head first, in a dive through the air. He struck head first, like a missile from a great spring gun.

Had there been the slightest warning Charlie Bear inevitably must have leaped aside. But warning there was none. He received the full blow, with one hundred and eighty pounds of solid weight behind it, full in thc middlc. He was flung backwards as a football player, tackled at a vicious onsweeping rush, is flung; he toppled and went crashing.

Glennister rolled free and wriggled to his feet. There was the great danger; handicapped as he was the other man might be up first. But

Glennister was ready and knew what was going to happen and thus had the advantage. The final thing to do, savage and brutal, was to leap again and strike with both heavily-booted feet, to strike a prone man in the head.

And that, as fate had it, was all unnecessary. Charlie Bear had fallen hard; his head had struck the edge of the open door. Where he fell he lay; a little pool of blood gathered and spread on the floor boards under his head.

Glennister's sudden attack had succeeded in all that he hoped for, and more. Yet everything yet remained in the balance. He was still bound and at any minute Starbuck might come. He had yet to find his way through the house and into the open. There, within reach could he but put out his hands, stood a rifle. At the moment he would have given ten thousand dollars for the use of his hands. Even for the unhampered use of his feet.

He heard a strange sound; a gasp. It seemed to come from above. Confound them; they had a spy up there.

"Oh, If I could only get to you. I have scissors to cut you free—"

Only a whisper, yet it thrilled through him like an angel chorus. Glee Hathaway up there—free!

"You can't get down," he whispered back. "How did you get up there? How can you get to me?"

"Through the ceiling in my room. Can you manage—"

"Hurry," he commanded. "No noise. Back to your room. I'll get there somehow."

"My door is tied—"

"No matter. Hurry and quiet."

He flung himself down. It was pitch dark again; Charlie Bear's candle had guttered out. Glennister began writhing across the floor like a great snake. He got his feet against a wall and shoved himself along; he rolled; he inched. But he went silently and still with a strange speed. He heard voices from the kitchen; Applegate, God bless him, was firing a volley of questions at Starbuck, and though the Indian did little other than answer him with monosyllabic grunts, their talk might deafen them to Glennister's weird progress.

He came to the Grizzly Room. A door was closed. He got to his feet and lifted the latch with his teeth. He lay down again; he rolled across the room; he slid gently down the three steps. He rolled, inched, writhed across the living-room floor. It seemed to him the widest room in all the world.

Dark, pitch dark. He was afraid of getting lost. He was afraid that Charlie Bear, momentarily stunned, would be up and after him. He feared he would never find his way to Glee Hathaway's room—

Through the silence, as sweet as any star ray in a dungeon, came the sound of singing. Glee in her room lifted her voice and sang. It was to him; it was to lead him to her. She knew how in the dark he would grow confused.

He came at last just outside her door. He could see her light under it, could hear her singing. He stood up; he found the rope extending across the hall, tied to her door-knob and the door-knob across the way. A flimsy bit of clothes line—and Jim Glennister a good hundred and eighty pounds! He lay across it, slowly putting his weight on it. The rope snapped and he half fell, half caught himself.

The voices in the kitchen came to a dead halt.

"What's that?" demanded Starbuck.

Glee's laughter rang out.

"Did you hear me stumble?" she called lightly.

She opened the door. Glennister slipped in. The door closed, the bolt shot home. For the instant in which their eyes met each saw a glimpse of heaven.

There was a sound of running steps. Starbuck was not satisfied that all was right. He came plunging by; they heard him cry out when he saw the dangling rope ends.

"Charlie Bear!" he shouted.

Never did a pair of scissors work harder, more frantically than those in the girl's hands. And seldom, surely, if ever, were scissors so dull. Starbuck beat at her door, then went charging through the house, roaring out to Charlie Bear. And presently came a weak answer.

"Oh," moaned Glee. "I can't—"

"Keep at it," he said quietly. "Cut away. We've plenty of time."

That steadied her. She worked in fresh desperation, gasping out little broken fragments of prayers under her breath. And at last, after what had seemed to both an unending eon, the rope fell from his wrists.

He took the scissors in hands which functioned only because his will was the will of men who triumph in defeat, and hackled away at the rope about his ankles, and in another moment stood free.

"They're coming!" she cried fearfully. "They're almost here. They have the rifles—"

He sprang to her window. Boarded up, it would require time to break through. He glanced up.

"The attic? Any way out?"

"Yes," she whispered. "A little window at the back—"

"Up we go. Quick!"

He went up in a flash to the table top, and through. Lying flat he put down his hands to her.

"Quiet," he commanded. "And quick. The dark is on our side."

A shower of blows was rained on her door. Two thoroughly enraged Indians were shrieking curses and threats.

"They'll have to get an ax," whispered Glennister. "Come. We've got our chance."

"This way; follow me," she told him, and gave him her hand. He caught it tight and they crept through the dark, tiptoeing.

They heard the attack made on the door. They heard the thing splinter and crash and fall; there was a brief silence, then excited voices. But when the voices fell to shouting, Glennister and Glee were slipping through the window which gave from the attic to the shed roof.

The soft, free night air in their faces; the clear bright stars making a soft glory of the wide, wide sky! And just yonder, holding out its arms to them, the great dark forest.

"Thank God for that," said Glennister softly. He was down on the ground; she came down in his arms. "Thank God—and Glee Hathaway."

Hand in hand they broke into a run. He barely heard her say, in a queer, quiet voice:

"—and Jim Glennister!"

THE STARS ARE BRIGHT   CHAPTER XIX

GLENNISTER felt as if his feet were made of solid india rubber; and as if the foot-manufacturer had left a handful of needles in them, scattered from toe to ankle. As he ran some of the needles worked upward prickling furiously—

There was a tremendous din in the house behind; yells, curses, ax blows and then a dozen shots, fired no doubt at random into the attic. Superior to all these came a mighty shout from Nevada Applegate:

"Good old boy, Jimmie! Good girl! Hurray! Whoopee-eee!"

"Where are we running?" gasped Glee.

"Where they won't get at us in a hurry. Where we can drop down and breathe easy a bit. Where I've got everything all ready for us. Come along. Those wild redmen may make a pepper box of your roof, but they're giving us the chance of a lifetime to step along."

"If—"

"There are no *ifs!*" he laughed. She had never known him so gay; laughter rang in every word. "You and your old scissors cut them all out of existence. Right now, henceforth and for ever, we're the captains of our own destinies. Hear old Applegate yelling his head off!" He had to stop a second to listen and chuckle. "He's a good old scout, even though he was born and raised a humbug."

They hurried on. The friendly forest lands appeared to waver in the starlight and to be coming half-way to meet them. They plunged into the infinitely welcome, fending arms with the feeling of coming home after long, weary journeying.

"What are we to do?" she asked. And of a sudden it dawned on her that all this while they had been hand in hand and even that her own fingers had clung with perhaps unnecessary tightness to his. She freed herself a little hurriedly.

"We're going to have a nice little stroll in the starlight," he told her gayly. "Was there ever such a night? Just a delightfully leisurely stroll; we've run enough. To rush along like that, break-neck speed through life, has its drawbacks. There's Wild River right over yonder; he's the fellow that indulges in all the mad haste in the world—and then you'll note, growing wiser, he begins down here to loiter and enjoy himself. We'll do likewise."

She looked at him wonderingly. He understood just what sort of an expression must be in her hidden eyes, and laughed again.

"We may even stop for a bite to eat, who knows?" he added. "Certainly I am going to massage my ankles and wrists—and I'm going to have a smoke. Thereafter—"

"Yes," he said eagerly. "We must remember poor Danny—and Mr. Applegate—"

"So we'll indulge in a moment or so of thinking," he conceded. "They've the guns in there; we've no sort of weapon. But—"

"We can't think of attacking them. It would be madness. Now that we are free we must go for help."

"Hm!" said Glennister. And, after a pause, "Yes, we'll think things over pretty carefully."

"If I only knew where you are going right now—"

He told her of his first nocturnal expedition that time he had come to see her at the old cabin among the redwoods, and of the canvas roll he had hidden in the woods against some such emergency as to-night's.

"My one oversight," he confessed, "was in not caching a rifle with it. But never mind; we'll right all small omissions."

"But to dare stop so near!"

Glennister chuckled.

"I have a notion that part of it is all right. Those two poor befuddled heathens are scared half to death by now—if I know Jet Norcross. They've got to make an accounting and a fearful time they've got to look forward to. They've let two birds fly—I hope you don't mind me calling you a bird?—and they're going to be precious careful to hold the others. Which means they'll stick close to the house."

"One of them might follow us—"

"Hope so," he said cheerfully. "Let them divide numbers and we rake them in one by one."

"But surely we're going to hurry off for help?"

"I, for one, am nine-tenths starved," he said by way of answer. "I'll bet you are, too? The stuff they handed me—and made me gobble up, hands tied—faugh! Come along; a little way further and we'll pause for a bit of a picnic!"

She followed him silently. Unerringly he led the way through the woods to the spot where he had concealed his canvas roll in the thicket. His fingers being still stiff and numb, he used a knife to slash the rope binding the roll; the contained articles he spilled out in a little heap, the blankets themselves he spread on the ground.

"Sit, my lady," he invited. "We'll dine; we'll remember that all wise armies march on their stomachs; then we'll relax and rest and plot mischief to all villains."

"You seem to have forgotten our friends, Danny and Mr. Applegate!"

He did not reply immediately. He was meditating upon her expression: "Our friends." Well, why not? He did have friendly feeling for both, come right down to it.

"No, I'm not forgetting them," he said presently and began busying himself with the parcels at which he fingered in the dark. "We're going to have them free and rejoicing in a jiffy."

"But, unarmed against two armed men? And with the others, maybe, returning at any minute? You alone against so many?"

"You and I against the world!" he cried joyously. "And now, eat! Here's a can of peaches, opened with a jack knife. Here is cheese and here a box of graham crackers. We dine like king and queen— and then we recall our sovereign duties to our loyal friends and, presto, we succor and reward them."

Despite all that she had lived through and had so

recently escaped, despite fears that had fled along with her, she was infected with his mood, so exuberantly confident was it.

"You're smiling!" exclaimed Glennister. "I—I can feel it!"

They ate, she but sparingly, Glennister hungrily and with gusto. She leaned back against a tree and looked up at the stars, seen here and there among the dark tracery of wide branches. Never had stars seemed closer to earth, more comforting.

He lighted a cigarette, cupping the match with his hands, hiding the glowing cigarette end against any chance watcher. He, too, leaned back against a tree, the same tree by the way, and his eyes went like hers to the stars. The woods were dark; the sky was bright with its glittering lights. All about them was intensely still and strangely, compellingly peaceful. Life had been such a rushing, mad and tempestuous stream; it was most pleasant to loiter a moment.

Presently he began speaking slowly and thoughtfully: "I am a bit ashamed, if you want to know, Miss Wonderful Dryad. A while ago, prisoner in my room, I saw how Norcross was running things; I understood how, because he had the power, he used it and treated you as he did. I would have given a whole lot just then to get his throat in my hands—and then I saw that what he made you suffer was little different from what I had inflicted on you. And that was why I was ashamed."

She did not speak, but a sudden gladness went thrilling through her.

"To you," went on Glennister in the same low, grave voice, "we two, Norcross and I, must appear to be pretty much alike. Well, maybe we are. Only I never guessed it before and I don't like to think it now. But what's the use? What's done is done."

Still she made no answer. For a long time, smoking meditatively, he was silent with her. Then he laughed softly.

"What's done is done and let it go," he said lightly. "What remains to be done is yet ahead of us." He rose and trod out the spark of his cigarette. "We face forward, if it pleases you?"

"Will you tell me something?" She recalled and had recalled many a time Judy's words concerning Glennister's capture. And now she asked: "Will you tell me how you fell into their hands?"

"The craft of Miss Judy," he said, and explained. And, by way of conclusion: "With Jennifer and me locked up in the dugout, there was nothing for it but be good and do as we were told." And that was all.

Impulsively she put out her hand to him.

"You did it for Danny's sake. Oh, that was fine of you!"

For a moment he held her hand tight in his. It was with a sigh that he let it go.

"And now, I tell you, we face forward. First of

all, have you any idea where Norcross went with the trucks?"

"No. There are two roads out; he could have taken either and could have gone—anywhere."

"And so we can't judge when he'll be back? But we can hazard a guess that he will make his trips as short and as quick as he can. He will have picked out a likely place to hide his plunder; and he will want to be back in a hurry to make sure that all is well here. The thing for us to do is to be ready for him at any minute from right now on until he comes."

"But how be ready?" she wondered. "They are all armed—"

"But not forewarned as we are, and so at a disadvantage after all."

"Oh, it would be so much wiser, so much better, for us to hurry for help!"

"It might be wiser; I don't know," he told her coolly. "But as for being better, never! This yet remains my game and Jet Norcross', and I have a hankering to finish it up my way and without outside interference. Wait a minute and you'll have an inkling."

He began questing about in the dark until his groping hands found a straight young sapling which satisfied him; some three inches thick at the butt, it tapered so that four feet above ground it was of a satisfying thickness to the hands that closed about it. He cut it down, lopped off the thinner end and freed it of branches. He balanced it tentatively; the green wood was heavy, his club was formidable as an iron staff.

"For a scrimmage in the dark, a pick handle or a club like this is worth all the rifles in the land," he assured her. "You're about to have the time of your life, Glee Hathaway, if you'll just hang around and watch and listen," he concluded grimly.

"The thing is impossible! It's madness!" she gasped.

"Not when you understand all details. Shall we walk forward a little way? I'd like to meet the returning trucks at safe distance from the house, so that no yells or chance shot may be heard. And also, I'd like to choose a place where the old road winds through the thickest and blackest of the forest. You'll stay a good way off, well hidden. If I should be grabbing a lion by the tail, you, anyway, remain free. You'll strike off through the woods—be sure you keep away from all roads and trails on which they might try to head you off—to the nearest ranch house. You could have word rushed to the sheriff, then, and conclude matters in your own way. Meanwhile, let's try mine."

"Haven't you any sense of fear?" she asked, fearful for him.

"Not to-night!" he laughed back at her, swinging his club so that it cut whistling through the air. "And, do you know, I begin to think I have found an added incentive to live, too! And I'm going to be telling you all about it—soon. After we dispose of Jet Norcross and his little Indian gang for good and all."

They swung along together through the dark, their feet now in the old road which the trucks had traveled. They came up over the crest of the ridge from which Glennister on his coming here had first glimpsed the old home; they went down on the further side.

"And here we wait," he said, coming to a halt. The road ran under thick, spreading branches; hardly the stars found a crevice to glitter through. "We'll see the headlights long before they get here; they'll make slow going of it up this hill. At the first sign of them you will draw off yonder— and if I make a mess of things, you'll keep on going."

For Glee Hathaway, standing there in the quiet road or stirring about restlessly, time passed by with dragging, torturing slowness. Waiting, for what? Waiting, how long? She looked in ever-growing wonderment at Jim Glennister who spoke to her quietly and cheerfully now and then out of the heavy silences. What was he thinking? Had he no proper understanding of this thing that he meant to do? Was he a man utterly devoid of fear?

"Now!" he said softly. "Here they come. Draw off and hide."

But she caught his arm.

"Please—"

He patted her hand and when he spoke his voice was graver than she had ever heard it.

"Why you should care what might happen to me, I don't know," he told her. "But I thank God that, after all that has happened, it may be so. Now, you are going? Oh, I promise you it is going to be so simple you'll wonder you ever doubted it."

She began drawing back as they arranged. Withdrawn a hundred paces from the old road she crouched behind a big fallen log. She could not be seen here and yet could make out, as well as the dark of the night permitted, what went forward.

She seemed to see a dark form moving along the road, Jim Glennister going to meet the truck. Its headlights flashed; the road was empty. She did not know where he was; he had simply vanished. The truck came on, the engine making a deal of noise with the laboring uphill pull. Vaguely she made out the forms of two men on the seat; she could hear no words from them. They came on in silence. It had been a long hard day for them. "You'll see; they'll be half asleep," Glennister had promised her.

Just the one truck? Where, then, was the other? Glennister had said: "They'll come one at the time, you'll see." And had laughed. It was his night to howl, he told her; all was to go well with him and with her; witness the stars above, how bright and serene and auspicious. The other truck was following, of course; once she fancied she

317

caught the flash of lights far away through the trees.

She watched this slowly moving one, fascinated. Suddenly she hid her eyes; it was too horrible, this thing that was going to happen! But she could not long keep her eyes averted.

Was there a third dark object in the truck? Was it slowly moving forward in the truck's bed, inching along toward the two other dark forms on the lurching seat? What a noise engine and crunching wheels made! One could hear nothing, could see so little. She started up; she stood on her log, forgetful of self, her hands wrung together, her eyes staring wildly. At last something was happening— the car was going crazily—crashing into a tree.

Glennister's club was swung high; it came crashing down upon a man's head and the man slumped and slid quietly from the seat. Up club again; swish and crash. The second man, with a little cry but no such warning as permitted of him catching up his gun, slid down. Glennister was in the seat; he had the wheel.

"Come!" he called softly. "It's all right. Hurry before the other car gets here."

She ran to him, crying out at every panting step, "Thank God, oh, thank God!" The car stood still in the middle of the road, the engine still running. Glennister stood up in it, stooping over something that busied him. He had brought with him the rope from his canvas roll; when he stood up two men, half stunned or stunned outright, lay bound securely.

"Into the seat, Dryad Girl," he called triumphantly. "On our way to the house and our friends before Jet Norcross shows up. We've bagged two of his Indians and have two more to bag in a hurry. And we've got two first class rifles all ready to do our bagging with."

She climbed up beside him, trembling like a leaf, sick with the horror of what had happened—yet strangely, singingly glad. Something did sing within her as he threw in the clutch and drove on. A strange time for her to feel within her heart that it is a fine, a glorious thing to be alive.

"The game is as good as played to the finish now," he said as they turned down into the meadow and saw a light marking the house. "Played and won. We're going to hand our aboriginal friends such a nice little prize package that they'll just stand stiff and stupid under it while we do what we like. You watch; watch again, little Glee Hathaway."

Where his words ended, he made the truck's horn continue for him. Its shrieking blast made the night hideous. He slammed on the brakes, killed the motor and jumped down. She, getting down, saw him leaning over the two captives he brought with him; and she saw that he had one of the rifles in his hand.

"Never a cheep out of either one of you birds,"

he commanded in a stern whisper, "or I'll stick a gun barrel down your throats and blow you all to pieces. Quiet, remember, if you want to see the sun come up."

He set his hand to the horn again. A door opened at the rear of the house; a burly form stood revealed in the dim rectangle of light. It was Charlie Bear; it must have appeared obvious to him that this was Norcross returning and he came out into the night, slowly, hesitantly. He had his report to make and it was no such report as would send a man hurrying.

Coming from the lighted rooms he saw none too clearly at first. Glennister strode along to meet him. And before Charlie Bear got his mouth open for the first word he felt a rifle barrel rammed into his middle and was commanded in a very low but none the less deadly voice:

"Drop your gun! Keep your mouth shut; never a word or I'll kill you! Up with your hands. Turn around. Now, back to the house!"

He had counted on stupefaction and met with it. He commanded obedience and received it. Charlie Bear, like an unwieldly automaton, trudged back to the house.

From within came Starbuck's voice, calling:

"Oh, Charlie! Who come?"

"Call back to him," whispered Glennister, driving his rifle sharply into the inert hulk. "Tell him to come here."

Chokingly, Charlie Bear grunted out:

"You come, Starbuck—Ouch! Come quick!"

At a run came Starbuck. And, like Charlie Bear before him, his progress ended abruptly with a gun barrel jammed into his paunchy stomach.

"Drop your gun! Up with your hands!"

"The two in the truck," cried out Glee. "They're trying to get away!"

"Into the house on a run," he called back to her. "Cut Applegate loose and send him out. Then Jennifer. I'll ride herd here until they come. Only make them hurry. We won't have any too much time before the other truck gets here."

She went by him like an arrow. She flew down the long hall, through room after room and burst in upon Nevada Applegate. He had heard something of all that went forward and was stamping about, shouting like a madman.

"What is it? It's Jim Glennister? He's got the top hand?"

She caught up a keen-edged butcher knife from the table and cut his ropes in wild haste.

"He has guns outside. He has captured the four Indians. Run, help him! Quick! I'll untie Danny."

Before the words were done she was out at one door, he at another. Sobbing softly in her excitement she raced through the house to Jennifer's room. It was locked but the key stood in the door. She had forgotten a candle; it was pitch dark in there.

"Danny," she called. "Oh, Danny are you here?"

"Now, God bless you, Glee," came Dan Jennifer's voice, no longer placid and calm but shaken mightily. "This way; I'm on my bed. Tied—"

"Never mind; never mind, Danny dear. It's going to be all right now. Jim—Oh, Jim is just wonderful!"

"Humph," said Dan Jennifer, who was very quiet while she cut him free.

"You're all right, Danny?"

"Yes, yes; I'm all right. But you—"

"Come, hurry! Poor dear Danny!" He was stiff with cramped muscles and staggered a little; she threw her arms about him, hugging him tight. "Our bad days are over, Danny. Oh, I know. But come; we must hurry to help. Jim has the rifles outside; you and I can shoot as well as the others—"

They made their way, she leading him, through the kitchen. And there they met Glennister and Applegate with four utterly miserable looking prisoners.

"We want a few feet more rope," said Glennister gaily, "to do a thorough job here. The other car is coming. And some of the kitchen rags Norcross spoke of. Applegate, if you'll be ready to drop the first man who bats his eye, I'll do the rope act. Come boys; take your turns and don't make any mistakes."

They muttered, but ever the bright blue eye of Nevada Applegate was upon them, and they were

322

cautious of going beyond vocal protest. Swiftly Glennister bound them, the ropes drawn tight, knots made hard and fast.

"That will hold them for a while—and we'll not be busy outside ten minutes," he said at the end. They could hear the motor of the second truck, growing steadily louder. "Jennifer, will you hold a gun on them? I wouldn't kill any of 'em unless I had to," he ended with a grin. "At such close quarters it will be enough just to blow a leg or an arm off!"

Old Dan Jennifer caught eagerly at the proffered rifle.

"I used to hunt Injuns, when a boy," he said, and again his voice was the gentle, serene voice characteristic of him. "Don't do any worrying about this end of it."

"Come on then, Nevada Applegate," said Glennister.

"Oh, but be careful!" cried Glee. "Norcross is not like the others. He—"

Glennister paused a moment and looked at her curiously. Across the width of the poorly lightly room their eyes spoke together. Then, without a word, he swung about and went out. At his heels trotted Nevada Applegate.

"Quiet now, and let me start things," said Glennister sharply. "Jet Norcross can be a bad hombre at a pinch. Leave him to me; you keep the other man covered."

They went across the yard to where Glennister

323

had left the first truck standing under the madrones. The headlights of the oncoming car cut a wide path through the night. It was coming on with a rush, sweeping down grade. Norcross, evidently, was impatient. Uneasy, too, perhaps; he had been forced to trust more than he liked to his henchmen.

"Hello," his voice called. The truck came to a standstill and he rose in his place, rifle in hand. "That you, Modoc?"

"Hands up—high!—or I drop you, Norcross!" rang out Glennister's sharp command.

From Norcross a curse of rage as, with no thought of obeying the unexpected command, he hurled himself to the side and so to the ground. And so swift was his act that hardly an instant seemed to have passed before he was firing.

"You Injun," yelled Applegate. "Sit still or I pot you!"

The Indian on the seat remained rigidly in his place. But from Norcross came spitting fire and angry report and screaming bullets.

Glennister had expected no better than this from Norcross—and perhaps had asked no other. For him and Jet Norcross there was but one way out. What must happen now was only what had been long on the cards, long deferred. His rifle, too, was at his shoulder; shot for shot his answer was given to Norcross.

"In the dark this way—it's all as luck wills it—only to-night—is my night!"

A bullet shrilled by his head; another whipped through his coat. What a doubtful wavering blot of a target Jet Norcross was! Glennister fired again; lost his target entirely—found it—

A sudden wild pain tore through his arm; the arm dangled at his side. He set his teeth. The left arm, thank God for that. He steadied his rifle with one hand; he kept on firing. His arm was growing numb. But—

But Jet Norcross had ceased firing.

"Got you, old-timer," said Glennister.

"Damn you," gasped Norcross, and the dark blot on the ground stirred and shifted and struggled to rise. But Glennister ran in on him and kicked the weapon from Norcross' uncertain hands. And Norcross, with a little sigh, fell back and lay still.

A slight, dark form which had lain very quiet in the truck, sprang out and started running.

"It's Judy!" shouted Glennister. "After her, Applegate! She's off with your roll! I'll take care of the other man."

"Hold on there," yelled Applegate after the running figure. Judy screamed back her shrill vituperation and but ran the faster. And Nevada Applegate, roaring threats, was after her with all the speed that resided in his rotund form.

From the house, running, came another slight swift figure.

"It's all right," called Jim Glennister. "Your bad days are over."

Of a sudden rifle shots began crackling again. Yonder where Judy fled and Applegate pursued, with him shouting at her, he fired as he ran; over her head, at her feet, to right and left, so that it must have seemed to Judy as though bullets swarmed like bees about her. She ducked wildly and ran on; he plunged after her, threatening to shoot her head off if she didn't stop.

There came a shrill scream from Judy; they heard her stumbling and falling. Glee, her hands to her ears, gasped out:

"He has killed her!"

A joyous shout from Applegate:

"I've caught her! She tripped and fell—Help! Hey, there, help somebody!"

But in the end, and all unaided, he brought Judy back to the house, a sullen captive.

THE GOLDEN COMPROMISE   CHAPTER XX

"And now that it is done," mused Jim Glennister moodily, "I'm am sorry for it!"

His prisoners were huddled in one room, Nevada Applegate mounting guard over them. Here before him lay Jet Norcross.

"Is he—dead?" asked a hushed whisper at his side.

Glennister answered Glee Hathaway without turning toward her.

"No. But my bullet must have broken his

shoulder and may have penetrated a lung. Just the same he is not going to die if I can help it."

There had been a day when he and Jet Norcross were friends. Oddly, the old days surged up in clear-cut detail before him while these latter days were mistily unreal. A few minutes ago he had meant to kill Norcross; he had shot to kill and had come very close to succeeding. His frown deepened.

"Will you help me make a bed for him in the truck?" he asked her, turning at last. "I don't want his death on my hands. I'll take him out now as far as the store; we'll have a doctor for him there; we'll improvise a hospital. I've a notion I can pull him through—and I'm going to do it."

"But your own wound?"

"As you have seen, only a flesh-cut in the forearm.—I'm square with Jet as things are. And there's no use rubbing it in."

There came a new look into her eyes which she hastened to hide from him. How she had mis-judged him before now! She ran gladly to do what she could; she, too, prayed within her soul that Jet Norcross would not die. She did not want his death on Jim Glennister's hands!

And so, half-an-hour later, Glee Hathaway and old Dan Jennifer were alone again in the old home. In the bed of the departing truck lay Jet Norcross, white and unconscious. Bound hand and foot his Indians went with him, one only of them allowed to ride unbound since he must drive. With them went Judy, very quiet for once. And Jim Glennister and Nevada Applegate, each with a rifle in his hand, stood guard over them.

Applegate at the last minute had run back for a final word. He grasped the girl's hands and squeezed them tight.

"I guess I was sort of a snake in the grass," he admitted, but his face beamed all the while. "I got wind of gold, and gold always pulled me like wild horses run away with a go-cart. I spied on Norcross; I followed him up; I tried to pump him, to buy him out or buy in with him—anything. And now? I'm coming back in a few days, never fear. And I'm going to chip in with you, somehow. I'll finance this thing for you, or I'll take a part interest—or I'll just lend you the money to work it and darn the interest!"

And off he ran. Glennister, for his part, had gone without a word. What did he mean to do? When would he return? Would he ever come back? She really knew so little of the man. "He was square with Norcross now." Was that the end for Jim Glennister? Was his interest over? Did he even remember the gold?

She must have known all the while that he would come back, that he would come soon, even before Nevada Applegate. For there was something which she was eager and impatient to do, and yet which she postponed until his coming.

Slow days passed, days of waiting. At last he came—as she knew he must. Evening had shut down. She and Dan Jennifer had had their supper and she was putting away the last plate. There came a gentle rap at the door and a voice—his voice—saying gayly:

"May I come in, Miss Dryad?"

She ran to the door, her cheeks flushed, her eyes dancing.

"Need you ask to return to your own home?" she challenged him, the door flung wide.

"Not mine, but yours," he told her firmly. "And I don't put my big foot across the threshold unless you can tell me I'm welcome."

So, laughing all the while, she replied to him:

"Will you step in, Mr. Glennister? You are quite welcome, sir."

In a flash he was across the threshold and had caught both her hands in his.

"I've missed you to beat the band," he said warmly.

She slipped her hands out of his and retorted lightly:

"It has been very quiet here since you left us!"

"Why didn't you say 'lonely?'"

They went together to the living-room where Jennifer sat brooding by the fireplace. The old man looked up and nodded; his eyes went back to the coals. He looked very old and very weary—and hopeless.

"I suppose that by now," said Glennister, "you

329

two would have solved the last mystery and found the lost mine?"

Jennifer looked strangely at Glee. She, with sparking eyes, ran to him and put a soft loving hand on the stooping shoulders.

"I have made Danny promise to wait; to stay in the house; not to look for anything until—"

"Until?" Glennister prompted her.

"Until you came back!—But it's all right, Danny dear. Everything is all right; and now that Mr. Glennister is back Can you wait just until to-morrow morning, Danny?"

Thus she mystified both men. But not a word of explanation would she offer.

"I only wish," laughed Glennister at last, "that Applegate was here! You'd see him go into con-vulsions, wondering."

Jennifer excused himself early and went off to bed. Glee Hathaway jumped up and went eagerly with him to his room; she seemed to be gripped by a growing excitement; she hurried him off and hurried him to bed and came back to Glennister, looking brighter and more flushed with eagerness than ever.

They sat by the dying fire for a long while. She would have no lights lit, saying how much lovelier the faint fire-glow was. Glennister tried to talk with her; she seemed absent-minded and answered seldom and then strangely at random. Presently he rose, saying a trifle stiffly:

"I'm off to bed—if I am offered the hospitality of your roof, Miss Hathaway?"

"No, no!—I mean, sit down a while. I want—there is something. Seeing is believing, you know!"

"I don't understand you to-night."

"I don't want you to understand anything, just yet. And then, I want you to understand everything. Please sit down—and wait!"

He sank back into his chair. An hour passed; another hour. She stirred restlessly now and then; there were times, so still did she sit, that he thought she had dropped off to sleep. He watched her all the while in the dim, soft light; he marked the curve of her cheek, the line of her mouth, the way her hair clustered in ringlets about her ears. More than once Jim Glennister sighed, all without knowing it. But she knew and looked at him through her fingers. And her mouth curved to a little smile.

"Look here—" began Glennister. It had grown very late.

"Sh!" she commanded. "Be still!—Listen!"

"What is it?" he whispered back, tense without knowing why. "Somebody walking! In the next room."

She caught him by the hand and drew him quietly after her to the door. There was but little light in the next room, the Grizzly Room, but light enough to see someone moving across the floor. It

331

was old Dan Jennifer, fully dressed, stepping along softly—and going straight toward that hidden door of which they both knew!

"There is a closet there," said Glennister. "I meant to tell you of it. Some papers—"

"Sh! Be still! And watch."

Jennifer made a direct line to the batten which concealed the catch; he pulled it forward, opened the door and stepped into the closet.

"What on earth—"

"Quietly now. After him."

"But he'll come out; he'll hear us."

"He won't come out; and he won't hear if we're the least bit quiet. Now!"

She almost ran across the room. When Glennister came to her he saw that the closet was empty. Further, there were steps going down, and up the steps came a light. Jennifer had gone down—somewhere—and had lighted a candle!

"Come on. After him," she whispered.

"But he'll see us."

"He won't see us. He won't notice. Come; hurry."

She slipped into the closet and went down the steps, Glennister more puzzled than ever, at her heels. At the foot she was waiting; she put out her hand to stop him, bidding him look about him.

A great excavation under the house! Rocks lying about; piles of dirt; something yellow, spotting every inch of a rock at Glennister's feet, winked up into his eyes. Picks; a wheelbarrow; picks everywhere! And old Jennifer, carrying his candle, moving along like one who knew his way well. Stopping here and there, fingering a specimen, setting it down to take up another, going on among his picks, arranging them with strange meticulous care—Jennifer seeming to gloat like a miser among his gold pieces—

"Look out! He's coming back!" whispered Glennister.

"Stand very still! Don't move!" she commanded, and he could feel her trembling with excitement.

Jennifer, walking slowly, his head turning this way and that, returned toward them. He came so close that they must have been revealed perfectly in his candlelight—yet no change came into his expression! He brushed by them, went on, started up the steps, extinguished his candle—and was gone. And, if anything on earth was clear, it was that he had not seen them!

Of a sudden, belated understanding rushed on Glennister.

"He is asleep! Good heavens—Coming here—It's the lost mine!—walking in his sleep!"

He struck a match. She had brought a candle with her and now lighted it. Her hands were shaking.

"I got the secret from an old diary of Grandfather Dick's. He wrote that one night he was down here when Danny came upon him—and that he found out just in time that Danny was walking in his sleep! How Danny first found the way down, who knows! But—Don't you see now how Jet Norcross told the truth when he said that it was Danny who led him to the gold? He has been visiting it in his sleep for years and years!"

He was for the moment stricken speechless. He looked about him with marveling eyes.

"Men do strange things—I never knew—All his life he has looked for this and all the time he has had the knowledge tucked away in some dark part of his mind!"

"And after all," she said eagerly, "it was Danny who found it and who made it possible for us to know. We are going upstairs now to wake him and tell him. Oh, it will be a dream come true!"

He stood looking at her thoughtfully. Not at the wealth that lay about them, but deep into her eyes.

"May I congratulate you, Miss Hathaway?" he said quickly. "To you goes the Hathaway mine!"

Her quick look flashed back at him.

"And you?"

He shrugged.

"I never dreamed it was right here. My rights, if any, were to the property outside. You will remember that I even deeded to you all my rights to the house!"

She flashed a paper before him and suddenly tore it to bits.

"It is not fair!" she cried. "You spent your

money, a full seven thousand dollars; you risked your life; you took two wounds—Oh! Do you think that I would hold you to a thing like that? You did not know that the gold was here, and I won't have it on such a misunderstanding."

"Look here," said Glennister soberly, but with a warm light in his eyes. "I told you at the time that I tricked you. There was a note which I found in the closet up there; it was from your father and gave you the house. The house was always yours. Norcross knew—"

"Where is that paper?" she asked him.

"Norcross got it; burned it—"

"But then—"

"I'm no confounded robber," cried Glennister. "The place is yours."

"I won't have it! I—"

They went presently to tell the glad news to old Dan Jennifer. It was just a few minutes later—and yet by that time they had managed, logically or illogically, but entirely to their satisfaction—to arrange a way! And the steps leading upstairs were now amply wide enough for the two abreast.

"Not mine—but yours!" Love had said.

"Not mine—but yours!" Love had whispered back.

"Then—ours!" had Love triumphed.

And they went to tell old Dan Jennifer—everything!

335

Center Point Publishing
600 Brooks Road • PO Box 1
Thorndike ME 04986-0001 USA

(207) 568-3717

US & Canada:
1 800 929-9108
www.centerpointlargeprint.com